Mary,

Thanks for supporting my new novel. Be sure to share with your brother.

Azarel

11/18/03

A Life to Remember

a novel
by Azárel

Published by
Life Changing Books
PO Box 423
Brandywine, MD 20613
www.lifechangingbooks.net

Life Changing Books and the portrayal of a person reading
are trademarks of Life Changing Books.

ISBN: 0-9741394-0-8

Cover and book design: Stacy Luecker, Essex Graphix
Edited by: Susan Malone and Chandra Sparks Taylor

This book is a work of fiction. Names, characters, places, and incidents are products of the author's imagination or are used fictitiously. Any resemblance to actual events or locales or persons, living or dead, is entirely coincidental.

Printed in the United States of America.

This book is dedicated in loving memory of
Anthony Malik.
Remember, I'm your guardian angel.

Also, to my two gifts from God.
Thank you for being so patient with me during this process.
Mommy is sorry for the many fast-food dinners and rushed
bedtime stories. Home-cooked meals are on the way!

Acknowledgments

I asked my Father for guidance so many times, unsure of how to compose the contents of this book. It is with His help that I was able to complete this novel. Thank You...Thank You...Thank You.... With You all things are possible and without You none of this would be possible.

I must give kudos to my everything. To my husband, Anthony, who has sacrificed so much. I could not have accomplished this monumental task without your unconditional love and support. I can now be a wife again!

I have to give a special shout-out to the people who provided me with the information for this work: Candice, without you I would never have thought about bringing this creation to life. Edward, Andre of Turning Heads Salon, Mousey, and Mike Coker, you were all invaluable resources who made this all come together. Thank you for helping me to see "life behind the walls" through your eyes and experiences.

Words alone could never express my gratitude for the incomparable group of professionals who supported me on this novel. Susan Malone, your dedication to the editing of this work and your red pen will never be forgotten. Chandra, I appreciate your diligence during the editing process. Thank you for rescuing me. Tonya Howard, my publicist, you have been and continue to be one of my biggest motivators. Thank you for introducing and leading me in all the right directions. Stacy Luecker, I am forever indebted to you. You've worn many, many hats in order to put this thing together. Your website design and artwork are incredible! I wish you and Essex Graphix the best (www.essexgraphix.com).

Blessing is the only word that will describe the phenomenal group of women and the best test readers a girl could ask for. Ladies, what can I say?

I truly appreciate the time you've taken out of your busy schedules to *continuously* read and critique this novel. To Joyce, my stepmom, I hope you threw away the first draft. Things were rough, but you helped me stay focused along the way. To my cousin Leslie, you believed in this from start to finish. And you've read it so many times you probably know it better than I do. To Leslie German, I can't express my appreciation for your dedication and the late nights you pulled in the final stages. To Emily and Cheryl (aka "Cel"), my color purple sister, you are first-class. No matter what I do in life I know both of you will be there. Don't go far. I plan to use my phenomenal ladies the second time around.

Much much love and thanks to my crew of family and friends. There are way too many to name, but all have either critiqued, promoted, or supported my venture in some way. Tam, my one and only sister, thanks for being there for me and the girls. We've been together through *all* of life's ups and downs. Mom and Bill, thanks for putting up with all my mess over the course of the last year. Daddy, you amaze me. It is you who taught me to have drive and determination over the years. You've never doubted this project from the start. Don, my brother-in law, your hard-core advice will take me a long way. I won't forget it. Lover and Gram, the best grandmothers in the world. Both of you have always been my biggest cheerleaders. No matter what I do, you're with me 100 percent. All I have to do is ask, and it's done. Toot, my Grandfather, I knew all I needed to do was tell you about this and you would get to work. Thanks! Jeremiah, my future cousin and accountant (hint-hint), keep promoting.

I can't forget my niece who kept the girls busy while I worked. Shaunda and Damon, you left me, but now I'm expecting you to handle North Carolina. The Kinneys and Woodruffs in Texas, I love your enthusiasm. The Vicks in the ATL—good looking out. From the Fords and Freemans in Maryland to the Williams' in Philadelphia, thanks for the word-of-mouth advertisement. Miguel Davis, thanks for your marketing techniques. I wish you much success on your clothing line (soulcitylimited.com). To yo' brotha, Maurice, I'm positive Drama Sports will take off. Thanks for your support.

Dora, Schalette, Alaya, Sundra, Jackie, Lisa, Danielle Daniels, and Danielle Adams, you gals are the best group of friends I could ask for. Your encouragement and continuous support rank number one. Kenya, I admire the way you jumped right in there to help make this a success. Much love. I can't go without recognizing all the distributors, book-stores, and organizations who made it possible for people to have access to this novel. I'm blessed to have your support.

To my readers, I hope you will enjoy this book as much as I have enjoyed bringing it to you. I don't take your decision to purchase this novel lightly. Visit me at www.lifechangingbooks.net and let me know what you think.

For all of those people I forgot to mention, please forgive me. You know I love ya.

Much love,
Azárel

Author's Note

Many prisoners and correctional officers will wonder about the events that took place in *A Life to Remember*. Most will say, "That doesn't take place in my institution". However, my intent was to acknowledge globally, some of the perverse activities going on "behind the walls."

Divine found himself in a situation where he needed to *change*. Hopefully, a lesson will be taught to anyone who reads this book. In a world where life is already difficult, many people bring additional heartaches on themselves.

To all the brothers incarcerated, whether you've been misjudged or you're locked down because of your own error, God gave you the ability to change. Remember, there is a huge commonality between those on the inside and those on the outside: *The Lord is the maker of us all, so don't judge!*

A Life to Remember

1

Reminiscing

"Hey C.O., if you get a chance, can you get me a grievance form? I need to write somebody up for this shit!"

Steaming, I yelled again after being ignored, "Can somebody get me a grievance form?"

I shouldn't have asked bald-headed C.O. Warren for nothin'. He's straight by the book. That's just like him, to park his three-hundred-pound, sloppy, lazy ass in that seat, and act like we don't even exist. Asking that bastard to do something is like asking Jerry Springer to stop having trifling guests on his show. And you know that shit will never happen.

Warren just sits his high-yellow freckled-face self around, like he owns the place. He doesn't give a damn about anybody in here, not the inmates nor his coworkers. I guess because he's in his late forties and has put in twenty-plus years, he thinks somebody around here owes his ass something. He just comes here to humiliate us, and collects a paycheck in the process. His attitude is as nasty as this food in here. I can bet he won't even turn my shit in.

Maybe I'll wait until the shift changes.

Right now I'm supposed to be meeting Niko out on the yard, but instead I'm making trouble for the C.O.s here at Dunnridge State Correctional Institution (well for the ones I don't like). C.O. is sorta like our way of bonding, you know giving them a nickname. Though I shouldn't even call Warren C.O., because he's such an asshole. All of the inmates on Block C don't believe me when I describe the freaky things I see these sorry-ass officers doin'. Not to mention all the corrupt shit they're involved in. Yeah, I'm a real troublemaker and would probably have a sharp-edged knife stuck in my back by now if it weren't for Niko, Mathematics, and Black.

I haven't always been like this. In my early twenties, I was a quiet, ambitious young man. My life was so boring back then—I thought going to the racetrack was exciting. Well, there's nothing really exciting about Portsmouth, Virginia. That's why knowing people like Niko has its benefits. During the week I worked hard and hung out every now and then. I spent most of my free time at the gym balling with the fellas, or rolling to the mall, or sometimes even checking out a movie. The weekends were definitely designated for fun.

I had graduated from Morehouse College in Atlanta and had a good job. Going away to college surely taught me lots of responsibility. Every semester I was on the dean's list and was a celebrity in the National Honor Society. Can you believe that? Yes, me! Not many people get to light that candle.

My studies came easy and didn't require extended hours like some goons I went to school with. College life was good. I moved off campus in my sophomore year with two other guys and started keeping my place real nice. Making it on my own gave me a sense of pride and respect. I was even beginning to think about pledging. Those Ques, draped in their purple and gold sashayed around campus like they were the shit; barking like stupid-ass dogs. On the real, they were just pups in a pound. I couldn't get down. And the pretty-ass Kappas macked all the chicks. But then, they weren't so damn cool or respectful either. Now, that I'm older, I know that mess is for people with an identity problem. I know who I am. So I pledged Me Phi Me and stayed to my damn self.

Grandma was proud of me and that was all that mattered. When I graduated she sat in the audience crying her little heart out. She cries for any damn thing and anybody. Hell, she cries for people she don't even know. She knew I would be somebody special, and I was determined to keep pleasing her.

After college I started working my tail off. My job was the next best thing to Grandma's baked macaroni and cheese. It was so easy, and came natural to me. I could figure numbers in my head so fast, at times I didn't even need a calculator. Starting out as a bank teller, and maneuvering my way into other responsibilities, I spent many hours working overtime to make everything perfect. My coworkers threw me shade most of the time. But I didn't care. My profession gave me joy, and that's all I was concerned about. Most of the fellas kept wondering why I was so happy. They probably thought I was making more money than they were. Well, I was. I can't help it if I'm smart as hell. I got so caught up in my job that I couldn't do anything but work.

My daily routine consisted of going to work, then

hanging out with the boyz from time to time. Even though girls would put the full-court press on me every now and then, at that time, I preferred being with the fellas. I had no idea that my life was about to drastically change.

In 1993, on the night of the Norcom championship basketball game against Wilson High School, everybody who was somebody was in the house. Believe me, they were all dressed to impress. If you had anything to show off, that was the place to do it—jewelry, clothes, a new car, or a new fling, it didn't matter what it was. While the guys sported their matching jean outfits, the girls rocked their daisy dukes and flipped do's.

Even though I was a college grad and had outgrown much of my childhood play, my neighborhood homies expected me to still swing through the games with them. I'd oblige. People sort of hung out with their cliques just kicking it, not really paying attention to the game. The excitement was watching what people had on and who they were with. Wilson games were always jampacked.

The fried chicken and french fries sold at the concession stand produced a crowd. In the last seven years, I don't know if Wilson had ever had a record better than 6/19. But people continued to pack that small-ass gym like sardines. I guess I shouldn't dog the school like that, but hell, the team sucked!

Believe it or not I looked like a nerd back then. I wore a pair of Ray-Ban glasses and owned every preppy sweater you can think of. Since I'm hairy, I've always had this mature, manly look. People say my thick eyebrows resemble those of a forty-year-old man. Some people might call me chunky. I think of it as having a little meat on my bones. With brown eyes, I've always thought of myself as being handsome, priding myself on my deep cinnamon skin tone. My physical features haven't changed much, but my lifestyle has.

The night of that game, I first met Niko. I had never seen the infamous Niko before, although I feared him before even seeing him. He stood on the sideline talking to Whop, one of my boyz. Niko was always the center of attention. He didn't do anything special. He had it like that. He commanded respect.

He was just standing there with his hands in his pockets. I walked over to let my crew know that I was going to the front gate to chill, when nonchalantly, Niko and I made eye contact. We just nodded to each another. I was thrilled that he even acknowledged me.

A week went by and I ran into Niko again outside of Club Malibu. He and his boyz were dressed in all the latest gear. I couldn't afford half the threads Niko had on, especially that glittery jacket. It seemed as though his entire outfit was perfect: a fresh pair of kicks, and the latest jeans and shirt. The diamond in his ear glistened every time he moved. When he and his crew walked up, people started whispering under their breath and pointing, the girls in particular. The line waiting to go into the club was about a mile long. When I finally got to the front, this ugly, fat-ass bouncer with a double chin said, "That's it! Too many people in the club, and we're not gonna let anyone else in for a while."

My boyz and I were blown. As we began to turn away, I spotted Niko on the sidewalk. He walked over and said,

"Dog, weren't you at the game the other night with Whop?"

"Yeah," I said, unsure about what to say next.

With confidence he said, "Come up front with me, I'll get you in."

Whop was my boy. We had been friends since high school. He was a little on the wild side, but nothing like Niko. Whop and Niko hung out together every now and then. I guess since Niko had seen me with Whop before, I was cool. I felt bad leaving my boyz but Niko's King Kong stare made it clear that he meant me and only me.

Inside the club, Niko got mad respect. Dudes from every part of town were slapping his hand and nodding. Niko ordered about twelve bottles of Moet at one time. Girls came from nowhere wanting a glass and shaking their asses. I wasn't use to no shit like that! When I would go to the club with my friends we ordered *Red Bull,* or the dollar special. Niko must have spent over a "G" ordering drinks for everybody that night. The way he macked was totally out of my league. Bottom line—I was impressed.

From that night on, we were boyz. I'd heard a lot of good and bad things about Niko, mostly bad. When we first started hanging, I often wondered, how can he dress so nicely without a job. He was only three years older than me, and certainly didn't talk with enough intelligence to own a business.

I had heard rumors about Niko being an enforcer for local drug gangs, but didn't know how true it was. Simply put, that was a nice way of saying he was a hit man. After meeting him I dismissed all thoughts. And, I was too scared to ask what he did for a living. You just don't go around asking people how they make their money or how much for that matter. After a while it didn't even matter because I was having the time of my life, hanging and partying every night for the next two years. The fun only ended when we got locked up. I'll never forget that date— September 8, 1995.

I have many regrets, but overlook them at times. God, the fun we used to have. Niko used to do wild, sporadic shit, like the time he asked me to ride with him to Baltimore to pick up something. I didn't ask questions. I simply hopped in the black Porsche with Pirelli tires and fly rims, listening to the cranking sounds ready to roll. I told Niko I needed to sleep on the way back. At least with a couple of hours of rest, I would be ready for work the next morning.

After about four hours on the road, I was so busy grooving to Dr.Dre and Snoop that I paid no attention to the fact that we had passed Baltimore. Niko was rolling at about ninety-five miles per hour the whole time. I didn't say anything at first. I wanted to make sure I wasn't hallucinating. After all, I'd been smelling the aroma of Niko's weed the whole time. Maybe I had a buzz from inhaling that shit. When the green sign appeared saying DELAWARE BRIDGE—3 MILES, I nearly lost my breath.

"Niko, where the fuck we going?" I shouted over the music.

"We're on our way to A.C."

"And just what is that? You told me we were going to Baltimore."

By the time Niko had finished explaining why we never even stopped in Baltimore, it didn't matter. We ended up walking into a casino less than two hours later. The smoked-filled rooms, glittery lights, loud sounds, waitresses prancing around in skimpy outfits, and loads of people overwhelmed me. With no idea what was going on, I walked close to Niko's side. Niko explained in the car that he was supposed to meet someone important in Atlantic City.

He never told me who, or what it was all about. Hell, I'm a naive country boy, not used to adventure. I just wanted to be in his presence.

Sure, I'd heard of Atlantic City before, but damn sure never been. When Niko slid the key in the room door I should have known we were going into some plush shit because you had to open two sets of double doors before entering the room.

The spot was laid. Mirrors all over the place. Two bars lined the large window that overlooked the city. The carpet was white as snow. I was a little apprehensive about walking on it. I started opening doors, rubbing my hands against the velvet wallpaper, and just sort of checking out the place. I didn't want to act like I wasn't used to shit, but this was totally out of my league. Niko picked up the phone to do some business. Using all his code words, which I was at this point somewhat familiar with, I knew we weren't going home anytime soon. I just needed to make sure I called my boss in the morning with some lame-ass excuse.

When Niko met his friend on the casino floor, I was mesmerized by the gambling. To see the amount of money people threw on the crap table made my pockets scream! I had seen Niko play street craps before, but this was off the hook. With about eighty bones in my pocket and since Niko was handling business, I wanted to win a little money. I put ten dollars on the pass line, waiting for the dice to be thrown my way. I figured that was the safest bet since I could throw anything but a two, three, or twelve to remain in the game.

Then some bald-headed man wearing a skin-tight suit, pointed to a sign that said minimum bet fifty dollars. A slap in the face would have been more acceptable. Everyone looked at me, as if I were holding up the game. Face flushed red, I dug deep only to pull out four tens. A Vanna White look-alike with long pink fingernails quickly swooped up my money and exchanged it for five green ten-dollar chips. I don't know why I did that stupid shit. In less than thirty seconds I rolled a twelve, crapped out, and Vanna grabbed my chips with the same quickness. I crept away from the table like Sam Sausage Head.

I sauntered around, checking out the spot when a lot of cheering and excitement boomed from one of the tables. As I got closer I realized Niko was playing at a hundred-dollar table! He stayed on the dice for about forty-five minutes, betting like it was his livelihood. He was winning hardways, field bets, and bets I'd never heard of. The guy he was there to meet just watched. By the time we left the table, Niko had won about twenty thousand dollars. He gave me a thousand dollars for going with him. Hell I was just happy to be there. Niko had that effect on people, and still does. You just want to be around him.

Just think, I'm not even upset about this ugly-ass scar on my face because I got it having fun with Niko. I didn't even know how to ride a motorcycle on that sunny day in May when Niko decided we were going to buy motorcycles.

First of all, I didn't figure a motorcycle into my budget, nor did I know I was going to learn to ride one. On the way to the shop we passed several packs of riders balling and looking slick. By the time we got to the shop Niko asked all the questions about the specifications of the bike and, of course, worked the price. I spotted the perfect wine-colored bike with silver chrome. But, before I could even get a chance to talk to the salesperson, Niko had purchased two bikes. That's right, one for me and one for him. I didn't have a clue as to how I was going to make it off the lot, or if Niko expected me to pay him for it.

The salesman gave me a short lesson, and Niko was ready to roll. I made it to the first light hesitantly, with little confidence. When the light changed Niko zoomed, like a prisoner making his escape. I couldn't pull it off. People rode by laughing and pointing fingers. I felt like crawling into a hole when a group of dudes went flying pass me ballin'.

The thought of speeding through town and hanging with Niko got my adrenaline pumping! I just couldn't learn fast enough. It took him at least fifteen minutes to come back to the area where he found me practicing in a parking lot. I laughed along with Niko, but didn't tell him I never made it through the light. He thought that he left me behind because his Zx 11 was much faster than my CBR 600. My bike was a baby compared to his, but I just wanted to be a part of his crew.

Needless to say, I eventually learned how to ride. Unluckily for me, one day we were balling down High Street when I flipped my bike over twelve times trying to keep up with Niko. It felt like sparks were firing out of my ass. By the time the ambulance came, I thought I had met my maker. That's how I ended up with this gruesome-looking scar right below the left side of my lip. That's okay, the scar accents my perfect set of white teeth. And even though this mark is with me for life, so is my dog Niko.

Niko did a lot of fun shit, but I'm most grateful because he introduced me to Sherese, the love of my life. Now Sherese isn't the type of woman Ella Mae Lewis, my grandmother, wants me to settle down with. In her opinion, my mother was pretty trifling, and that's why she wanted to raise me, so I could set some high standards for myself. She said my mother used to run around with different men and didn't have time to look after me.

From what I'm told, my mother had no goals or dreams for us. I probably wouldn't have gone to college if I were raised by her. I don't know to this day if my grandmother took me from her or if she abandoned my ass. But Grandma has been taking care of me all my life and cares about my well-being. You see, she's from the deep south. That's where I got my southern accent. It almost sounds like that L.A. shit. Anyway, down there they've got all these morals and principles they think people need to live by. That's why she wanted me to have someone who's educated, like myself. But that's not what I fell in love with. I have a degree in finance and Sherese has a degree in the streets. It was love at first sight. And, I'm going to be devoted to her forever.

As I sit here and reminisce, I can see Sherese counting out Niko's profit from a job they did together back in the day. For Sherese to be a girl, she's pretty damn smart. I mean not just common sense but she's a critical thinker. You don't find that in most girls and surely not the ones from the hood. She never let Niko talk no mess to her either. Whatever the deal was supposed to be, she stood her ground. Although, we were never formally introduced, I wanted her! She was full of excitement and danger, something I wasn't used to.

Sherese was conceited, but had every right to be. Her petite frame has curves like a salad-dressing bottle. She's heavy in the chest and baby definitely got back. The cutest set of dimples enhances her mahogany skin. But what really hooked me was her silky long hair. She's famous for wearing a part right down the middle and just letting it all flow. We made the perfect couple!

If I could change anything about Sherese, it would be her friendliness. She speaks to everyone, and that pisses me off. I couldn't stand being out with her, and some guy would say, "What's up, Sherese?" I wanted to be able to introduce her to somebody, instead of her already knowing them. She made me feel like I was her only love, but I didn't like that friendly shit at all. I used to say that I wanted my girl to be a virgin so she could never say she had been with anyone else, but I didn't have time to hang out at the junior high schools.

As time went on, Sherese began to trust me, which was out of her character, and I became infatuated with her. As we grew closer and closer, my life began to change more and more. Her sex was the best! I always think about the night we were on our way to the bowling alley. Cars were less than an inch from us on all sides. The steam from the heat rested on our bodies while we waited patiently in bumper-to-bumper traffic. For a Tuesday night I couldn't understand where everyone was going.

She stared at me with her soft, luminous eyes. Playing with the radio, I avoided her at first. The aroma of her body cream began to fill my senses. I wanted her so bad! Not sure if she wanted me, or was teasing, I relaxed. But, when she came blazing across the seat I knew the feeling was mutual. Kissing passionately for several minutes, she slid her hands down my pants and commenced to stroking my dick. I knew it was time for me to pull on the side of the road. Before I could actually get my car in park, Willie had expanded an additional two inches. At that point Sherese jumped on me and began to straddle me like a horse in a rodeo, causing me to explode inside of her within minutes. I must say that was the best fifteen minutes of my life.

After that night we were together on a regular basis. We used to lay up on her mother's couch, cuddling and smooching. Oh God, and those back rubs, how can I forget! She should have gone to school for that shit. Maybe even worked in one of those day spas. I sound crazy in love. But, we've got a flame that will never go out. You see, the love we have is boundless, immeasurable. Hold up—this is starting to get depressing. That was 1993, seven years ago, now look at me. I'm thirty-one, Niko is thirty-four, and I guess we're lifetime friends considering we'll be here in Dunnridge, better known as the Dungeon, until 2007. That's right! The judge gave us twelve years. But, Niko looks out for me because I really shouldn't be in here. You see I'm innocent! (That's what they all say on Cell Block C).

Anyway, right now my innocence isn't important. What's important is the fact that I'm supposedly here for seven more years and my crew is running shit for now. Needless to say everybody in here wants to be down with our clique. We're envied by all the gangs: Bloods, Crips, and the Five Percenters. About sixty no-good, scum-of-the-earth inmates are housed on my unit block. That's a pretty good number considering most prisons are overcrowded. They all know exactly who to fuck with and who not to fuck with. When I walk around, all eyes stay on me. People are frightened by my posse. It's what you call respect. Block C ain't to be fucked with. Even the riot squad gets chills when it's time to roll up in here.

2

Daily Drama

Let me use my connections to give Lieutenant Graham this grievance form before C.O. Bennett gets on post. It's like pulling teeth, but it's worth the payoff. Maybe he can do something about that bitch since he's the head nigga in charge! She'll do everything in her power to keep me from turning in this form. But that's okay, she's not going to keep harassing me. I'm gonna make sure of that, 'cause I'm the man. I don't know what made her think she could fuck with me and get away with it. Doesn't she know that correctional officers don't mean shit to me, or anyone else around here? Well, C.O. Bennett can officially kiss my ass!

I'd like for Niko to catch her ass alone just like the Crips did Officer Hawkins who used to work here. They raped her ass so long, I know she wishes like hell she never fucked with those dudes.

Bennett better think about the fact that C.O.s can't carry weapons, aerosol restraints, or batons. All they have to rely on for help when shit hits the fan are their coworkers. And sometimes that ain't shit.

Most correctional officers around here try to maintain
safety and apply appropriate and fair rules for everyone.
They realize that they're in here ten hours a day with a
bunch of fools. They also realize the potential problem—
that the worst citizens of Virginia are being grouped together
to carry out their sentences. That's why some officers try to
make the best out of the situation. You might find some
C.O.'s who will extend your phone time or let you stay
outside on the yard a little longer. Outside recreation is like
a treat when you're locked in twenty-two hours a day. But
of course, to get a little, you've got to give a little.

When one gives you extra time when it's freezing outside,
it's truly a gift, because most C.O.s will cut your time
because they're cold. Don't get me wrong, some jerks will
mess with you for no reason. Like that damn Bennett. She
has a chip on her shoulder as soon as she hits the block.
You can see her coming with all that damn gold on lookin'
like Mr. T's little sister. And, she's guaranteed to twirl that
ring on her finger, knowing damn well nobody's gonna
marry her ass. She complains too fuckin' much to have a
man. Always complaining about her working conditions,
or not being appreciated. Her five-foot-one, chubby ass
needs to run a mile or two every day. Maybe if she stops
bringing soul food meals to work she might lose a few
pounds. She's been labeled as one of Graham's penitentiary
pets. Always bringing him fatty meals to work. Both of 'em,
fat as hell.

Bennett is conceited. I haven't the slightest idea why.
For starters, she's dead wrong for gelling down her short,
nappy-ass hair. Second, she's homely as hell and has a
Mississippi-mud complexion. And, to add insult to injury,
she's got to be 210 pounds of solid pork, all at the age of

twenty-four. She just sways her plump, full-of-lard ass around the unit, with a grim look on her round face.

Bennett tries to be hard, knowing that when shit happens, she's the first C.O. to blow the whistle. Even though I know she's a devil in disguise, I try not to fuck with her because she's real religious. It's hard to believe because she has so many negative characteristics. You know, when you think of a Christian, you think about peaceful, caring people. People who would go out on a limb to do good. People who get enjoyment out of seeing others happy!

Well, Bennett is unsympathetic, insensitive, and thoughtless. These aren't personality traits of a Christian. Not to mention, the red lipstick. What is that all about? She spreads that trashy color on her lips every day. Maybe a good man will change her ways. Bennett has only one attribute. Therefore, I can admire her for one reason and one reason only. I always see her reading her bible and studying scriptures. I can respect that, even though I can't stand her ass.

The one thing my grandmother always taught me is not to play with the Lord. As a matter of fact, I miss going to church, listening to Reverend Grey preach the word. It kept me doing the right thing, and I was always giving praise to the Lord for all the positive things going on in my life. I also miss getting up on Sunday mornings smelling salmon cakes, grits, and the buttermilk biscuits my grandmother used to cook. On the usher board during my late teens, I wore my little pendant and everybody needed my assistance. You know Grandma was proud. Now all I simply look forward to is grabbing a Snickers from the commissary.

See, I consider myself a good-natured guy, for the most part, but prison changes a person. Over time, I've started to curse, use improper grammar, and dress thuggish. It's not the person, it's the environment. But, I can admit my shortcomings—I've regressed! Grandma always said, "If you live in the jungle long enough, you're bound to start acting like the animals." She's right.

I've always been deceitful, but now I've had to learn to add skill to that deceit. Being incarcerated makes you do that. It's a game of survival. Either you make it, or you don't!

"Divine, what's up? I been waitin' on you," Niko said, in his deep baritone voice, interrupting my train of thought.

The sound of his words carried through the day room as I walked toward him. His presence stopped all nearby conversations. Noticeably, inmates moved quickly to other areas. It's typical. When he's in motion, his broad shoulders produce the most thuggish walk in Dunnridge. Not to mention the way he strides along as if nothing or no one else exists. Niko has a pointy nose, accented by moist skin. His look is almost royal until you look at his unkempt dreadlocks. Size has to be Niko's most significant feature. He's at least six-three packing 280 rock-hard pounds. He's always been tall, but since we've been in, he's gotten buffed.

People think he's on steroids because his body is ripped. His daily routine is to workout all day and put fear in the hearts of everything that moves in Dunnridge— except for me, Mathematics, and Black of course. I try to keep up with him, but I can't hang. He does over twenty reps of barbells and skull crushers on a daily basis. He needs to lean up off the chest presses. The man got bitch tits. This nigga doesn't even tremble, bench-pressing 375 pounds. Fearless! Shit, I guess if I did all that, I'd have a six pack too!

I replied, with a frown, "You better check yourself, fool. I'm taking care of these chump officers up in here."

Collecting his thoughts, Niko began to hit his fists against one another as they customarily do when he's thinking. "Man, you still mad at Bennett because she strip-searched you in front of the faggots yesterday?"

"It's not the fact that she strip-searched me, it's how she did it and who she did it in front of."

"Man, it's over. Let it go!" Niko laughed.

"Oh, you think it's funny?"

"Nah, I'm thinking about how Squzzy and Shaunte were prancing around clapping for you." Niko clapped his huge hands wildly portraying Squzzy and Shaunte.

"It's all good, 'cause I'm getting ready to turn in this grievance form. You know how things work in this here prison. All an inmate has to do is make a written accusation about a prison guard and then suddenly the officer is under investigation.

"I guess it's fucked up for the officers but it's good for me. I told you I'm the man. She'll leave me alone after she finds out her ass is under investigation. Plus, you know I added sauce to make it sound good."

"Man, you petty."

"Call me what ya like," I said in total disagreement.

Standing beside Niko smoking one of his nasty cancer sticks, Black, was intrigued by my trickery. I swear he must inhale three packs a day. We should call him Newport instead of Black. But, I guess the name Black is fitting considering he's darker than a black Magic Marker, and ugly as sin. His looks are quite deceiving though. Everybody thinks he's a cold killer. Probably, because he's bulky and rugged. Plus, when you hang with Niko, you automatically catch a ruthless reputation. But, Black isn't really like that.

Happy-go-lucky is his m.o. until it's time to rumble. He's actually one of the more laid-back ones from our crew. But don't get on his bad side. That nigga is bipolar. I mean some shit that's uncontrollable. And, nobody can calm him down.

Black rolls with us on occasion, but prefers to spend his time alone. Raised in Brooklyn, New York, he moved down here to Virginia in his early teens. He still acts like he just left New York. It helps give him his hard-nosed status around here. I mean he goes the whole nine, from the gold tooth to the accent and the northern slang. He's a good dude though. I'm glad I've got him in my corner.

"What's up, dogs?" Mathematics asked, walking up on the conversation.

Black slapped his hand. "Whaz'up, kid?"

Niko balled up his two fists, wrapped his arms around Mathematics and patted him on the back.

Mathematics and I showed each other brotherly love with some dap.

"Mathematics, you looking real slick today," Niko said, shaking his head up and down. "Yeah, I used to be like that, but I grew outta that shit. Everything I had on had to be top notch. Now, I don't have a reason to look good."

"For yourself," Mathematics said, positioning himself as if he were posing for a *G.Q.* photo shoot.

"Man, who am I gonna impress? The four cement walls

in my cell? Or let me guess, that nice-looking toilet in the corner of my room."

Everyone got silent for a moment. Where was Niko going with all of this? Finally he laughed just a little, giving us the okay to laugh too.

"Divine, you remember when we used to wake up in the morning tryna decide what expensive shit we were gonna buy for that day? It wasn't nothing for us to go out and spend ten to twenty thousand on some bullshit!"

"Damn," Black said.

"Ooh," I said, grinning, "remember those honeys we met down Virginia Beach?"

Niko slapped my hand as hard as he could. "Yeah, that worked out well."

"They didn't have anywhere to stay, so we did our civil duty, and let 'em stay with us." A woody rose in my pants just from the thought of a woman. *Sad!*

Everybody laughed, until Squzzy's flat feet hit the exterior of our circle. He, she, it—or whatever you want to call him—was parading around our crew, leaning back slightly, stretching out one foot at a time. Slinging one foot in front of the other slowly. He walked like a diva, switching so hard that I'm sure he'll need a hip replacement by the time he's thirty.

In his squeaky, high-pitched girlish tone, he said, "What the fuck do y'all niggas have now! Y'all always talking 'bout what you use to have. Where is the shit now?"

Seeing Niko raise up on his tiptoes meant trouble. With his eyes turning blood-shot red, I silently hoped for a positive outcome for Squzzy. Meanwhile Squzzy enjoyed the media.

Obviously upset, Niko shouted, "Fuck you!"

"When?"

Shaunte, formerly known as Shaun, Squzzy's loyal flaming friend and confidant, decided to cheer Squzzy on at this point. Wearing fitted jeans that seemed to say, "Help, I can't breathe," Shaunte took center stage. Twisting his body up and down the floor, snaps were heard all around the room. Chants and cheers celebrating Squzzy echoed throughout.

We all laughed except Mathematics. Niko just shook his head. This was the one and only battle I've ever seen him back down from. Squzzy does this kind of shit all the time. His appetite for attention goes way beyond that of a woman possessing a Weight Watchers membership. Just look at those skintight floral pink pants. They look like they've been painted on his petite body and will split in the seams if he tries to sit down.

"Yo, Scuz, why your lips always so damn shiny? Lay off the gloss," Black said with a grin.

Rubbing his well-manicured finger in slow circles around his mouth and swinging his braids, Squzzy smacked his puckers and responded, "First of all these lips are listed as a deadly weapon."

"Man, get your ass outta here."

"Second, why are you all of a sudden calling me Scuz? You didn't say that last night!"

Black held his palms out with an "I don't understand" look. Empathy quickly changed to anger.

We were laughing hysterically!

That's why I don't want to get on the wrong side of a faggot. They will spread lies about you and think nothing of it. And, I know how Squzzy can get. At this point, he knew Black was pissed, so he ended a winner, and made a flavorful exit. He and his sidekick Shaunte started kicking up their legs, singing "Fox-ay Shaun-tay Fox-ay Squz-ay."

By the time Squzzy's heels made their last click, Niko and I had been thoroughly entertained. Black no longer had the desire to smoke, which was rare. Conversation was limited. I could tell by Black's newly humbled attitude that he didn't know if we believed Squzzy. But, that's how faggots operate.

Now Mathematics, inmate #926104, never said one word the whole time Squzzy was around. He just moved back and watched him perform. The sight of a man posing as a woman fills him with disgust. And just think, Dunnridge has a whole crew of men acting and looking just like women.

Mathematics is smart, eccentric, low-key and has an I-don't-give-a-damn attitude. He's one of those pretty boys I would normally despise if we weren't cool. With light-brown skin he carries himself as if he were being watched at all times. Highly observant and slow to move, he makes you feel like an idiot. You would think he plays for the Knicks or the Bulls the way he towers over everyone, but we know that's not true. You could tell he lifted weights, yet he wasn't a big brute like Niko. Of average weight, Mathematics stands about six feet six inches. He's next to perfect. His fine black hair really sets off the look. He even looks good with that prison-made black do-rag on his head.

Don't think I'm gay or no shit like that. And, don't think I'm saying he looks scrumptious just because I've been in here for nearly five years 'cause you know, to some of these guys Jeffrey Dahmer started looking good after a year of not getting any from a woman. Hell, some of these nuts felt like that after a couple of weeks. Anyway, the do-rag makes Mathematics look good. He wears that thing all the time—except when he gets visits. And he definitely gets more visits than anybody on Block C. Sometimes I get jealous, but then I stop and think, that man got ninety-nine years.

Mathematics fell under the three strikes, you're out law. If you're convicted three times for the same type of offense, then you'll probably spend the rest of your life in prison.

From what he told me, he would've been straight if he hadn't been greedy. Mathematics had it all planned. During his twenties, he was making major paper on the strip by Chesapeake Street. Now this is one person who knows how to make money. How do you think he got the name Mathematics?

He was one of the lucky few who had a Colombian connection out of Florida. They were fronting him fifteen keys a week! Mathematics never had to give up a dime until he sold all his shit from the previous week. He was making loot! Chesapeake was locked, and Mathematics was the major supplier for the entire area. Just think, he was getting each kilo of cocaine for eleven thousand dollars. He then turned around and sold it for nineteen thousand dollars. Talk about monthly income! You do the math, as Mathematics would say.

The man had it all, well what any uneducated person might think is everything. He had fly women, clothes, cars, a laid house, and loads of money. Tashonda, his baby's mama, knew how to spend that money. She hooked their house up with all that fancy Italian furniture, imported marble floors, and limited art editions. Oh, for those of you who don't know what that is—it's when an artist paints a limited amount of a particular painting (such as one hundred) and they are numbered 1/100, 2/200, etc. Tashonda definitely didn't know how to buy art. She was simply a pro at spending money. She bought top-of-the-line everything. If a new T.V. was out, they had it. A new car, they were driving it. Appliances, household furnishings, you name it, they had it. As far as he was concerned, Mathematics was on top of the world.

Mathematics was the sole provider for his whole family. Nobody worked, they just sat around plotting on different ways to ask him for money. They would ask for anything from a Happy Meal at McDonald's to a presidential Rolex. Everyone seemed to think they deserved some dough because he was making it, especially his brothers. Every other week they had a dilemma or a situation. Just another reason to ask for money. You know shit is fucked up when they got to ask him for five dollars to fill up their tanks. They depended on him to get all of their needs and wants. I mean everything. To this day they still don't have a damn job or any desire to go to college. I guess Mathematics was making so much money that it didn't occur to him that his family lacked intelligence and the desire to work.

Being a whiz with money didn't keep him from getting caught in the game. He'd been locked up twice before. Both times for drug-related charges. The first time he actually got caught, he had a kilo of cocaine in his backpack and still said it wasn't his. He served four years.

The second time he got off easy. His high-profile lawyer got his A-1 felony—a crime that carries a substantial amount of years—reduced to a class E felony, in which a shorter sentence is given. He must have gotten his law degree from some fancy ivy-league school. Mathematics refused to plead guilty to that charge at first, until the guy transporting the drugs for him started breaking down and telling everything on the stand. Mathematics' lawyer advised him to plea-bargain for a two-year bid. I would think that after being locked up for six years of his life, he would stop dealing.

Greed was his closest friend. You know he had enough money to live off for the rest of his life even if he never worked again. Hell, he's been hustling since he was twelve. He started off as a lookout for the older guys in is neighborhood. He eventually moved up to becoming a runner. He was so smooth as a child he ended up getting his own strip locked down by the time he was seventeen. Word has it that he has more than a million dollars buried underground somewhere but I don't know how true that is. Don't get me wrong, Mathematics and I are real tight but he would never tell me no shit like that. I'd send my grandmother with her wooden shovel to dig that shit up! And Mathematics knows it! I guess that's why he doesn't discuss it. I don't even think Tashonda knows about it, if it's even true. Anyway, his plan was to get two million stashed away and then get outta the game for good.

Why wasn't one million good enough? That's the problem with most Black people making illegal money. That shit keeps calling you until your ass gets caught. You feel like you can't do without, or you have to live a certain lifestyle. I've got to give it to Mathematics, he tried.

As time went on he stopped splurging on the finer things in life, which nearly killed him. He said he put himself on a budget, which practically destroyed

Tashonda. And check this out—his two brothers stopped speaking to him. Despite all the living demons trying to keep him spending so he would have to keep hustling, Mathematics told me, he saved, saved, and saved.

Unfortunately for him he couldn't rid the demons fast enough. One summer night, he was driving one of his favorite cars, his black 500 series Mercedes Benz, which was sitting on a set of phat rims of course. With the windows tinted, and the sounds of Tupac blasting, Mathematics barely noticed 5-0 rolling up on him from all corners. He was cool, calm, and collected because he was ridin' free. He never rode dirty. Hell, he said he even turned the music up louder and was bobbing his head as if everything was all right.

The police cornered him from all angles, surrounding his car. He wasn't even fazed by the fact that the police had drawn their guns saying, "Get the fuck out the car now! And place your hands on the front hood, now!" Mathematics said he got out the car slowly and lackadaisically placed his hands high above his side ignoring the instructions on purpose. The officers pushed him on the ground facedown with his hands behind his head. The only thing Mathematics kept saying was, "You're making a big mistake."

Well, what he didn't know was that his cousin Drake— a small-time dealer who worked for him—had gotten caught earlier that night. Scared stiff, Drake sang like a bird, telling about Mathematics' entire million-dollar operation. Mathematics later found out that Drake had been threatened with king pen drug charges and tons of conspiracy charges. He was so scared, he told everything from who Mathematics' supplier was to how much cocaine he bought on a weekly basis. The narcotics officers knew exactly where to find Mathematics' stash and immediately went looking for him. Now, everyone makes mistakes, but had it been me, I would have made enough money to buy my own business and stopped selling that shit.

Immediately, Mathematics was locked up, denied bail, and was well on his way to serving ninety-nine years under the three strikes, you're out law. Just think about it, he's thirty years old, and spending the rest of his life in Dunnridge. By the way, Drake, being a first-time offender, got off on probation.

3   Desperation

In the cold, dark quiet, moaning and groaning comes from the next cell. The sounds repeat in my ears over and over. If I didn't know Niko, I would never believe he would be banging another guy in the ass! How disgusting is that? I mean Niko's latest prison girlfriend isn't even attractive. As a matter of fact, Deuce has dreadlocks just like Niko and barely resembles a girl. The shit is actually scary with his muscular build, although not as defined as Niko's. Deuce is sad. He's got a bad case of bitchitis; Trailing behind Niko like a hen-pecked husband. With his lightly tan blotchy skin he sports blemishes from his cheeks to his chin. He carries a set of deep baggy eyes, which makes him look like he hasn't slept in days. Plus, his walk disturbs me, all hunched over like the Hunchback of Notre Dame.

Now things can't be perfect around here. But I can't fight off the hatred in my heart for oversized men wanting to get fucked in the ass. I can sorta sympathize for the scrawny, puny fellas who don't have a choice. But Deuce is simply sickening.

What's really nasty is the fact that the dreadlock duo hates rubbers! You can buy a condom for about two dollars from the inmates sneaking them in here. When all else fails use the traditional rubber glove. That's some wild shit, when you put a glove over your dick just because you can't afford a condom. But anything goes in the Dungeon. Rubber gloves are customary. The crazy part is Niko can afford and has the connections to get anything he needs. He gets so much respect around here he could have anyone he wants.

A lot of these young punks are just waiting to get with him. I guess they know they would be taken care of— financially and physically.

I've seen some of these crazy fuckers acting like they married and shit. Whoever is doing the fucking is also spending the money and doing the protecting. It's like being somebody's husband—buying food and toiletries from the commissary or merely getting shit from the outside. I guess that's why Niko plays the role well. He had more than six hundred thousand dollars taken from him after he got arrested. All of his accounts were frozen and seized. That shit was devastating, but he still managed to have quite a bit of paper left. Sneaky devil!

Niko got about four punks with their eyes on him now. I don't think he wants them because they've been passed around a little too much. You know—used and abused. Like Squzzy and Shaunte, nobody wants them. So why Deuce? Someone who bullies people around just as much as he does? Maybe he settles for him because they're cellmates. If that's the case, I'm glad I got a cell to myself.

Niko can get any fresh meat that comes in this block. Like that kid Flip from Raleigh, North Carolina. Flip was nineteen when he came here, doing time for his first offense on a nonviolent crime. A small, frail thing. Shit, one hundred and thirty pounds probably exaggerates his weight. He was the smallest dude we've had on our block in a while. I'm sure for Niko that was like taking candy from a baby. Some homosexuality in here is voluntary, but Flip was forced into it. When he first came here everybody knew someone would get him. He looked like he was made from papier-mâché, and his voice was way too meek for prison.

Flip had some basic problems from a few of the inmates when he first got here. Nothing major, just a few people trying to chump him. He was passive, so Niko decided to look out for him.

After the first couple of weeks, I guess Flip thought he had Niko's protection. Niko showed him the ropes, and Flip began to trust him. Many of the other strong salad tossers had their eye on Flip, too, but knew he was becoming a servant for Niko. He was running his errands around the prison and stuck by him like Krazy Glue. Soon Flip was performing all the wifely tasks of being in prison, such as laundry and cleaning. I knew he'd flipped when I saw him washing Niko's drawers. I just wish he had realized it. Eventually Flip was a sex slave for Niko, and nobody did a damn thing to help him. During his first couple of weeks in the block, he didn't make friends with anyone but Niko, and gave the C.O.s a hard time just like Niko. Flip went from stealing cars to being a faggot.

What was he supposed to do? Take the abuse and torture from Niko or suffer multiple gang rapes once Niko became his enemy. I guess he could have told the C.O.s, but who wants to risk being labeled a prison snitch. Snitches get stitches. The C.O.s wouldn't have been able to protect him anyway. Don't ever let anyone tell you anything different from what I'm about to tell you: Accountability around here for C.O.s is nonexistent. But Warden Weaver would have their asses for an escape on their shift.

Hell, some guards overlook prison rape on purpose. They see it as society giving inmates the punishment they deserve. Some are weak and afraid to approach the powerful inmates inflicting the pain and some just don't give a damn. I've seen it all before. I've witnessed correctional officers laughing directly in a prisoner's face, especially younger inmates. Some guys are able to escape all of this drama by buying the C.O.s or an inmate's protection. I just wish Flip had bought his protection with money and not his body.

He could've snitched on Niko, however, the only thing that would've happened was for the incident to be treated as a crime. Niko would've been charged for rape, had his security level raised, and given a longer sentence.

Once Flip told his family about his homosexual relation-ship with Niko, they were opposed to pressing charges. The myth is that once you have to spend a major portion of your life in prison, extra time doesn't make a difference. He was lucky his family was one of the few able to pull some strings to get him transferred.

Flip's sentence was for three years. Although he was moved to serve it on another block, he still served it as a homosexual. Rumor has it that Flip tried to get into protective custody, but was denied several times. Nobody took him seriously because of his intense buddy-buddy relationship with Niko at the beginning of his sentence.

It's quite typical for young boys to enter this block

as heterosexual criminal offenders and leave with the experience of forced or voluntary homosexuality.

8——*

I always thought that when two guys have an intimate relationship, one portrays the female and the other, the hard-core male. In this case, Niko and Deuce have a masculine physique. I mean, how could a man get an erection and force himself inside another man's ass? That shit is mentally ill.

It's just a shame that Niko is going out like that with a man. If he weren't my main man, I'd be calling him a faggot by now. But, that's my dog and I'd whip anybody's ass if I heard them calling him faggot. It's not right to judge people but I don't condone that gay bullshit. In my opinion if you stick what God gave you as a man into another man's ass then you had homosexual tendencies all along. You got to be desperate to go to that extreme.

Now don't get me wrong, it's not just Niko doing this shit. Most of the men around here will take advantage of any opportunity to fuck someone. It happens all the time. But most people are afraid to let anyone know they are digging up in a man.

Niko don't give a fuck about what people think about him. He openly stands up for Deuce. He once approached Carlos for fondling Deuce. I guess Carlos never thought he would tell. Niko came up to him in the mess hall one day. Now Carlos is no slouch. Not to mention he's down with the Bloods. With his medium height and muscular build, he sat with his boys at a "Bloods Only" bench. The color red brightly stood out throughout the long bench-style table.

The mess hall swarmed with inmates. Some ate peacefully; some were getting their food taken.

Carlos was in the process of jacking somebody's dessert and dared his victim to say no. When our crew stepped foot in the door, as usual, Carlos' boyz surrounded him like the secret service guards the president. By the troubled looks on their faces Carlos jumped up, ready for whatever kicked off. His crew stood right behind him. Like men ready for battle, we positioned ourselves directly behind Niko.

Even though Niko is the man, Carlos knew he needed to stand up for himself if he planned on continuing his membership with the Bloods. He had a reputation to uphold for his crew, just like Niko did.

We had some arsenal ready that Niko had made in metal shop, but decided not to use it. Way too many eyes and ears surrounded us. With me, Mathematics, and Black behind him, Niko got up real close in Carlos' face. Carlos planted himself firmly in one spot. If his eyes could talk, I'm sure they'd say "fuck you." Studying Niko like bacteria under a microscope, Carlos never lost eye contact. The C.O.s headed our way and we all disassembled as if nothing had happened.

We were all questioned individually, but no one said anything. Not even Carlos. Everybody knew Niko was just protecting his property. I didn't think we should have put ourselves out there for Deuce. The situation could have gone down differently.

Thankfully nothing happened. Deuce is simply not worth it! Hopefully Niko will leave him alone soon. He would be better off paying one of the lady C.O.s to give him a little piece of ass, rather than bone a man. They fake like they're not down with that shit but Mathematics told me plenty of stories about the sex he gets from the ladies around here. Some of these bitches are in love with his ass. And, they're cute too! He's got this one babe who has been meeting him in remote areas on the regular. Obviously, she can't get enough.

I asked Mathematics the formula. He tried to be debonair as usual. He said, "You got to learn how to treat 'em." My expression proved that my question went unanswered. Mathematics said, "School's out! In time, son, in time."

His secret is worth the wait, but I'm not fucking with these C.O.s. I'll leave that for him.

If Niko doesn't want to deal with C.O.s instead of Deuce when he gets horny and desperate, he could at least bang some cardboard pussy instead of a masculine ass hole. Cardboard pussy is the best there is in prison. It's easier than trying to find a partner who is willing or simply settling for punk booty. Finding the right spot, or paying a guard to pretend they hear no evil, see no evil is not worth it. With this method, it's just you, your dick, and your cardboard pussy.

So I lie here thinking about Sherese and listening to those exotic sounds next door that are driving me crazy. I started caressing my shit, and knew it was time to prepare my cardboard pussy. First, I set the tone by tuning in to the quiet storm on my Walkman. They throw it down on Tuesday nights!

Yes!

They are playing: "Let Me Make Love to You" by the O'Jays! I started singing *"I won't hurt, I won't hurt, I'll treat you ever so gentle."*

I positioned myself on my bunk, while yanking my pants off as quickly as I could. My nakedness sparked thoughts of missing Sherese's touch of intimacy even more. Oh, how I wish I could be with my baby right now! I would give anything to feel her hands rubbing all over my body. Ahh. . . and massaging me in all the right places! Her kisses are so gentle and wet, just like her pussy.

I can no longer hear Niko, but I know exactly how I'm feeling at this point. I've got a burning desire for my baby right now! I've got to have her. So I take out a picture of Sherese and pull out the round, brown cardboard object that came from the middle of the toilet tissue roll that is hidden inside my mattress. My willie starts to get excited as I stuff the cardboard object with small pieces of toilet tissue. I form the tissue perfectly as if carving a sculpture. Carefully, I place just enough tissue to fill the inside of the hole. This makes it nice and soft inside. My willie starts quivering just thinking about the texture inside my cardboard pussy. Every now and then, I look over at Sherese's picture and tongue-kiss her.

Soon I'm ready for the final touch. I spread vaseline inside the cardboard, all over the tissue, until it covers all the space inside the cardboard object. The vaseline insures me a smooth and slippery feeling. It's almost as good as the real thing. Of course, not as good as Sherese.

Well, time to get my swerve on. As I ease my dick inside the cardboard pussy, it feels like a warm woman's body. I am panting and making passionate love. The hole is a little tight because I'm blessed with a fat one, ten inches long to be exact. My temperature starts to rise while my veins welcome the warmth of the blood taking over my willie. I have an orgasm within seconds!

Sensations are felt all over my body. As I exhale with relief and satisfaction, C.O. Bennett abruptly starts banging on my cell with her walkie-talkie, interrupting my shit.

She looks me directly in my face and says, "Get up and clean your nasty ass. If you weren't such a scumbag you would be on the street able to be with a woman."

"Fuck you," I respond, trying to start trouble to keep the attention off Niko in the next cell. I'd rather her harass me because I finished my business. But Niko is probably still going at it. "Why can't you let a man handle his business. I ain't bothering you or asking you to satisfy my needs."

"You need to repent."

"And what do you need to do, Ms. Perfect?"

"You're on your way to hell on a skateboard," Bennett says, looking at me with disgust as she starts moving slowly east toward Niko's cell.

I watch her closely as she slows down for a moment, looking directly into his cell. Her eyes get big, and her eyebrows crinkle just a little. Maybe Niko has finished, or maybe she is too embarrassed to say anything.

As suspect as it may seem, she keeps on walking not saying a damn thing to Niko. With a confused look, tongue-tied even, her anger could cut wood. The smoke seeping through her horns could not be hid as she walked away. But still in awe, she didn't say anything. Why in the hell doesn't she just look in my cell and keep moving?

No, she had to stop and fucking chat awhile. She's a bitch. What kills me is the fact that she's Dunnridge's Dr. Jekyll/ Mr. Hyde. One minute she's praying, and in the next second, she's cursing like a sailor. I've heard she has some deeply rooted issues. Rumor has it, a couple of years ago she caught her ex-boyfriend in bed with her best friend. That thing must have devastated her. Since that time she's not sure who she wants to be.

One good thing came out of her betrayal. She got saved! You would think she would've become a better person by now. Instead, she reads the scriptures, but doesn't apply them.

I have mixed feelings about Bennett. Sometimes I think she might have some hidden hatred for men just because of what her ex has done to her. Then at other times, her spiritual light shines through.

I've seen her give toiletries and clothing to inmates who don't have any family or support from the outside. Once she was on duty during church service and said a prayer for the inmates, which put tears in the eyes of everyone in the room.

Even though she has two personalities, what really puzzles me is why she let Niko off so easy. Maybe she's scared of him, or maybe Niko paid her to ignore his sexual escapades. I'm gonna ask Niko about that shit tomorrow.

Right now I need to write Sherese and Grandma a letter before I go to sleep. I miss my two favorite girls so bad. One of them needs to send me some loot right away so I can maintain in here. Grandma knows I'm not supposed to be in here so it devastates her to see me like this. I feel bad asking her for money, because she's still spending all of her retirement checks on expensive lawyers. She's trying to find any loophole there is to get me out. But hell, deodorant and hygiene supplies are on the low side, and my cigarette stash has seen better days. I need my cigarettes bad, not to smoke of course. You never know when they might come in handy.

4

The Rumble

The banging of steel bars at 7:00 A.M. indicates that a count is about to begin. That's when everybody has to line up outside his cell and be counted just like they do in fucking kindergarten. The C.O.s want to make sure nobody got lost in the middle of the night or died on their shift. This is some serious shit because every inmate has to be accounted for.

As Niko stood there I didn't give him a sign that we needed to talk. The count took extra long because some chicken head decided he didn't want to get out of the bed, so the count wasn't right. I felt bad for the dude. He picked a bad time to pull this shit. C.O. Warren headed the count. He was known to open up a can of whoop-ass, for those who needed it. Especially when someone interfered with his normal, restful routine.

Warren is famous for acting like he's too superior for petty incidents. He's been trying to get promoted for the past ten years, and most of the time acts like he's already an administrator. His frustration is evident when he feels the need to flex his authority. But still in all, his experience, has gotten him nowhere. He's being prostituted and doesn't even know it. Lieutenant Graham only calls on him to handle extreme cases. And that shit don't work either 'cause Warren goes too far when dealing with minor incidents.

Stepping into the short white man's cell, Warren tossed him up against the wall like a rag doll. I knew things would escalate. He commenced to whipping his ass like he stole something. Warren yelled, "Didn't I tell you to stop fuckin' with my count?" His baldhead was pressed so deep in the inmate's chest, dude gasped for air.

"Man, why you tripin' on like me like that?" he cried.

"Stop crying like a pussy."

"Damn, man, my bad. Would you just stop whipping my ass?"

"Get up. I run shit around here," Warren said.

Before that dude could move, Warren dragged him out and pressed his face to the ground with his shoe. He took him straight to solitary confinement. He'll probably whip his ass a couple of times on the way there. That mother-fucker looked like a fool in front of everybody. I guess we won't be seeing him for a couple of weeks. C.O. Warren ain't to be fucked with.

"Count's clear," said C.O. Bennett.

I'm glad that bitch's shift ends in a few minutes. I started toward Niko's cell. By the time I arrived, he was gone! It bothered me all night that Bennett overlooked what he was doing with Deuce. Did he pay her, and if so, how much? I can't even imagine her taking money considering she's always concerned about doing what's right. Miss God is Good All the Time. I can't stand a hypocrite. Point blank, I want the same privileges Niko gets. After all, we're friends for life. I'm his right-hand man and he's mine.

About forty minutes had gone by before I gave up looking for him. I checked the mess hall, the showers, and the yard. No need to scope the library because reading is like kryptonite to Niko. Can he even read? Where could he be? This shit was puzzling and starting to frustrate me. It's not like he stepped out for a moment or rolled down to the corner store.

I patiently waited in the rec area. He had to come through at some point. I stood by the stairs, lost in thought, when I noticed Bradberry saluting some fellas.

You'd think he got his papers straight. His overwhelming excitement perplexed me. As he strolled in my direction his face shone with a smile as wide as Bennett's ass. His extended hand was met with the rhythmic words, "Divine, it's been real, man." His baritone voice forced me to freeze in thought. It took a minute for his words to register.

I asked, "What do you mean?"

"I'm outta here."

So his lawyer did get his papers right?

"When you get out, check me, Divine."

"Bet."

"I'll leave you my info," Bradberry said.

"Sho 'nuf. Protect yourself, dog. The streets are dirty!"

"I ain't comin' back this way," Bradberry said. "Even if it means I gotta sweep streets."

We embraced like frat brothers. I can't deny, I was jealous as hell. I could've won an Oscar for the way I pretended to be happy for the brotha. It should be *me* who's leaving. He committed a violent crime. I didn't.

Moments later, I saw Mathematics coming my way, sort of pimping and swaying all together. He was cool like that.

Equality, an arrogant inmate from Richmond, yelled out to him, "Aye, you got me."

Mathematics turned slightly as if he were trying to see who Equality was talking to. All along, he knew he was speaking directly to him.

"You got yourself, player," Mathematics said as he kept walking.

You see he's like a razor, too sharp, you'll never catch him wheeling and dealing out in the open.

"Man, what's up?" Equality said, with his hands spread above his shoulders.

Mathematics just kept on walking toward me. This gigantic, hairy, monster-looking dude grabbed me by my neck. His cartoon character muscles sent chills through my spine. What the hell is going on? I had done a lot of cruddy shit to people since I'd been in, but I had never had any problems with Crazy Ed. What was he fucking with me for? Looking like the Incredible Hulk on crack. I'm not even his equal. The only advantage I've got over this nigga, is that my legs are even.

The force of his blow caused us both to hit the concrete. We rumbled and rolled, me on top of him, then him on top of me. Boos and cheers bellowed from the spectators. At that point I had to make a power move. I tried to pull a Mike Tyson and bite his damn ear off. Once Ed realized I was going for the obvious, he pulled a move on me like a professional wrestler. Next thing I knew, I was in a head-lock. He cuffed my head under his right arm. While hovering under the funk, I spotted the craziest tattoo I'd ever seen. It sat dead in the middle of his shoulder. Who would wear a man with a chainsaw chopping someone's head off? A psycho!

Man, don't let him have a shank! This joker wants to
kill me! My shit got taken in the last shakedown so all I
could do is try to stay alive. I saw a couple of guards out of
the corner of my eye. By the looks of it, the lady C.O.s are
just as scared as I am. While I was taking a beating like
Rodney King, they waited for backup. My arms served as
a shield protecting me from Big McNasty's blows. I needed to do some real damage to this dude. My reputation was
at stake. People respect me because I roll with Niko. This
greasy, crazy motherfucker is making it hard for me to
handle mine.

By now everyone was on the scene. At least twelve
officers stood and made no attempt to break this shit up!
Black's shiny gold tooth caught my attention. Kneeling on
one knee he watched everybody else. He paid no attention
to me at all. I guess he was making sure I didn't get
jumped. Mathematics stood outside the perimeter of the
circle. Chewing in slow motion, he looked like he didn't
have a worry in the world. If some deadly shit started to
happen, he'd look out for me, I'm sure.

All the guys in the area started standing on chairs,
chanting for their favorite fighter. This is probably the closest
they'd get to a Pay-Per-View fight. Some made cigarette
bets, while others watched for mere entertainment. Odds
favored me to win, I'm sure.

"Represent Divine," a Niko wanna-be yelled while
cracking his knuckles.

"Yeah, right. Crazy Ed is whipping that ass," another
inmate shouted from the crowd.

Ignoring the chants and comments, I continued to
stand my ground. I'd like to think of myself as tough, but
this guy was not letting up at all. His eyes had a ferocious

look that would kill me even if he didn't.

About five minutes passed before officers broke up the fight. A few people lingered, but most rolled out. Blood covered my face and clothes, and a stinging sensation seared my body. "Let's go to the infirmary," a manly lady C.O. ordered, walking up to check the damage. Besides the bumps on my head and the bruises that would show up by morning, I should be okay. I declined.

"I'm okay," I said.

"Now, I'm not gonna press you. It's your life!"

"I'm straight," I said with bass in my voice.

Looking down I noticed my shirt was ripped and the watch Sherese sent me was gone! At that moment, I contemplated my decision. Maybe I should get checked out. Naw, I thought. No one will ever get a chance to say I was laid up.

All of this could have been avoided. Why didn't I get help sooner? Maybe the officers took their time because the shift ended at 8:00 A.M. and it was now 7:45. Or maybe they were just worthless-ass C.O.s. I'm sitting here getting my ass kicked and they take their sweet time stopping this shit. I'm a lover not a fighter.

Well, at least they didn't put me in lockdown. Once, C.O. Warren arrived on the scene, he let both of us go without punishment—a gift in disguise. He probably just wanted to go home. It's my lucky day!

Warren started yelling like a drill sergeant, "Move it! It's over!"

Niko burst through the crowd roaring like a beast.

"What the fuck is up! You must be out your fuckin' mind. As a matter of fact, you might as well consider yourself dead!"

Ed was completely silent. His face spoke the words *but I'm tryna help you.*

Niko just wouldn't stop talking shit. He kept patting at his broad chest real hard while moving his head up and down. "Nigga, this is the street with walls. You better recognize quick!"

Ed stood there speechless. Niko stepped close enough; Ed could smell Deuce all over Niko's breath.

"You've just fucked yourself, dog," Niko said.

Spit landed on the tip of Ed's nose.

"Man, you don't understand," Ed pleaded.

Niko rose on his toes. Ed knew what was up.

Ed stepped back, "It's squashed," he said, giving Niko five feet.

Meanwhile, Black was circling the outskirts, chanting. "Y'all don't want none of this. Y'all don't want none of the boogie down Bronx. Y'all don't wanna see me!"

Ed's crew responded, "Punks jump up to get beat down."

"What?"

"Yeah, what?"

Mathematics approached Black to whisper in his ear.

Black's frown turned into a sinister grin. Together they turned in their rival's direction. After a hard-core nod, Black ended with, "Country-ass bammas!"

Mathematics started to pull Niko and Black away from the confusion moving closer toward me. Bennett walked in shortly after, asking what had happened.

C.O. Warren started to tell her and stopped abruptly to ask, "Where were you?"

"I was in the powder room," she said.

"Oh, right when it's time to go. Can't you piss when

you get home?" Warren asked sarcastically.

Bennett looked at Warren and shook her gelled head, which looked like she ironed it this morning. "I've got to start sending out résumés! Anytime you can't use the bathroom in peace, I know it's time for me to move on."

"Yeah, right. You love it here. You get all the special privileges."

"What?" Bennett said.

"Just think, none of the other female C.O.s get to wear lipstick and fancy earrings. They'll get written up. But you, nooooo. You have no need to worry."

"Prayer, it works!"

"I'm gone. I'll let the next shift put the rest of these fools in order," Warren said as he picked up his jacket.

"Good teamwork!" she said, smirking.

Warren sauntered away. Bennett soon followed him out with one of her usual disgusting looks.

Even though I was bleeding and messed up badly, I had to ask Niko about last night. I felt like limping away, but everyone would be watching. I acted as though everything was normal and working well. On the real, my body was aching like shit! If the fight hadn't gotten broken up, I would have been in deep shit. But, I'll never admit that to anyone. Not even Niko.

"Niko, did you see Bennett looking in your cell last night?"

"Yeah," Niko responded with hunched shoulders.

"Well, What happened?" I asked.

Niko turned slightly. "That nosy bitch looked in and gave me a nasty look but she didn't say nothin'."

"Dog, I saw that shit, that's why I was anxious to talk to you. I thought you paid her to overlook your sexual activities," I said as we took a few steps forward.

"Man, she tiptoed by and gave me a nasty look because she's jealous," Niko said, snickering.

"Jealous? I don't see why she would be jealous. You're not her type."

Grabbing his jewels, he said "That's what you think. She's sweating me hard. Where do you think she and I were while you were getting your ass whipped?"

I frowned. My boy degraded me. He had no idea he had just killed my self-confidence. "Man, I was trying not to catch a charge right in front of all those witnesses. In a more secluded area, you know I would have shanked his ass with the quickness."

Niko turned in the other direction as if to say, "Whatever, nigga, you just got punked."

Embarrassment forced me to switch the subject back to Bennett. "Oh, so you tellin' me you hit that?" Niko's lip dropped.

"Naw, I'm cool!" We both laughed.

Niko continued his story about Bennett. "She said she was pissed off last night because it hurt her to see me inside of Deuce. Plus, she does a lot for me in here."

"Like what? You holdin' out?"

"Naw. Lately she's been bringing me all this shit up in here that I normally can't get. How do you think I got that vaseline that I gave you? And this morning she gave me some fish that she cooked yesterday. That croaker was good!"

Mathematics was just looking and smiling. He had ignored our entire conversation. Now all of a sudden, we're speaking his language, and he wants to add his two cents. I guess the ladies have that effect on him.

"That small stuff doesn't even compare to the things I get from these C.O.s," Mathematics said in an arrogant tone.

His comment made me think about the undercover cell phone he's got in here. I started thinking back to last week when White Boy Jimmy wanted to use the phones. All day motherfuckers kept treating him like shit. Jimmy simply wanted to use the phone to call his lawyer. He kept saying, "All I need is five minutes to tidy up some business with my lawyer." But, every time he was next to make a call, someone would walk up and tell the person on the phone, "Oh! Don't forget I got next," or "star, remember you owe me," or slap hands with the person while passing them cigarettes as payment to be next. Jimmy patiently waited, afraid to speak up. If I was cool wit' 'em I would've made a way to give him next, but I got tired of watching that bullshit and went back to my cell. Eventually everyone thought Jimmy had given up because he wasn't out in the lounge waiting on the phones anymore. The joke in the mess hall was "let my little Jimmy make a call—pleaseeeeeee."

Later that night Jimmy took all the jacks (headsets) and phone cords. No one knew he had even done it. He laid low while things were in a tizy. The inmates went crazy like in a bull-fighting stampede. As he read one of his porn magazines, he heard the men shout, "I need to use the horn!"

"Who did this dumb shit?"

Another shouted, "I'm gonna kill the motherfucker who did this!"

Inmates were throwing shit, banging on the walls, and acting like lunatics. This one guy said, "Someone is playing with my livelihood." This idiot would continue to make collect calls from the phone book until some vulnerable old lady would accept. I guess he would eventually swindle money from them. One guy kicked the wall and threw a temper tantrum.

Warlike voices boomed all over the block. Somebody squealed to a C.O., but none of 'em cared. I bet if they were looking for a weapon there would have been a unit search. Nobody even suspected Jimmy because he was typically peaceful. A quiet guy who kept to himself most of the time was serving a ten-year bid for real-estate fraud. Prison is no place for those type of people. If I were Jimmy I would've said, "I'm in here for murder!" Then you get respect.

As the evening approached, Jimmy came out of his cell with all the parts swinging back and forth over his arms.

"The next time I need to use the fuckin' phone, show a little respect. How in the hell am I supposed to use the phone if y'all keep putting your damn buddies in front of me? Well, y'all didn't think that shit was so funny when nobody was able to use the phone today. Sounding like a bunch of babies. I just need the damn phone, pleaseeeeeeeeee."

Jimmy threw the phone cords down in the center of the floor. I told Mathematics to go ahead because I knew that earlier in the day he had an important call to make. Mathematics pulled a cell phone out that I knew wasn't his.

He said, "It's a loaner," and laughed.

I'm assuming that had something to do with the connections he referred to earlier. When I think about it, I never see Mathematics on the pay phones. This nigga got wireless access and gets plenty of visits. Damn, he's the envy of all men.

Jimmy got stabbed up about an hour after he returned the phone cords. He lived but there wasn't a damn thing the officers could do to help him. Just like when the C.O.s told the phone-starving inmates, "Nothing can be done about finding the phone cords." That's how it is in the Dungeon.

5

Looking Good

Mathematics got dressed for his usual Wednesday morning visit. Everything had to be perfect. I watched him carefully clip his toenails, nails, and remove his homemade do-rag. Not a stitch of hair was out of place, leaving no room for brushing. That's what happens when you have a good grain. Because this nigga is so pressed about what he wears, choosing his gear is like solving a damn chemistry problem. Even though our dress code is strict, Dunnridge will at least let us receive approved items. We can't wear navy or black. These colors are too close to the C.O. uniforms.

Tashonda had sent him all new gear in his quarterly package. He couldn't decide between the fresh khakis and pressed Prada shirt or his gray FUBU sweat suit and black Jordans.

Quantity is such a big issue around here. But, as long as we stay within the requirements, everything is cool: two pair of jeans, two sweat suits, two sweatshirts, two sweaters, six pair of underwear, six pairs of socks, and five pairs of shoes. *Boring!*

Mathematics definitely has a hook-up because he gets loads of stuff every quarter. He had everything you can think of in his latest package. The hottest kicks and top-of-the-line sweat gear.

Grandma tries to send me what she can, but it's never what I really want. Don't get me wrong, I may not have Mathematics beat, but I'm representing. Sherese sent me some off-brand kicks and sweat suits. Not name brand, but they'll suffice. She attached a note that read: THESE WERE THE ONLY THINGS I COULD SEND BECAUSE I'M LOW ON MONEY.

After reading that garbage, I definitely didn't want to hear that shit, because when I came in here I left her with all of my savings. So she better have some money to send me. Let me stop triping, she's still my boo, no matter what.

"Divine, how do I look?" Mathematics asked.

"Like a million bucks, dog."

"Thanks. I hope Tashonda feels the same way." He started glowing just thinking about it. "It sure would be nice to get a few feels."

"I know that's right!" I said as we slapped hands.

"I told her to wear something sexy."

Someone shouted, "Number 926104, you've got a visitor." Mathematics smiled as he strolled toward the long hall leading to the visitor's center. *Lights, camera, action!* The runway exploded when Mathematics stepped one foot in front of the other. His smooth flow would put Pimp Daddy Don Juan to shame. Pausing to take a deep breath, he tugged slightly at his collar, to assure its proper place. Seam by seam he checked himself from head to toe.

So self-absorbed, before he knew it, the checkpoint broke his concentration.

I'm jealous! I wish I could get visitors during the week.

Oh well, might as well stop dreaming because neither Grandma nor Sherese has a car. They normally catch the shuttle bus that comes here from Portsmouth on Saturdays, and it's not in service during the week. I hate being way out here in the country. It's not convenient for anyone. Who really has the time to spend two-and-a-half hours on a country-ass bus coming out here?

Even the correctional officers complain about how long it takes them to get to work and how they can't run out for lunch. Most of them live fifty to one hundred miles away. Forget about going out to eat. The closest fast-food restaurant is fifteen miles from here in the town of Dublin. No one wants to live or even drive through this rural area.

I remember riding that big blue bus here with my legs shackled to the pole. That was the most uncomfortable ride of my life. We stopped at different correctional facilities on the way to pick up more inmates. Each time someone new got on the bus they looked liked they were scared shitless.

Niko and I rode here together so we felt like we owned the bus. It took us about five hours to finally get here after stopping all those times and from traveling up and down the country roads. Who would put a prison way out in the middle of nowhere? All you can see are hills and countryside. I felt like a neighbor of the Waltons.

When I finally got here, it was like entering an enchanted castle. The facility had to be at least two hundred years old. The aged, elevated towers reminded me of a fairy tale, but scary. Vines grew wildly up the sides of the building. The disturbing part was seeing how these deeply rooted gates slowly creep open one at a time.

"Inmate Jones, you've got a social," shouted one of the older male C.O.s, in his formal voice.

Oh shit, that's me! I hurry to my cell to throw on something presentable. I decided to brush my teeth just in case it's Sherese. Ah, winterfresh breath! She'll appreciate the sentiment. I can't wait to hold her in my arms again. This physical separation shit will kill a man.

Not too bad, I thought after taking a few looks in my half mirror. My face is a bit fucked up from my little brawl the other day, but I'm still cool. I slapped some grease in my hair and was ready, until I checked my clothes. I wouldn't go through nearly all the trouble Mathematics did. I threw on a T-shirt and a pair of light-blue jeans, and quickly used the bathroom. I know all the shit I'm getting ready to go through before entering the visiting room.

People thought I was late for a meeting the way I jetted down the deserted hallway. All sorts of questions popped in my head. *Is it Sherese or Grandma? How did they get here? Why on a Wednesday? I hope nothing is wrong.*

I got to the prisoner's entrance of the visitor's room and the bony, male C.O. working the post said, "You know what to do."

They give you the freedom to walk down the hall that leads to the visitor's room by yourself, but when you reach the door, they humiliate you. Great philosophy for rehabilitation!

I took all of my shit off one piece at a time. Each strip of clothing was checked like I was a smuggler. I stood naked in the dreary cold area with chill bumps forming all over my body.

"Spread 'em wide."

I did. Once again I split the buns. I got an instant attitude. The way he probed and prodded, I felt like a woman getting her first GYN exam. The officer searched for anything inappropriate, like drugs or money. He had on a rubber glove as he lifted my sacs and checked them carefully. It was degrading as hell but every inmate felt like it was worth it, just to get a visit. While I lifted my tongue and opened my mouth wide, I couldn't help but think about Sherese wrapping her warm arms around my neck. I would be happy to see Grandma, too, but I couldn't slide my hand up her skirt.

My hair was the last thing that needed to be checked before I could enter the room. I kept moving forward just a bit trying to look into the big brightly lit room before I actually walked in. Adrenaline surged through my body. Anxious wouldn't even describe what I'm feeling.

As soon as I was given the okay signal to enter, the first person I saw was beautiful. Was I dreaming? Or did the sun come down and land right in front of me?

It was C.O. Riley. Her lightly caramel skin tone glowed when she greeted me with a warm smile. Just imagine a voluptuous black sister with the perfect body, 36-24-36, damn! I smiled back at her while undressing her with my eyes.

I never thought I'd see the day when I could say something good about the uniform of a correctional officer. But when I saw her dressed in that dark blue, button-down, cotton short-sleeve shirt, it didn't seem that bad. The tightly fitted top drew my attention to the gold nameplate she wore near her breast, which read, Alecia Riley. Fitting perfectly, her matching khaki pants accented her round booty. She didn't try to wear fancy hairdo's or come to work dolled up. Her shoulder-length, sandy-brown ponytail was just right. She looked like a natural with no make-up, no earrings, and clear fingernail polish—my God! Even though the patent-leather black shoes tainted the flow of her ensemble, her beautiful image remained.

I hadn't seen her in more than three days. I guess she'd been working the day shift in the visitor's center. I'm sure Mathematics was happy about this.

Now Riley is real cool and everybody knows it. Smart and well respected by the inmates and her coworkers, she's got the face of an eighteen-year-old, but carries herself like a mature professional.

I suddenly came out of my trance when she nodded toward my visitor. I looked on each side of the room and began to walk down the center aisle. The room was filled with chatter. Chairs lined the wall on both sides. People sat packed like sardines. A chair had been placed in front of each visitor for an inmate to sit. I passed Equality, Science, and Little Joe as I looked for Grandma or Sherese.

Black yelled out, "Yo, Divine."

I look over and see him sitting with an unattractive young lady. I pointed my finger and smiled. Finally, I got a chance to see the girl he talked to, tying up the phone lines, 24/7. Hell, that's wasted money. That sista was busted. Thank God for Sherese!

"I see ya, boy," I shouted.

"Yo, you buggin' out, kid," he yelled back.

"Nice work. I see why you're always on the phone."

"That's right, kid," he said, touching the girl affectionately on her right leg.

It's not like she was gonna stay in this motherfucker overnight. She'd be gone in about an hour, and he'd be running up somebody's phone bill all over again.

I kept walking, searching for my folks. I didn't even see Mathematics and I knew he was in there.

C.O. Riley yelled, "Keep going all the way down to the end."

I continued to walk, looking at how many white boys had visitors. They were everywhere, talking, laughing, and playing with their kids. Some sat so close to their significant others, you'd think they'd need each other's air to breathe. I even spotted one couple tonguing each other down, right in front of their kid.

I got to the back where it was dim with only four chairs set up. Mathematics sat in one chair with Tashonda on his lap. She was giggling and laughing in her expensive Vera Wang halter dress. Her hair was freshly done. Jet Black spiral curls with plenty of bounce hung about ten inches below her back.

"Baby, why didn't you wear my favorite sweat suit?" she said rubbing her air brushed nails all over Mathematics' face.

"I don't do repeats," he gloated.

Spreading over half of her shimmery gloss on Mathematics lips, she ignored his boasting. Even though Tashonda is black, and shapely like a true African American woman (phat), she reminds me of a Spanish muchacha.

A few inches away sat a dark-skinned thin woman. At first, I simply glanced at her, unsure of who she was. After noticing her schoolgirl wave, it was confirmed that she was there for me.

She said, "Hi, I'm a friend of Tashonda's. Mathematics asked me if I would sign my name for a visit with you since I came down with her. I hope you don't mind. He just wanted you to be able to visit with all of us today."

"It's cool," I said, acting like this was my first date.

I looked over at Mathematics but he was busy sticking

his tongue down Tashonda's throat.

"Since my man's all tied up, let me do the honors. Hi, I'm Divine."

"I'm Stacey, the pleasure's all mine," she replied.

"How were you able to request a visit with me? You're not on my list."

She responded, "The lady up front said it would be all right."

"Oh!" I said, surprised.

"You must be special around here," she said crossing her long legs.

"True dat," I said, nodding in agreement.

Riley is mad cool, I thought, *with her sexy-ass self.* Glancing down at Stacey's thighs, I caught myself. *I can't cheat on Sherese.*

My attention was re-focused when Stacey asked, "What happened to your face?"

"Oh, I had to help a friend out," I said.

"Well, you sure are a good friend," Stacey said, smiling from ear to ear.

We continued to talk and get to know each other, when out of the corner of my eye I noticed that Tashonda was sitting on Mathematics, slowly rotating up and down. It didn't seem like they were screwing because Tashonda kept a straight face as if everything was normal. But Mathematics could not keep his composure. His eyes rolled so far up in his head until I could only see white. That nigga looked like he was having an epileptic seizure. I knew exactly what was up then. Stacey and I acted as if nothing was happening.

I told her all about Sherese and how we were going to be married once I got out. She didn't seem interested.

Changing the subject, Stacey asked, "What did you do to end up in a place like this?"

"I'm here because of a friend who put me in a situation I couldn't get out of. I'll be out of here by next year if everything goes as planned. My lawyer knows I'm innocent."

Stacey smiled. "That's funny. Mathematics is singin' the same song. What, are you all a part of the same choir?"

"A lot of people in here say that but I'm telling the truth."

"True dat," Stacey said, laughing as she mimicked me.

She and I chatted for about forty-five minutes straight, paying no attention to Tashonda and Mathematics. She told me all about her career as an insurance investigator. She really seemed to like what she did. Stacey even went back to her college days. I really liked her personality, although, I was not too happy about those braids. They looked like they were coming up on an anniversary. My baby Sherese would never be caught having a bad hair day.

"Stacey, I'm really glad you came. It gives me a chance to have a conversation with someone who seems to be intelligent. You think you'd come again?"

"That could be arranged," she said, nodding as if she were happy about our visit too.

Before I could say everything I wanted to say, a whistle blew from the front. Visiting hours were over. Most of the convicts were getting their last-minute hugs and kisses. Stacey and I were just sitting there. She looked at me like she wanted to kiss me, but I tried not to look directly in her eyes. She told me that their flight was gonna leave in about two hours. Hell, it took about thirty minutes for the cab to make it back to the airport from here.

That's crazy because the flight time back to Norfolk

was only forty minutes. If you could afford to fly, that's better than driving two and a-half-hours. Tashonda truly loved Mathematics because I know it cost her an arm and a leg to make it out here today and she brought a friend.

Well, I know Mathematics is slingin' his shit inside, but damn, is it *that* lucrative? He's so discreet that he never talks about his business ventures around here. One thing is for sure—drugs cost more on the inside than they do on the outside. I know for sure, Black pays double the amount. Shit, those niggas are fools, spending their last on some bullshit like that. It's all right though, if Mathematics is benefiting, it's all right with me.

People were starting to head to the door to leave. Tashonda and Mathematics were getting their last kiss, which was way too long. All of the visitors and inmates watched them. I just knew one of the C.O.s was gonna break that kiss up. Tashonda's overly large soup coolers drowned Mathematics' lips and all the skin around his entire mouth. It was way too X-rated for the visiting room.

"Get a room!" the bony C.O. yelled, bringing attention to the kissing bandits.

Within minutes, all of the visitors were escorted out. We had to sit there until they all left, because of course we had to be searched all over again.

Four different officers stood up front as the last visitor left. They all lined us up to humiliate us once again during the search process. C.O. Crawford, who has more soul than any white man I know but tries way too hard to be black, came straight to the back where we were. He had been drinking again. The potent smell of alcohol filtered from his breath. When I first met Crawford, I could only think about one thing—white trash. He's a scruffy-looking man who can't keep his shirt tucked in to save his life. But after getting to know him, I saw a different side of him. For starters he looks like he's been on earth longer than thirty-nine years. I didn't believe him at first, until he showed me some I.D. Jack Daniels and his friends were getting the best of him.

Crawford stood shabbily in front of us, prepared to begin the search. He said, "I'll start back here."

I took everything off and started to shiver. He gave me a quick search and sternly asked me to open my mouth. After being cleared, I walked to the front, dreading my return to hell. I turned back to see if Mathematics was coming behind me when I saw him drop something into Crawford's jacket pocket. He was probably paying him for that nice setup. It was like being in the VIP section of prison. It must have cost a lot too, considering he probably had to pay Riley and Crawford.

By the time Mathematics got to the front, his lips had formed a huge pucker. Ain't this a bitch, they were directed at my dream girl Riley.

Damn, is this nigga gonna save some for us? I thought to myself, wanting to punch him dead in the jaw.

6

The Yard

Entering Block C brought me and Mathematics back to reality. All of the different gangs were assembled closely together. If I were the superintendent of prisons, I would make these jokers hang with people who committed similar crimes. All of the motherfuckers with breaking-and-entering charges would be together. That way they could steal one another's shit all day and night. All the inmates with kidnapping or rape charges would hang out and swap sadistic stories. Maybe even bang one another a few times. It's pretty sad when a grown man can't get a woman voluntarily.

I don't know what I would do with people like Abdual and Eddie who got life for first-degree murder. What fool put them in a medium-security facility? Who's to say they won't have a flashback and snap somebody's fuckin' neck?

Now Black, since he's my man in all, I'd cut him some slack. He can't help himself. He's in for multiple gun charges. What would you expect from him anyway? He's from the Bronx. Well, used to be anyway. He's a fake New York. Been in Virginia for fifteen years, still rooting for the Knicks.

Let's not forget about Bones. He has murdered more than fifteen people in the last five years. An enforcer for the Quigley street boys, he was caught only because of snitches. Nobody actually saw him do anything. He didn't admit to anything either.

The Quigley street boys consisted of six neighborhood thugs who sold more than forty thousand dollars worth of cocaine per week, on Quigley Street in Norfolk, Virginia. They were making so much money, drug dealers from all over town wanted to sell their product. They all wanted to be down. That's where Bones came in the picture.

His job was to bump off anybody not in compliance with the no-drug trespassing decree put into place by the Quigley boys. Bones was given specific instructions on how to handle anybody trying to sell on their turf and was paid very well. Every now and then he slipped up and gave us a little bit of information, but overall, he was still claiming to be innocent. He had two years under his belt and ten to go. He'd done a peaceful bid so far, but with a name like Bones he might end up in some shit before it's over.

Then I look over at Lawrence Day who's got forty-four years as a habitual offender. He's sixty-five years old and didn't seem like he would hurt a mouse. But, that quietness could be deceiving. Word had it that he has a rap sheet ranging from armed robbery to intent to kill. He never talked to anyone about what he was in for. Anyhow, he probably wouldn't tell us.

Oh! How can I forget Crazy Ed, who was staring at

me with his crossed-eyed self. This joker was in for armed robbery with a dangerous weapon. I think he actually killed someone, but the prosecutor couldn't prove it. How did he pull that off? That nigga can't even see straight—seeing four of everything.

He had nine years to do anyway. I wished Niko would go ahead and take his ass out. Why did he jump on me yesterday anyway? I started getting depressed looking at these bars, concrete walls, correctional officers, and incarcerated fucks.

"These motherfuckers are around here playing cards like they're at camp. I need to be out of here soon!" I screamed.

Niko walked up behind me saying, "Stop crying like a girl. I wanna be out of here too. Has your grandma been working with the lawyer to get our case reheard?"

"I'm not sure I wrote her a letter asking her to check on it."

What I didn't tell Niko was that Grandma was probably working on it, but only to get me off, not him. But I didn't want to break Niko's spirit by telling him that. It's hard enough trying to make it in here as it is. It's not my fault that Niko doesn't have anyone on the outside looking out for him. All the friends he had before he came in are either locked down or have disappeared.

When I used to tell him to keep in touch with his father, he would tell me his father was the reason why he turned out the way he did. His dad had been in and out of jail all of his life. He never tried to teach Niko about right and wrong and never persuaded him to stay in school. His father would probably never have a chance to make things right. For starters, Niko knew that he tried to give his mother money to get an abortion—two times.

The first time she told him that she had simply spent the money—who knows on what, considering she was a pipehead. The second time he gave her money, she told him she didn't want to give up her baby. She kept the money anyhow. She said she was going to use it to buy baby clothes and accessories. Just knowing that your daddy tried to kill you twice can be harsh on anybody's relationship.

Before Niko was four years old his mother was on drugs hard. He didn't say whether it was crack, cocaine, heroin, or what. All I know is that it had an effect on the way Niko was raised. He lacked proper food, clothing, and love. He wasn't getting any care from his dad either because he was busy running around being a womanizer. He did sound worthless.

Niko's dad eventually took Niko away from his moms right before his fifth birthday. This devastated him, as it would any five-year-old being separated, even from a bad mother. Niko's dad acted like he was gonna be different; like he was gonna be there for him. For the first couple of months his dad took him to parks, bought ice cream, all the fun stuff. However, he didn't think to enroll him in school. How bright is that?

As time went on, I guess parenting got rough because soon Niko found himself being dropped off with his daddy's mama to live for good. He needed to thank God for his grandma. I definitely thank Him for mine. While living with his grandma Niko got plenty of love and good care. However, she was too old to keep up with Niko. He said he used to cut school, steal bikes, or anything else he could get his hands on. By the time he was fourteen he was working as a runner for a neighborhood drug dealer. He was barely making it to school at all.

Niko's dad never really came around much so he never tried to persuade him to do the right thing. His grandma tried real hard up until the day she died. Niko was only fifteen the day of her funeral. He took it hard, but not nearly as hard as the days to come when his moms passed away also. He couldn't get any comfort from his dad who was locked up at the time, up north somewhere. Niko was all alone and has been on his own since he was fifteen.

By the following year he had completely dropped out of high school and was in and out of detention centers. Niko really felt the pressure when he tried to get a job and couldn't because his highest level of education was eleventh grade. Nobody is going to hire you without a high school diploma. Now he's an uneducated convict without any family support. I'm all he's got and I'm feeling cruddy because I don't know how to tell him that my lawyer isn't working for him.

Me, Niko, and Black headed for the yard. C.O. Crawford and Mathematics stood talking in hushed tones. Nothing really looked suspect but I thought back to what I had seen earlier in the visitor's room. What did Mathematics put in Crawford's pocket? Why were they all of a sudden so tight?

About three-fourths of the way down the corridor, Mathematics caught up with us. He maintained his suave disposition. It's amazing how someone destined to live the remainder of his life in a shit hole can have such a smooth attitude. Something was going on but I couldn't put my finger on it.

Before we could head out, we were strip-searched and

there were several guards searching the grounds for
weapons. Most shankings happened outside because of
the open space. Inmates like to hide weapons under the
benches or in holes. I'm just anxious to get out because it's
been raining all week. Not to mention the fact that all the
housing units will be out at one time. I can't wait to see
Slick. I think he's in Block D. I heard that joker is the
man.

I could feel the humidity in the air as I got closer to the
door. Aah! There's nothing better than blue skies and the
freedom to walk around outdoors. With anticipation getting
the best of me, I stretched my arms high in the air,
impatiently bouncing like a five-year-old. It didn't matter
to me that it was hot and sticky.

Once I got outside, the first thing I looked at are the
officers in the towers outside the perimeter fence. They
sitting up there like they high and mighty with assault
rifles and shotguns. Now these motherfuckers bring you
back to reality. When I look at them, I realize where the
hell I am and who's in charge. I don't understand why they
have so many towers with guards watching us. It's not like
we can get very far. The fences are about thirteen feet high,
and if we do make it over the fence, there's nowhere to
run. Basically, we're in the middle of nowhere.

I know one thing: it's hotter than two hells out here.
I think I'm gonna just sit here near my crew and take in
the sights.

It's amazing to see everyone grouped together. The
Whites, Blacks, and the Mexicans stay separated like
they're segregated. Is this year 2000 or 1950?

Now Jake, who I think is the coolest white inmate in
here, is standing by himself today, which is rather strange.

I would never go over to talk to him because people will be watching. I don't want it to look like we're buddies. So I'll just keep my eye on 'em. Something is shady. Maybe he's got a beef with his crew. I shouldn't be worried anyway because there's got to be at least nine officers on post out here today. That's excluding the firing squad up top.

Suddenly, I see Mathematics looking at some Mexican real hard who's making sexual connotations to one of the lady C.O.s. She's only been here about two months. I don't know her name but she's kinda cute. Although, I don't normally check out red bones, I like the ones like C.O. Riley. Mathematics is probably upset because he wants her. The new C.O.s are easy bait. They don't know the ropes that well and are more likely to accept flattery and bribes.

Most of the seasoned officers know that if they're seen being too talkative and friendly with us, they won't be trusted among their coworkers. On the other hand, if they don't talk to us and treat us with respect they might get their ass whipped or shanked when shit goes down. It's a hard decision to make. I would definitely look out for C.O. Riley if anything kicked off!

"Hey Divine, you ballin' today?" Mathematics asked.

"Nah, I'm gonna sit right here and watch," I said, throwing my leg up on the bench.

"What's up with you? That shit ain't normal," Mathematics said.

"I'm playing," Hodge said, walking up within our circle.

Niko snapped, "Who the fuck asked you?"

Hodge is a wanna-be. He tries to be down with our crew, but fuck that. He's a trustee and we don't trust him. Obviously, if he's hired by the C.O.s because they have faith in him, then there's a strong possibility he may have snitched on somebody to get that job. I'm not taking any chances, and my crew ain't either.

"We already set." Mathematics said calmly.

Although everyone could see that we were short one guy, it didn't matter. The basketball game was on. Hodge just stood there on the sideline pissed, looking like he lost his best friend. About three C.O.s started coming near the court. It's standard just in case anything kicks off. I looked back over to my left to find Jake staring at his crew and watching their every move. Something was going down. I just didn't know what. I was laying back on the bench relaxed but decided to sit straight up. I saw Jake get up and move toward the weights. It wasn't unusual for him to be there. But today was different.

During the game Niko was extra aggressive. He loves to dominate. He was dribbling the ball back and forth between his legs, showboating. Now Mathematics showed off as well, but his game is consistent.

Black and the other guy on our team are modest players. They just didn't seem to be getting the ball much. The game is kinda tense anyway 'cause we're playing the white boys. They beat us the last time and that shit really pissed Niko off. They won by luck anyhow. I don't know how Niko's gonna to take it if they win today. If I were them, I'd let his ass win.

Niko impulsively stopped bouncing the ball, and knelt down to fumble around with his left shoe. Everyone looked directly at him, trying to figure out what the problem was. His shoelaces were tied, and everything seemed to be in order, but something was clearly troubling him. "What's the holdup?" Mathematics asked.

Niko stood, threw Black the ball, and walked about

three yards over to some off-brand scrawny dude smoking a cigarette.

"Raise up out those kicks, punk!" Niko said with a treacherous look upon his face.

The guy looked down at his shoes, not really sure about how to handle the situation. His cigarette fell from his hand as he held his palms out, dreading what was about to happen.

"Why me?" he asked, trembling.

"You questioning me?"

"Uh, no. . ."

"Nigga, no!"

"I mean. . ."

Before the guy could finish, Niko was so close to his face at this point, their noses were touching. Inmates from all over the yard suddenly stopped to watch. I could see two guards coming this way. Within seconds, the off-brand was bending down removing the brand-new crisp Jordans from his feet.

Before Niko could even do away with his old shoes, things were right back to normal. Everyone went back to their activities as if nothing happened. By the time the guards arrived, the "punk" was already exiting the yard barefoot. If that had been me, I would've at least fought for my shit. He'd never be able to keep anything after sucking up like that!

"Yo, let's go," Black yelled.

Niko took his time lacing up his new white kicks, ignoring Black in the process.

"Now, I can show off my skills," Niko said, looking down admiring what now belonged to him. The game was back on. I don't know if psychologically Niko thought his game was now better, or what happened, but, he was on a roll. Hogging the ball was his specialty anyway.

From the corner of my eye I noticed a strange face coming our way. The fellas were so wrapped up in the game, they barely noticed him.

"What y'all working wit'," some crusty dude from Block A asked.

He just swayed his way near the court like he was down with us. I didn't really know him so I stayed silent. I don't know whether he needed food, drugs, or cigarettes. I don't have shit for 'em. I knew Niko had gotten a weapon from him a while back in exchange for some cigarettes, but that was the extent of that relationship. Besides I couldn't imagine what he had to offer. By the looks of his gear, not much. He should know better coming around here bartering, looking like some shit. His sweats looked like they came from the Dollar store. Who in the hell sent him those fucked-up sneakers?

Mathematics put on his mean face saying, "We straight, player." He looked at Mathematics, not wanting to buck at all. They obviously had done business before. I can't blame dude. It's all about survival. Try to get what you want by giving somebody else what they need. He's definitely in need.

I could see Jake walking closer to the court from the corner of my eye. Nobody else seemed to notice him. Not even the guards. He was holding something in his hand down by his side. I couldn't make out what it was. It was long, round, and white. The next thing I knew Jake jumped on Hodge who was standing less than three feet from me. Everyone on the court stepped back. Normally, if it were a gang hit everyone would've jumped in.

Simultaneously, the whistle blew, gunshots rang out in the air, and three C.O.s nearby dismantled the fight quickly. They had both of them down on the ground with the heels of their shoes digging in their necks.

All the guards in the tower were standing up ready to act if needed. The guards on post were getting all the other inmates on the yard facedown to the ground.

I wonder why none of Jake's boyz acted concerned. Lying on the ground beside me was a rolled-up piece of white paper. It was the same object Jake had in his hand when he walked over. I thought he had a shank. I saw one of the C.O.s bend down to pick it up. He looked at it and shook his head. Jake and Hodge had already been taken inside and we were next. They'd fucked up our recreation time over a petty-ass fight!

Knowing that I was gonna have to be searched to re-enter put a damper on the mood and a frown on my face instantly. It seemed like some fuck-up always messed it up for us. My time is valuable! And, my yard time is precious! I'm like a young child wanting recess.

Before I knew it, all available officers were out on the yard searching us for re-entry. There was no real system in place. Officers were scrambling about the grounds. Since blocks A and D were out with us, there were about 180 of us total.

The yard was filled with chaos. We couldn't tell who was gonna be searched next, or for that matter, who was gonna do the searching.

Once we were checked by an officer, we were free to go back in. I was lucky enough to see Bennett waddling my way, acting as if she had been called away from some important assignment.

"I'll frisk this one," she said, turning her attention to Niko.

A nearby female officer chuckled. "I guess I'll take this one."

I was appalled! What was she trying to say?

With a quick frisk, I was on my way back to the reality of my life. On the way inside I asked one of Jake's boyz what was up with that whole ordeal.

He told me Hodge was running a football pool and that Jake was in the pool. Jake had obviously joined Hodge's gambling ring without the approval of his crew. I guess his boyz didn't want to fuck with nothing outside their own clique.

Well, Jake obviously won and Hodge didn't pay up. He told Jake he wasn't gonna pay him and there was nothing he could do about it.

That Hodge is a dirty dog. That's why he was trying to play ball with us. He probably wanted Jake to think he was down with us. The only bad part about it, was that Jake would never get his money. Simply because to earn respect around here you've got to kill, or at least send 'em to the infirmary. That was just a simple catfight. From what the paper showed, he owed Jake seventy-five dollars.

It was near lock down when Skip came by selling sandwiches. I wasn't real hungry, but I knew the brotha was trying to make money. Otherwise, he wouldn't want to work in that nasty-ass kitchen.

"What you got?" I said.

"Tuna, fresh from the sea, and I got Spam," he said.

"Now you know I don't eat no damn swine."

Skip laughed. "That's what they all say until it's late at night and your stomach is growling. Plus, nobody's around!"

I took the tuna sandwich out of his hand and handed him a pack of cigarettes.

"Get me later, dog, just know, it's now two for one."

"Naw, you ain't gonna clip me. I'm paying now!"

Skip pushed the cigarettes into his overloaded pockets and kept on moving. The sandwich was a little mushy, but fuck it. It beat being hungry.

7

Blowin' Up the Bottle

I don't know what I'd do without my books. Call me a nerd, square, or whatever you like. I consider myself a scholar. Most people around here hate on that! It's not easy being intellectual. You get respect when you say "you shanked somebody," but you get laughed at for reading. Something is deeply wrong here.

Rehabilitation is not taking place. The classes we take are some bullshit! They're supposedly designed to help me acquire knowledge and literacy, but folks up in here don't take it seriously.

They don't think about what's gonna happen when they get back on the streets. For now, it's all about survival. The scary part is if you make the wrong move, you may not make it out. *Ever.*

Most of the inmates who joke on me about my reading habit don't even have a high school diploma. And what really makes it bad is instead of participating in more GED training, they're taking wellness and recreation classes.

Finally, disregarding thoughts of the negative remarks I

would be getting soon, I opened my book of the month #1 *Guide to a Successful Life*. I love self-help books! I'm thinking about writing one called *Ways to Survive in the Pen*. Amused, I smiled as I began to read.

I read for about an hour until my eyes felt heavy as stone. I tried to keep them open as long as possible, but after too many tosses and turns, it was time to chill.

I slid a sticky label I had taken off my hair grease between pages thirty-six and thirty-seven. Satisfied about my daily knowledge, I closed the book, ready for some good lounging.

Just when I thought I'd be able to rest, some fool decided to initiate a random drug test. For what? Everybody knows who the users and the dealers are. It's a waste of time. The good part for me was that only letters J, K, and L had been called. That meant two things: One, only a handful of us would be tested, and two, whenever anything was done around here alphabetically, me, Niko, and Black would be together. We all have last names that begin with J—Jones, Jenkins, and Jacobs.

I don't know where Black got a last name like Jacobs. He's black as tar, walking around with a name like that. But, it's all good. He's my man!

At the testing center, I could see one of the young male guards standing there passing out cups of water. I didn't recognize him, but it didn't matter. I wasn't gonna blow up the bottle. I've always had clean urine. Under no circumstances did Grandma raise a weed head!

I went back for a refill on the water when I noticed

Black behaving a little jittery. I got up close enough to him to ask, "You straight?"

"Not really."

"What do you mean?"

He looked around nervously, with his hands in his pocket.

Questioning him like a parent, I asked, "Why aren't you drinking?"

"I don't think I'm gonna take the test."

"So, you're gonna refuse?"

"Yep," Black said with certainty.

I hesitated for a moment, then said, "Do what ya got to do!"

Black's mind was already working, scheming on how to maneuver out of this.

"Can you see who's working the other side of the door?"

"Nah."

"Shit. I'm in trouble."

Next, the hefty officer called Niko to the front.

Niko proudly walked up, like he had won some sort of prize. "Don't you have a bigger bottle?" he asked with a chuckle as he looked at the six-ounce specimen bottle.

"Get in here," the officer said from the inside.

His tone was familiar, but I just couldn't figure out who it could be. C.O. Braswell or Crawford? I knew for sure, it wasn't Warren. He never worked random piss checks. For one, he thinks he's too good and two he's selective when it comes to working certain posts.

Within seconds, Niko came out, pants half-buckled and baggy as usual. "Y'all ain't never gonna catch me blowin' up the bottle!"

While he continued to release overconfident expressions throughout the area, his gaze remained focused on the young officer signing inmates in, and handing out water. "Keep on doing these bullshit test! Wasting your damn time. Wasting taxpayers money too!"

I laughed at Niko's simple ass. He'd never paid taxes a day in his life, and now he was concerned. While Niko continued to talk, I cheered him on, making his conversation seem worthier than it was. Black, on the other hand, uninterested in his comedy kept his focus. Unable to relax, Black paced, agitated and fearful of his fate. When Niko walked past him, they exchanged a few words.

Next thing I know, Niko passed him something in the palm of his hand. Suspect was written all over their faces.

My attention was sidetracked. The fat guy named Pierce, who had gone in after Niko, was being thrown up against the wall. One of the C.O.s had already radioed for assistance. The sound from the interference on the radio kept us from hearing clearly.

"We've got one refusing down here," the younger C.O. said.

"I'll be right down," a female voice said.

Several minutes later, Bennett's fat ass swayed through to take control of the refusal violation. Apparently, Pierce had refused to piss in the bottle. Everybody already knew he would get about thirty to sixty days in the hole with no privileges. Just imagine no phone calls, no recreation, and worst of all, a shower every seventy-two hours. Risking all that to get high. What a fool!

Pierce was handcuffed behind his back and taken away by Bennett. We all stared at her as she walked by, but she made eye contact with Niko. Her eyes were fixed on him completely until she was several yards away from the testing area.

"Damn, what was that all about?" I asked.

"Love, nigga."

"Yeah, whatever."

My bladder was working overtime. I wanted to be called next. I started twitching around and moving my legs.

The C.O. looked me directly in my eye and pointed his index finger directly at Black.

"You, next!"

Before Black's rugged body disappeared behind the closed bathroom door, I knew he was in for a long, lonely week. He had obviously been smoking that shit again. Whether it was lockup for two weeks or two months, it didn't seem to matter. He never learned. The bad part about it was that he smoked whatever he could get his hands on—weed, cocaine, heroin, it didn't matter. Discrimination was not in his vocabulary.

Black's face was a glittering glowworm. He came out like a champ who'd just won the heavyweight title. His beam was a look of triumph.

Either something real slick had gone on between him and Niko, or the Lord was looking out for his tar-baby ass. He was smiling from right to left, with that sparkling gold in his mouth showing.

When he yelled out, "You next, kid," I knew everything was okay.

I grabbed the plastic bottle with confidence, and stepped inside the toilet area. Brown, a little pint-sized C.O. who had been working here for years, was running the show. I didn't see him too often and was unsure about his game. He could be for us, or against us. Or he could be one of those fifty-fifty playing motherfuckers.

"Man, you dirty?" he asked.

"No. . . No. . .," I replied, sounding relieved.

"It's better to tell me now," Brown said as he concentrated on my face.

"Like I said, no!"

"Oh. . . I see, you wanna try your luck instead of paying. Your boy did."

I laughed my way out of the conversation and handled my business. I knew I was clean. Why would I let a little pip-squeak like Brown chump me for services I didn't need?

I was still zipping my fly as I strolled past the last two people drinking water and intolerantly waiting. I laughed. Maybe I should've been a C.O.. Entrepreneurship around here is a motherfucker!

Walking back through the recreation area, I realized what had taken place wasn't just the usual *random* drug test. Lieutenants and captains were on site, and the dogs were called in. Shit was about to hit the fan. A little uneasy walking back to my cell, I took shorter strides to prolong reaching my destination. People get set up when this kinda shit goes down. It's a C.O.s' dream! They've been known to plant shit in cells during drug raids.

I decided to plop down on the couch and wait for all hell to break loose. I chilled out for about thirty minutes watching everything that was going on. I was amused by most of it, until C.O. Warren and C.O. Riley walked up behind me and flipped the couch upside down.

I ended up on the ground with my face buried in the

filthy floor. I knew Riley didn't really want to do that. It had to have been Warren's idea. There was no sense in filling out a grievance form, because a captain saw the whole thing and didn't seem to care one bit. I made about two baby crawls and slid out of the way.

As the officers ripped through the couch searching for drugs, I noticed a needle stuck inside the bottom cushion, which was now lying on the floor next to me. I started to sweat. I didn't want them to think it was mine. Had I been set up that quickly? That's all I needed!

I contemplated snatching the needle, but, what would I do with it? At least if they pulled it out the cushion and they tried to say it was mine, I could fight it. It would be extremely difficult for them to prove it was mine.

Riley's fingers were getting hot. Her hands were conducting a full-fledge search in close proximity to the needle. She was so close to finding it, if it had been a snake, she'd be bit by now. With a twinkling of the eye, Riley pushed the needle all the way into the cushion, and continued to search every portion of the couch. I nearly fainted.

Meanwhile, a huge commotion erupted in the cell area of Block C. With Riley around, I felt safe and decided to see what was going on. Once I passed the first cell, I knew this was serious. Officer Bennett had on rubber gloves going through every letter, every box, and every item in Bones' cell. Yellow tags everywhere represented the need for a detailed check. Because there were more than ten yellow tags, two more officers were called in to help Bennett.

Bennett sneered with excitement as she meticulously searched each item.

Ooh, if I could have one wish, that bitch would go

down! She thinks she's so damn fly. Oh, and she has the nerve to wear that gold ring on the outside of her gloves! She definitely thinks she's better than us!

Bennett picked up Bones' deodorant stick. The dog's bark became louder and louder. Bennett, irritated by the dog, kept moving away from the hound. She took the top off the deodorant stick and sniffed. She lifted her hands in the air and shrugged.

"Give me that," C.O. Warren said, snatching the deodorant from her hand.

"Okay, super C.O.," Bennett said.

"Hon, you push the deodorant all the way to the top, then pull it completely out, lift up this plastic piece, and violá!"

"My Lord!"

Everyone was amazed! A small stash of weed lay inside the deodorant stick. Creative! Bones was shaking his oval-shaped head in a daze. As he was lead out of his cell, he insisted, "It's not mine."

"Yeah, I know," Warren replied.

"Look, let's make a deal."

"What kinda deal?" Warren asked with peaked interest.

Bones whispered close to Warren's ear. With enthusiasm Warren grabbed Bones by the arm and jetted out of sight.

He'll have a new home in the hole for a few weeks, I thought. They may even try to make an example out of him since so many white shirts are on the block tonight.

Officers were pumped at this point. Word was out that Graham was giving comp time to anyone who found drugs or paraphernalia. Like lightning, all available uniforms were off to the next tagged cell. Regrettably for my crew, Mathematics' cell was the target.

Now I would be willing to bet my savings that Mathematics wouldn't get caught with anything. He was too smart for that. Besides, I think he keeps his stuff in a neutral place, so ownership can never be pinpointed.

On his bed like he didn't have a worry in the world, Mathematics sat while the facility's number-one dog barked ferociously at his locker. At this point, grins could be seen on the faces of several officers. The locker had already been tagged, the dog was signaling, but Mathematics lay composed.

"Open it up," Graham said, positioned in military stance.

"Boy, no wonder that mutt is barking, I smell it already," C.O. Crawford said, getting excited.

"What is it?"

"Hell, I don't know," Crawford said rushing toward the locker.

"Search everything!" Graham commanded.

The dog continued barking for more than thirty minutes, while four officers went through every shred in Mathematics' locker and room. They came up completely empty.

Warren stuck his head in the door after returning from walking Bones to the hole. "Those dogs ain't worth a shit. If you want something done right, you've got to do it yourself."

"We searched the entire room thoroughly, and still came up with zip, zero," Crawford said.

"I guess so," he said with poise as he walked over to the locker.

"We already searched!" Crawford yelled, sick and tired of Warren. Crawford stepped aside as Warren took charge.

"Who's bright idea was it to search this cell anyway?" Warren asked.

"Nobody. It was the smell," Bennett answered, rolling her eyes.

"The smell," he repeated with disdain. "The dog was barking because of a scent. Not a current smell. Obviously something was in here once upon a time, but not now!"

"What a night," Bennett said. "Can we end this?"

"Wait! Lieutenant, I got a tip," Warren called out.

"Is it reliable?" Graham asked.

"It's worth a try," Warren said, acting like a pressed cop trying to make his monthly quota.

"Who is it?" Graham asked curiously.

"Bones. He checked off in exchange for some extra privileges. He told me to check Black."

"Who?" Graham asked, irritated by the lack of drugs found.

"Black, you know nobody goes by their real name around here."

"He's already been searched," Bennett said.

"When?" Warren asked in disbelief.

"Within the last twenty minutes," Bennett responded on her way out the door.

"If you say so, hon."

"Great, let's wrap this up," Graham said.

"Ain't nobody gonna help me clean up this shit?" Mathematics asked, flipping his mattress back on the spring.

"Wait on it," Warren said, exiting the cell.

8━┱

Before saying my prayers, I couldn't help but to reflect on what had happened today. This is a cut-throat place. Nobody cares about anybody. Obviously, someone initially sent out a tip, otherwise we wouldn't have gotten a random drug test along with the dogs, all in the same day. And to make matters worse, officers wanting to catch us over some comp time is sickening. Isn't there any kind of loyalty around here? Yeah, I forget, with C.O. Riley. I'm going to do something real special for her. I'm just not sure what.

8

Dejection

There's nothing like new meat coming into a prison. The look on their faces reminds me of one of Freddy Krueger's victims. I know firsthand because I've been in their shoes. Just imagine hearing all those prison horror stories about getting killed, shanked, fucked, or becoming somebody's woman. Then you actually get here and you see cross-eyed Crazy Ed, muscled-out Niko, and a faggot with lipstick on, all staring at you. You have no idea who your cell mate is going to be or if you're going to live. Now *that's* horror. Think about your worst fear and multiply that times three.

As the new inmates walked through the corridor I kept praying that I wouldn't get a cell mate. The rule is two to a cell, but I've been lucky for the last six months. This eight-by-twelve is too small for two grown men anyway. Once you factor in the desk positioned up against the wall, the two lockers and the toilet, there's barely any room left. I've had the pleasure of having the top and bottom bunk to myself for so long, I've become selfish. Besides, I like being alone. I don't have to look at any naked men or pretend like I'm strong at all times. I can cry when I want to, and nobody will know about it.

When you've got a cell mate you have to portray a certain image or everyone else will find out your soft side. A soft side could mean trouble.

I remember clearly, like it was yesterday, my first day in the Dungeon. Exhausted from my long journey, I was in no mood for what was in store for me. When I got off the bus, C.O. Hawkins, who is no longer here, was doing the briefing. She gave us basic information about what was going to take place. We listened to her ramble on for about fifteen minutes straight. Then, our next piece of literary torture was Lieutenant Graham.

We were all lined up side by side in our orange jumpsuits when he walked in wearing his freshly starched white shirt, dark blue khakis, and his brown outdated glasses, which he still wears to this day. He didn't strike me as a correctional official because of his short, oversized physique. I expected a big muscle-bound control freak to be in charge. Instead, we got a rational, non-discriminating lieutenant.

I couldn't figure out whether he was black or white. After getting to know a few people I found out he's mixed. Although, at first, taking him seriously took some patience. His big stomach and whiskers growing in place of a mustache caused me to snicker the moment I saw him. He's so short that when he walked past the row of inmates, between his thinning hair, I could see a circular bald spot dead in the center of his head.

After checking us out carefully, he finally decided to speak. "Welcome to your new home! I'm Lieutenant Graham, and this is Block C, my block! On this unit you will follow my rules. We will not tolerate any unnecessary behaviors. I can tell you now, you will be transferred to another block. I run a tight ship, but it's one of the best units in the Dungeon. Be thankful you're here and not on another block."

He paused for a moment walking back and forth studying each one of us. Nobody said a word, not even Niko.

"Now I'm not going to sit here and post all the rules for y'all. You're grown men, and a counselor will be assigned to you. Let me just say this. No drugs, no sex, and no violence will keep you from doing hard time. My officers will treat you with respect if you treat them with respect. I believe in open lines of communication. Therefore, when and if you have a problem, fill out a grievance form, and I will investigate the situation."

Before I could even digest Graham's speech, another officer came in to take over. He was what I had anticipated—tall, bulky, and young. He gave no salutations and no introductions.

"Follow me to receiving. There you will have a shower and a physical."

"I already had a physical," Niko snapped.

"And, you're about to have another one," Sergeant Corning said as he got as close as he could in Niko's mug. They stood face to face, equal in height. A light pale-colored birthmark circled the side of Sergeant Corning's cheek. The perfect spot for Niko to whack his ass! But, he kept his composure.

Niko wasn't used to submitting to a white man. And definitely, not an uneducated one. Niko backed down immediately. At least he was smart enough not to get in trouble his first day.

Corning continued, "For those of y'all who have the same concerns, even if you had a physical in county, you will still get one here in the state. You got it!"

Nobody responded.

"You got it!" he repeated, walking closer, invading my comfort zone.

My first impulse was to haul off and hit this cracker. But after waiting several seconds, I said, "Yeah," in my lowest voice. Two or three others responded, but not Niko. He was pissed. He was rebellious as hell against authority then, just like he is now.

My memory is a little blurry about what happened after that. What I do remember is taking off all my clothes and being sprayed down with some type of solution. I haven't the slightest idea what, but it wasn't soap. The purpose was to cleanse me before my physical.

Now the aged nurse who gave me my physical had more to say than Graham. She hit me with question after question.

"Have you ever had any of the following? High blood pressure?"

"No."

"Dizziness?"

"No."

"Fatigue?"

"No."

"Cardiac related problems?" the nurse said, slowing down as she flipped to the second page.

"No."

"Are you currently taking any prescribed medication?"

Because she had picked up speed once again and asked so many questions, I couldn't think. I needed time to digest it all.

She sternly repeated after not getting a response, "Are

you currently taking any prescribed medication?"

"No, ma'am." (That's when I still had manners.)

"Are you allergic to any medication?"

Before I could answer she added, food, toiletries, etc.

"No, no, no, no."

She pulled her glasses slightly below her eyelids, giving me the evil eye, and continued. "Do you or anyone in your family have a history of cancer?"

"No."

"Depression?"

"No," I said, answering the questions quicker than normal. Nurse Mouth Almighty had worn me out.

"Diabetes?"

"No." I caught myself. "I mean yes."

"Who?"

"My dad."

"Okay. Have you ever been tested for HIV?"

"Yes."

"Good, because you'll be tested again." The nurse said as she whipped out the longest needle I'd ever seen.

"Wonderful," I remember saying in a sorrowful tone.

I was so exhausted, I probably could have gone to sleep anywhere, but that didn't matter to the officers. The next thing I knew I was in line for more blood work, urine samples, TB shots, and Hepatitis shots. The hemorrhoid check was more painful than the shots.

After several hours of questions and speeches, I was led to an area where I was eventually given three institutional outfits, soap, a pair of sneakers, hat, coat, boots, and a blanket. An evil-looking Hispanic inmate handed out materials, which caused me to be a little hesitant about asking for a pillow. I'm glad I didn't. I would've been wasting my time. Most of the time your cell mate would already have it when you got there. You've got to earn that pillow, or sometimes even buy it.

Next, I was off to my cell. We were broken up into groups, so Niko and I got split up. The two other people in my group were dropped off first. Inmates from all races were staring at us like we were the only piece of steak at a meat market. On impulse, I changed my upright, confident walk, to a rough and tough stride. The vibe I gave off said, don't fuck with me. Not a sign of a smile seeped through my killer look. But inside I was on the verge of shitting in my pants.

In front of my new cell, I stood mortified! I couldn't believe my eyes. I had seen prison movies before. I knew not to expect some friendly man to stand up and welcome me in, but I also didn't expect to see a tall, slinky, feminine man lying on the bunk with rollers in his hair. I was ill. "Please take me somewhere else," I pleaded with Corning.

Squzzy rudely interrupted. That was the first time I had heard his soprano voice. "Come on in here to our little castle." He got up, opened a locker for me, and threw me a pillow from his bunk.

"Thanks," I said, feeling even more uncomfortable.

"Sure, and let me tell you, we're gonna get along just fine."

Sergeant Corning displayed an instant smirk. I was numb. I didn't know what to think or what to do. Corning didn't introduce us. He simply told me a few rules—information about the showers, commissary, meals—and then left. My stomach started to knot up. I couldn't wait to tell Niko.

While I placed my items in my new locker, Squzzy made small talk. "Let me tell you how to make it around here, child."

"I'm straight."

"I'm just giving you a little free advice."

"Thanks, but no thanks," I said, giving Squzzy a hint to shut the fuck up. It didn't work.

"Associate yourself with the right people if you want to stay out of trouble."

"I bet, like your crew," I said, giving him the most disgusting look I could produce.

Unbothered, Squzzy replied, "Child, let me tell you, all y'all niggas are just alike. Acting thuggish all day with pants hangin' down, but with glass slippers under your beds at night!"

"Whatever."

"Huh, you'll see."

"I'll be fine. You'll see."

That night, I couldn't get to sleep thinking about all the drama and Squzzy's final words: "You'll see."

It kept ringing in my ears over and over, even though I could hear people whining in their cells and making crazy, retarded sounds. I wasn't afraid though. I'm a trooper. And Niko was surely handling himself.

Everything worked itself out because Squzzy never tried any mess with me. We were cell mates for more than four years. And, even though I've had to put up with his—or her—faggy friends, giving each other braids and swapping lipsticks, at least I've never had to worry about any power struggles like other inmates.

8—⚷

After reminiscing for more than an hour, before long the inevitable arrived in front of my cell. Short and stout, his middle-aged skin was so yellow he looked as if he had a touch of jaundice. The people working in receiving must have given him the largest jumpsuit they could find because his gear was way too big for him.

His body odor hit the door before he did. And now after seeing him, I couldn't figure out if he was afraid of the barber's clippers or if he was boycotting. My new cell mate looked around for a minute all too comfortable. I expected him to be nervous. I wanted him to be scared shitless. Maybe he had been in before.

I kept silent, not wanting to appear too friendly, not knowing this joker's background. He might think I was a pushover.

He threw his few items on the top bunk, mumbling, "I'm definitely not gonna be sleeping on this top bunk for long," and walked out, never saying one word to me.

I stayed on my bed thinking about Sherese. Class would be starting shortly. Also, the mail call would be coming up later. Hopefully I'd be getting a crisp money order from Sherese or Grandma or even a positive letter from my lawyer. Something good was coming in the mail today. I could feel it!

On Tuesday when the mail came, I was disappointed because they called Mr. Jones, and I assumed it was for me, forgetting that Crazy Ed's last name is Jones too. Unfortunately, he got to the podium first and informed me the mail was for him. What's strange is that his attitude was totally different toward me that day. This was the day before he decided to jump on me like a cheetah attacking its prey. I hoped we wouldn't keep having mail identification problems. His stupid-ass family members needed to put a first name on the mail so there wouldn't be any confusion. I didn't want to have any more run-ins with him. I was still waiting for Niko to shank that nigga!

My new sleep mate walked back into the cell and started setting up his things. Hopefully someone would be sending him some more personal items, although, he did have a carton of Benson and Hedges. That was like having three hundred dollars. In jail a carton of cigarettes will get you anything you need. The first thing this guy should get is a hair cut because that weak-ass fade wouldn't make it in here.

He started talking to himself: "*It's the Law; Save Me; The Prisoner's Mind; The Investor's Guide for Buying Stocks; How to Buy Bonds.*"

He was reading the titles of the books on my desk, I was thinking as I hopped up to defend my property.

"I'm Divine. I know this is a bad way to start off but don't fuck with my books and keep everything nice and neat like it is now!"

Not only were my books my prized possession, but I also needed to make a harsh first impression. He didn't give me a chance to make him feel new and uncomfortable when he first came in. My cell is always spic and span. One thing Grandma taught me is next to godliness is cleanliness.

The rookie broke western. "I'm Bishop, and fuck you and your books! And by the way, I'll keep this mother-fucker however I want."

"Oh, this is definitely not gonna work."

"Oh, it will. I promise you."

"Man, you're crazy," I said, feeling like I needed to find Niko. And quick.

"Is that my pillow down there?" Bishop asked, pointing to my hard-earned pillow.

"Hell no!" I snapped angrily.

Bishop left the cell with a nasty attitude. He was in for a shock if he thought he was gonna act like that and get away with it. He'll be murdered by next week. Who did he think he was messing with?

I looked around the room to make sure all my stuff was in place. Setting a trap is real brainy on my part. This way, when I got back from tutoring I could tell if he had messed with my shit.

On my way out to class, I saw Bishop having a confrontation with another inmate about the T.V. He'd only been there thirty minutes and was fucking with people already.

"Hey, turn back," the bulky inmate said.

"It's my turn now," Bishop replied as he sat with his back toward the guy flipping channels.

"Man, who do you think you are?" the inmate said, raising out of his seat.

Calmly, Bishop looked the guy dead in the face. "I'll change the damn T.V. whenever I want. Now sit down. We're watching *Gilligan's Island.*"

I wasn't going near them. I didn't want anyone to think Bishop and I were friends. The inmate sat back down. Bishop better be glad the inmate was a punk. I'd seen people go down over changing from somebody's favorite T.V. show.

Once, Science cracked this dude over his head with a weight bar. I didn't even know how he managed to get that weight near the recreation area without anyone seeing him. Science asked the guy nicely to turn back. I guess because he didn't say it disrespectfully, dude thought Science was a punk. Clearly, I remember the dude sitting there watching a damn talk show when Science nonchalantly walked up to the back of his head and knocked him to the ground. Guards came from everywhere and wrestled Science to the floor. Lucky for him, the sergeant in charge that day didn't give a damn and let him off without punishment. If that had been Corning, Science would have been in deep shit.

Nonetheless, he never tried to run or resist and never denied hitting an inmate with a blow to the head from a weight bar. I don't know what he likes to watch on T.V., but for sure when he is in front of the television he watches what he wants. Believe me, nobody says a damn thing. As for the guy who got chumped, he ended up getting seventy-five stitches in his head and suffered a massive head injury.

For Bishop's sake, most of the dudes that run the T.V. had obviously left the area to go to daily academic programs.

Some people take up carpentry, electricity, plumbing, or attend academic school. I guess you could say I'm giving back while I'm here because I help guys get their G.E.D. It makes me feel good and I'm still making Grandma proud while I'm in here. I don't know what they're going to do when I'm gone. Maybe I'll come back and volunteer.

Now, people like Mathematics don't have the option of choosing a program. The state chose one for him: Alcoholics/Narcotics Anonymous. If they only knew that shit wasn't helping anybody, they'd stop the program. Hell, I guess they're providing somebody with a job.

If Niko weren't my boy I'd recommend he be mandated to the sex-offender program. Just think, he works in the metal shop. What idiot gave him a job working with metal? I ain't mad at 'em. It just means our crew will always have access to weapons. I just don't see the logic in putting someone like Niko in that environment, especially, with his violent reputation.

ο—

Class was quite irritating for me. I didn't know if it was the fact that these fools really didn't want to learn, or if it had something to do with the reality that my crazy ass new cell mate was alone to rummage through my shit. If he touched any of my things I was gonna have to straighten him immediately. My pillow better be just where I left it. And, I damn sure hoped he wasn't looking at my pictures of Sherese. I didn't even want him looking at Grandma.

"Divine, can I see you for a moment?" Ms. Williams asked in her pleasant voice.

Ms. Williams was a well-dressed African woman in her late twenties. Because she was a teacher and a civilian prison employee, she could sport her many tailored suits with the miniskirt look. On a scale from one to ten, in terms of beauty, her dark-chocolate skin helped to give her a nine. As far as mathematical knowledge, I'd give her a ten. Her intelligence was an understatement. I was especially impressed by the way she enunciated every word from her luscious lips. About five-four, she was well refined and poised.

I like her. I'm grateful that she allowed me to be a tutor for her math classes. As soon as I requested the job, she checked my math scores and hired me, no questions asked. Most of the guys liked her, too, but not because of her personality. They rushed to class just to see her walk around in those tight skirts. As a matter of fact, she was the only female teacher in the academic department.

"Yes, you called me," I said, standing in front of her desk, blushing.

Taking off her wire-rimmed glasses, she said, "Write these problems on the board."

"Sure," I said, grabbing the paper willingly from her soft hands. I held on to her hands as long as I could without seeming too sensual.

"Oh, Divine. . .excuse me for a moment," she said as a C.O. looked inside the classroom window. "Everything is okay," she said, smiling as she signaled to the Asian guard. "As I was saying, Ray needs some extra help. If you could—"

"Say no more, I'm on it."

Even though I wasn't in the best mood, I played games on my mind. I'd do anything for Ms. Williams. Just the smell of her sweet perfume got me motivated.

Helping Ray drained me mentally, and before I knew it, we had already seen three out of four of our classes. With only forty-five minutes to go, I was tired. When the last set of inmates entered the room, I felt as if I'd been swamped by a bunch of idiots.

"No hope for this class," I said jokingly, setting some papers on Ms.Williams' desk.

"There's hope for everyone, Divine," she said, smiling. *I think she likes me.*

By the time Ms.Williams had erased the board, our last class was already coming in. Most sat slouched in their seats, not once getting their materials ready. Unenthusiastic, I didn't feel like tutoring anymore. Who would Ms. Williams assign me to? Some unwise character probably.

Ms. Williams stood in the front of the class giving instructions. Reid, a tall, elderly white man sat with a bizarre look on his face, had his mouth wide open while he glared into space. I waved my hand back and forth, trying to make him notice me. It didn't work. He didn't normally pay attention, but his stare was now fixated on Ms. Williams. His right hand was in his lap as his mouth released saliva. The wooden desktop covered the majority of his arm. He took some precautions, but after seeing his hand shaking back and forth, I realized what was happening. I moved my finger up and down, signaling the guard who had peeked through the window. My eye contact led him in Reid's direction before he even entered the room. With a nod of my head, the pervert was caught!

"Excuse me, ma'am," the C.O. said as he lifted Reid out of his seat by his collar.

Ms. Williams didn't respond, nor did she even realize Reid was using her to get his rocks off. How disgusting. Right in the middle of class. No discretion at all. Class continued as usual. However, I must say, I'd earned my ninety-five cents!

When class was dismissed I hurried back to my cell. Everyone traveled in slow motion. Most of the officers on the shift were moving about the block. This was the time of day when everyone was out of their cells and stirring about. It would be time to eat dinner soon, I thought, after hearing my stomach growl. I hurried past people rushing to my cell. When I got there Bishop was lying on his bunk facing the wall. Was he asleep? Had he been kicked off the T.V. already?

"Mail call, mail call!" shouted one of the correctional officers. Everybody who thought it was remotely possible for them to receive something started hurrying to the main podium. Lieutenant Graham called out last names: "Bell, Green, Hartford, Jacobs, Lewis, Joyner, Jones."

He kept on calling names for about five minutes. Black, excited about receiving his letter, moved in zig-zag motions. As he sung to himself, he made up lyrics about gettin' paid. When he opened his mail, a frown appeared on his face. He found a receipt inside from a money order his mom had sent him. Obviously the three-hundred-dollar money order that had been taken out when the mail was checked and placed on Black's account, wasn't enough. Seeing those receipts when you got your mail was like hitting the numbers around here. What did Black expect? A "G"?

Graham noticed me standing patiently, and finally said, "Divine, you're the Jones I'm talking about."

I kept silent and swiftly grabbed my letter. Happily, I started walking back to my room. All kinds of racket could be heard. "Yeah, boy. My baby looks out," one inmate boasted, shaking his mail in the air. Another inmate said, "Look at my girl," gloating over the pictures he had gotten.

When I saw the words *I will always love you* and red lips imprinted on the envelope, I got goose bumps before I even opened it. Mail makes you feel loved because you know someone had to be thinking of you when they decided to write. I hope those damn officers that go through the mail looking for contraband didn't read my love letter. They probably sat in a room and got off on freaky letters. I didn't even care at this point, as long as my baby was thinking of me, I was okay.

Bishop turned over and watched me as I ripped the envelope open and unfolded the letter. I love this sweet smelling paper. Sherese must have sprayed some of that vanilla fragrance I love. She knew that turned me on. Bishop probably resented the fact that he hadn't gotten a chance to receive mail yet. I started to read out loud with hopes of making him jealous. Green with envy, I thought.

Dear Divine,

I hope everything is going all right with you. When I spoke to you on the phone last week, I had so many things to tell you but I couldn't bring myself to talk about it at that time. I haven't been doing so well. I've been real depressed lately and haven't found a way to tell you what's wrong. I know it's difficult for you, as it is for me to be separated for so long. I feel like we've been away from each other for such a lengthy time now, that we're out-growing each other. You have been on my mind so much lately that it's hard for me to sleep. When you were out on the streets it was easy for me to be faithful because we were always together. Now it's hard because you've been locked up for five years, and I'm all alone. You should be able to realize that I have feelings and needs too. This doesn't change my love for you. I just want to let you know things aren't the same anymore. I know deep down in my heart, you're a good person. I've cried for hours trying to figure out how to tell you this. That's why it hurts me to say this, but I need you to know that I'm three months pregnant and I'm not getting rid of the baby. I'm so sorry for disappointing you. I didn't mean to hurt you. I guess this is one time I didn't use my head. Please don't hate me. I hope we can remain friends. Write me. Please don't call.

Sincerely,
Sherese

P.S. If there is anything you don't understand about the court transcript I sent you last week, write your lawyer.

There was a brief shortness of breath. Then I felt my heart pounding at about one hundred miles per hour. I was certain I was having a stroke. Maybe even heart failure. My eyes began to fill with water. Then, I burst into tears. I didn't even care that Bishop was looking right in my face. Sherese was my everything, and now she was pregnant by some nigga! I ripped her pictures off the wall in a rage. Shredding her letters into pieces, I threw things around the cell she had previously sent me. People started looking in my cell trying to find out what was going on.

"I know you're not gonna let some hoe make you cry like a baby in front of all these grown men. You're showing your weakness and that ain't good," Bishop said, turning away from me.

Shocked, and looking at the back of Bishop's head. I couldn't believe he had made that statement. He barely knew my name, and now he was giving me advice. This clown was fresh off the bus and portraying the lead man. I calmed down and laid on my bed thinking about how my life had been turned upside down and how Bishop saw me cry like a punk.

I started to put things into perspective only because Bishop turned over to look me dead in my face. I played it off like I didn't notice. "Get it all out now," he said with disgust. "Then let it be over," he said slowly and firmly.

I started rambling like I had a deadline to meet: "I can't believe Sherese did this to me. I knew that bitch was too good to be true. Everybody in here told me to forget about having a woman to yourself once you get in here. No. . .I didn't want to believe it! I can't understand why she just couldn't tell me she wanted to be with someone else. Fucking cunt! She's been making all these so-called plans for us to move together and get married when I get home. Now she's writing me saying she's knocked up!"

Bishop, trying to sound half interested said, "What did you expect?"

"Nah, man, it's not like that. She's been selling me wolf tickets all along. Sherese has probably been fucking around since I've been incarcerated. I'm sure she was lying all those times when she would write me about how her pussy throbbed for me. I truly believed that she was saving her body for me. Everything she said was probably a lie!"

I started pulling out all the pictures and the stacks of letters I had received from her over the years. I even found a picture of the wedding gown she wanted to buy.

After rambling on for several minutes I turned and said, "Bishop, the worst part about this ordeal is that Sherese has had a lot of contact with my lawyer lately. I don't even know what transcript she's talking about. She probably lied about sending it because I never got it."

Bishop tolerantly listened to me vent. While he moved to the floor becoming more personable it seemed as though something stood out about him. Maybe it was his style. His hands covered his face as if he were in deep thought. "It will take some time, but you'll get over it," he said, in the most caring voice he'd uttered so far.

I wondered what he was in for. If I asked, he'd most likely say he was innocent.

Switching gears, Bishop asked, "What are you going to do about having an outside contact to keep in touch with your lawyer, now that your girlfriend has another priority in her life?"

"My grandmother will step in and take care of everything. Sherese was just helping her anyway. I definitely need to find out about that court transcript. As a matter of fact, I'm going to tell my grandmother to get a copy of the transcript my lawyer sent to Sherese. I can't even pronounce the lawyer's name. Mr. Broth-en-stein or some shit like that."

"Do that," he said, like he was taking charge.

"I need to call Sherese and let her know my grandmother will be over to pick up my fuckin' money. I won't get pimped! Under no circumstances will she bear another man's baby and spend my money. I should have listened to my grandma about that freak a long time ago."

"Are you going to eat?" Bishop asked, raising up from the floor.

"I'm staying here. Besides, I'm not even hungry."

"You mean you're lovesick," Bishop said dryly. "I'll bet you after a couple of hours you'll come to your senses, but it'll be too late to eat then."

"I'll pass."

When Bishop left, I was all alone. Niko, Black, and Mathematics would be wondering why I didn't come to chow. Yeah, I went off in a rage, but I was not really sure how many people heard me. They may have thought I was chumping Bishop. At this point it didn't even matter. I was in love with a freak who didn't love me back.

Once the lights went out, I lay on my bed unable to sleep. Time had already flown by because the count lasted about two hours. At first the rumor spread, there was a jail break because one inmate couldn't be found. Dogs howled and loud sirens continuously sounded off. Every inmate portrayed his own lying-ass story about what was happening. The helicopters raced above and dogs howled, but that was it. No one really knew what was going down. We were safe and sound in our cells and the C.O.s on post inside didn't give up any information.

I can't imagine anyone from my block trying to escape. I would feel like an idiot trying to run. First of all, if the motion detectors didn't go off, I still had to get over that tall-ass fence without getting shot up.

All we really know is that all available officers and the local sheriff's department spent about an hour searching the grounds and surrounding areas looking for the missing inmate. This was one time I felt bad for the nice officers like Riley and Martin. I heard they had to travel on foot through the swampy wooded area near the facility.

We were all locked in our cells until they finally confirmed that the count was official and now correct. Just imagine, after all of that, nobody had even escaped. The warden should have been smart enough to think about the track record of this place. Although several inmates had escaped, most had been returned. Only two people had managed to escape successfully in the last five years. I believe one person had help from the inside, because a big hole discovered in the fence could only be cut by a high-powered tool.

All kinds of things raced through my mind. I lay awake until 4:00 A.M. thinking. How long had Sherese been cheating on me? Am I really getting out of this place? What's the scoop on Bishop? Why did he even listen to me, he hardly knows me? What's in the transcript Sherese sent me from my lawyer and why didn't I get it? Why didn't the lawyer send me a copy?

9

Bewildered

"Jones, get up, Lieutenant Graham wants to see you *now!*" Sergeant Corning yelled. Was I dreaming? Bishop's loud bangs on the bedpost interrupted my catnap. Oh, shit! Lieutenant Graham wanted to see me, probably about that complaint form I filed on Bennett. I jumped from my bed and threw something on as quickly as I could, thinking about what I would say. You know how it is when you tell a lie; it's hard to remember what you originally said. Plus I'd only had one hour of sleep. It was 5:00 A.M.! I needed to call Grandma as soon as I finished getting Bennett fired.

I found myself staring at Corning. I thought, *here's a wealthy man who doesn't have to work, still on the clock in the wee hours of the morning.* He's been dreaming about being a white shirt, but he's been going above and beyond lately. He has so much money from the lawsuit he won when his wife passed. I can't understand for the life of me why he wants to have a long-term career here in Dunnridge.

The block was quiet, except for undomesticated Mike

who talked to himself on a regular basis. I had no idea he started his chanting this early. When I walked past his cell, I saw him banging his head on his knee while sitting Indian style.

"I'm not doing it!" he yelled. "Somebody else did it," he said slowly as he looked directly at me.

He's as crazy as a jaybird.

What's really unusual is that a few inmates were awake and looking out of their cells glaring at me. Had they been awaken for complaints also? Oddly, they seemed upset. Science, peering from his cell, shook his oversized head from right to left. I know people aren't mad at me for snitching on that bitch. She should have thought about what she did when she made me strip in front of Squzzy's crew last month. And we know the type of search she gave me was illegal and abusive.

In Graham's office, Bennett's tears flowed like the Nile river. Her face was beet red with her head sunk into her hands. And once again she needed a perm.

Corning showered her with encouraging words as well as a few pats on the shoulder. She couldn't bear to look at me. I guess that bitch knew this was it and I was now in control of her ass. I'll bet she won't be swaying out of here today. Ever since I've been in, she's harassed me and made me feel like I'm nothing, degrading me every chance she gets. I hope she gets what she deserves.

Graham and Corning have their eyes fixed on Bennett. She'll probably lose her job, that's why she's laying on the crying so thick. The mood is dreary and dull. I hope nobody feels sorry for her. I don't.

I watched Corning closely for a few moments. He poured Graham's coffee carefully as if he had been trained as a butler. Penitentiary pet, I thought. He did everything for Lieutenant from making phone calls to delivering him fried chicken from Bennett. Graham loved fried chicken with his overweight ass.

"Sit down, Jones," Lieutenant Graham said. The office was plush for a prison. Plaques lined the wall, and pictures covered the stylish desk. And why in the hell did Graham need a mahogany desk like he worked at IBM? Or for that matter, a Persian rug?

"Jones we've got a serious situation on our hands," Graham said.

"It's not that serious," I said curtly. "Bennett was wrong and I filed a complaint."

Bennett thundered out of her seat as though she had a bolt of energy and bum-rushed me. She had gotten to my face when Corning snatched her off me and said, "You have to stay focused; you can never let the death of an inmate get you down like this."

Graham handed Bennett a tissue. "Calm down," he said, speaking in a soothing tenor.

"I'm okay," Bennett said, gaining composure. She quickly patted the tears away from her eyes. Although her face still illustrated sadness, she embraced some self-control.

I clapped slowly as if I admired her performance.

As the room settled for a second, Graham asked Corning if he could escort Bennett out of the room. She shouldn't be left alone. I, on the other hand, was in a daze.

Niko must have been killed, otherwise Bennett wouldn't be so upset. A million things started going through my mind. Sadness because I lost my best friend. Fear because I no longer have protection in here. And triumph over Bennett because I bet none of these officers realized that she was crying because she was fucking Niko. They probably thought the good Christian woman was saddened because a life had been lost. Who had the balls to kill Niko? I know I'm not powerful enough to take revenge by myself. Niko was the bad influence that got me here.

Oh shit! I was called to Graham's office because an inmate had passed. Do they think I killed Niko? Or did they think I had some pertinent information? I was so caught up in my own personal problems last night that Niko and I didn't even talk before lock down. Wait a minute, I saw him during the count last night, right before lockdown.

I blurted out to Lieutenant Graham, "Deuce did it. Niko was alive during the count and was then locked in the cell with Deuce. I'll take care of him."

Graham said, "Divine, Niko isn't dead. Last night during the count we figured out that Ed Jones was missing."

"Ed Jones?"

Graham with his arms folded spoke to me like a teacher shaming a student. "Yes, you know exactly who I'm referring to. The guy you had an altercation with last week."

"Oh, yeah."

"Your Alzheimer's is going away, huh?"

"I know who he is," I said, shrugging.

"When was the last time you saw him?"

"I don't remember. And what's with the third degree? What, you think I did it?"

"I didn't say that," Graham said, walking over to sip his coffee.

"But the expression on your face is saying it."

Graham started explaining what happened. "All officers

were put on patrol last night when we realized Ed was missing. The search started in the woods covering a five-mile radius. But during that time, Jones' body was found in the showers. He had been stabbed twenty-seven times. We didn't notify anyone until we initially started the investigation. We understand that you and he had some problems, which led to the altercation last week. The people we have interviewed so far have implicated you or Niko as the killer."

"Then why was Bennett crying?"

"She's upset," Graham said casually.

"Yeah, I know, but do you know why?"

"Some of my officers need counseling after the death of an inmate."

"She's not crying. . .Oh, forget it." Frustrated, I said, "Lieutenant, I thought you called me here to investigate my complaint on Bennett, then I get here to find out I'm a suspect for someone's death who I didn't even know was dead. This is definitely a fucked-up place."

Suddenly, Corning peeped in the door and gave Graham a signal.

"Excuse me for a moment," Graham said as he stepped outside the office.

Sergeant Corning came back in to baby-sit me for a while.

Thank God Bennett didn't come back.

I nestled down into one of Graham's plush comfortable chairs and ran all kinds of scenarios through my head. Exhaustion took over, but going to sleep was out of the question.

Graham left me in his office for more than an hour and a half. I guess trying to decide how to proceed with the situation. He seemed a bit overwhelmed. Officers came in and out. It seemed as if other situations going on irrelevant to Ed Jones' murder took precedent. I made myself right at home, checking out Graham's awards, which lined his wall. Interestingly enough, Graham was slim as a young officer. He'd actually been working for the Department of Corrections since 1968. I counted nearly twenty awards of recognition posted throughout the office. Needless to say, Graham was an honorary employee. Most of the inmates seemed to like him. Probably because he was a fair guy.

When Graham finally returned he had on his captain's hat, as if he were on official business. "Divine, I want to advise you that while this murder is being investigated you will be put in protective custody."

"Protective custody. . .?"

"It's for your own good."

"Not really," I said.

"After the morning count everyone will know what has happened and the prison will be in an uproar. And most likely, Ed's crew will want to retaliate against you and Niko."

"We can handle that," I said, hitting myself in the chest. "Bring it on."

Graham continued, "Oh, by the way, if you have any visits you will be shackled the entire time. You will not be allowed to use any of the facilities where inmates are free to roam. All of your meals will be brought to you. Do you have any questions?"

"Nah," I said, blowing a little breath out the side of my lips. I was so pissed off I pulled a bitch move when I slightly rolled my eyes.

The shift was changing. Graham walked to the front of his door as the officers were punching in. He said, "Officer Garcia, I need to see you immediately."

When Officer Garcia walked through the door, I realized, the newest C.O.—the one out on the yard a couple of days ago, stood in front of me. The Jennifer Lopez look-alike sat down nervously, not giving me any eye contact. Her starched blue uniform was extra tight. If I weren't in this fucked-up situation, I'd surely spend some time monitoring that body.

As Graham finished conversing with officers outside his door, he turned to Crawford for assistance. But before he could give him instructions, he abruptly stopped talking while his eyebrows raised with speculation. He placed his right hand under his chin, moving his thumb back and forth.

"Crawford, do I need to test you?"

"No sir," Crawford replied, tucking his shirt in and standing as straight as possible.

"It doesn't seem like you're mentally alert enough to handle these inmates or help your coworkers if they need it."

"I'm okay. I promise you, I'm straight."

"Consider this a warning! And get yourself together. Take a few days off if you need to."

"Yes, sir."

Changing tones, Graham respectfully asked Crawford to get me settled in while he tended to some important business. I felt like Graham's son when he asked, "Do you need to tell me anything before you leave?"

"Yes, I need to make a phone call. Looks like I may need another lawyer."

Disappointed, Graham pointed toward the door. Once

out of sight, he yelled, "On your way to your new residence, I'll allow you the opportunity to make one call."

Graham instructed C.O. Crawford to let me make a call. However, when we got to the pay phones the headsets were gone. That shit pissed me off! I was in desperate need of a phone call.

I couldn't believe this shit! First Sherese wrote me a sweet letter letting me know she was screwing someone else, then I found out my lawyer had sent vital documents through that whore and I never got them. To top everything else I might be a suspect in a murder I didn't even commit. All I wanted was to make a fucking phone call, which was totally impossible because some nut had taken all the headsets! As a matter of fact, I shouldn't even be here because I'm innocent!

C.O. Crawford just stood there looking at me. "Divine, I know you're upset, brother, but I've got to do my job. I'll see if you can use the phones in protective custody."

Passing through the block, my boy Mathematics' sat chilling. Others were in the room, but ignoring them, he played Mr. Antisocial.

This was typical when Mathematics wanted to make one of his many transactions. Sitting in the middle of the recreation area, he watched *Sanford and Son* on the tube. More than fifteen inmates had gathered around amused by the show. We caught each other's attention, but didn't speak. Crawford slowed down signaling Mathematics. Kyree, a brotha serving only two years, said, "Man, you watching this shit?" Mathematics kept silent. I expected him to acknowledge at least one of Crawford's many attempts to get his attention. Maybe he knew something strange was going on with me and didn't want any part of it.

Kyree asked again, "You watching this?"

"Shut the fuck up," Bishop said pompously.

As Bishop entered the room, everything went still. At that moment no one moved. Mathematics quickly looked at me, then without consideration, raised up as if he were about to leave. I assumed he was waiting for a sale. Maybe I was right because all of a sudden he had a change of heart. Putting his headphones on, he plopped back down in the seat and waited. Moving slowly back and forth as if he were enjoying the music, he never once looked in Bishop's direction. People slowly dispersed from the room. Mathematics noticed it, but continued to wait.

I was happy Crawford was so lax about getting me to my new home. Mathematics acted as if he didn't notice Bishop, me, or Crawford. That's how he is. He takes this shit serious.

Meanwhile Bishop sat in the chair across from him that he had taken forcefully from some sucker. He stared at Mathematics, waiting to get some type of look or response from him. It didn't work. His face was completely balled up like someone had done something to him.

"Yo! Whuz up, kid," Black said, slapping Mathematics' hand. He jumped over the chair landing directly next to him. Looking over his left shoulder in my direction, he said, "Divine, why Crawford got you on a leash?"

"It's a long story," I said. Shit, I'm glad somebody noticed that I exist. After being ignored by both Bishop and Mathematics, I was beginning to think I was insignificant around here.

By now, Crawford had given up any hopes of talking to Mathematics. He escorted me closer to the outskirts of the recreation area.

Black looked at Mathematics' shoes. He checked him up and down. Excited, he said, "Yo, money, who sent you those kicks?"

"You know Tashonda tries to keep me in all the latest shit. I think she forgets I got to wear my work gear the majority of the day. I guess she doesn't realize we being worked like Hebrew slaves."

Black laughed as he looked over to notice Bishop changing positions. He was now looking directly in their faces as if he were invited to be in the conversation. Black turned to the side to block his view as much as he could. He really didn't want a beef. He wanted some drugs.

The tension was so thick at this point you could cut it with a knife. Mathematics stood immediately with his shoulders sitting straight up and chest poking out. He knew if he didn't step to Bishop, he would be considered a chump. He didn't want any trouble, but wasn't afraid of it. Bishop was almost to his feet when a quad of officers showed up quicker than lightning. They didn't make a move or insinuate anything. Everyone knew a beef was on.

"This area is closed," C.O. Brown said, motioning for people to vacate.

Mathematics figured Bishop was just jealous because he couldn't run him. He never really came in contact with Bishop unless Bishop came his way. A beef was the last thing he needed anyway. Hell, he was all about making money. Mathematics and Black walked away talking much shit. They slapped hands when they were far enough away from the C.O.s to be seen—except for Crawford, who sneakily watched Mathematics every move.

Bam! It was done. The transaction had taken place even though Bishop almost fucked it up.

Things were really going well for Mathematics. I was proud. He was making plenty of loot and selling everything from heroin to weed. The best part about his business was that he had a set of dudes buying directly from him. He didn't like distributing his shit to sellers. Most weren't as smooth as he was. Besides he didn't want to chance anyone getting caught and snitching on him. That nigga is paranoid, that's why he rarely used the pay phones. He always claimed the phones were tapped automatically. He wanted no part of it.

Tashonda had started to visit weekly. Last month she came six times, which meant Mathematics was rolling. Someone on staff had to be helping him.

As we entered the weasle block I put all my thoughts about Mathematics behind me. Protective custody reminded me of a ghost town. The dimly lit unit wasn't like Block C at all. No recreation going on over there. It was not noisy or congested like the block either. Even though I didn't play cards seeing a game or two being played wouldn't hurt. The rusted iron gates were almost antique. And, the floors were laid with dingier flooring than we had on Block C.

Six cells are situated side by side, settled on the far right of the room. To my left an office desk with loads of junk and junk foods was the focal point of the block. One raggedy TV was facing the cells, hanging from the ceiling with a good view for everyone. Way down at the end it looked like showers.

Trying to get a closer look into the cells to see if I could see anyone made me feel like a stalker. I had no idea what it would be like or how long I would have to be here. I didn't even know if anyone over here had heard of me. I was sure they had, I thought, boasting to myself.

I heard the C.O. telling Crawford which cell to put me in. Walking down the dirty, gloomy path of misery, I saw Niko. He was lying on the floor with his knees nearly up to his chest. I could barely decipher the crazy sounds and mumbles he made under his breath.

"Niko!" I called. "Niko, Niko!" Over and over I called out as I was continuously being nudged past his cell toward mine.

10   Wishful Thinking

The heat in this place is unbearable and there's absolutely no one to talk to in here. I yelled out, "Niko, Niko." No response.

The light-skinned, unfamiliar guard abruptly appeared and asked me if I was okay.

I snapped, "Okay. Nothing is okay. I need to use the damn phone."

The officer surprisingly replied, "I'll see what I can do."

Once he turned away, I started to reflect. This was not the way my life should be turning out. I went from having a degree in finance to sitting on the floor of a jail cell and worse than that I'm in protective custody. This place should be condemned! It reminded me of those spots back home that got closed down for rat infestation. I couldn't believe I was still here. I should be a stockbroker or mortgage lender. I shouldn't be here under any circumstances.

How I wish I could be back at my old job, U.S. Savings and Loan. I was the man, didn't have a worry in the world.

I was well on my way to being bank president. I couldn't believe I was so stupid to fuck that up.

Magically, the officer working this wing arrived on the scene like my fairy godfather.

He said, "Mr. Jones, don't you need to use the phone?"

"Yes, yes," I repeated. I followed him back past the cells and out to the front of the wing.

He even offered me some of the salt-and-vinegar chips he was eating.

Declining, I hurried to call Grandma immediately.

When I reached the phones, I was ecstatic to see all the parts in place. As I dialed the number, chill bumps perked up all over my arms. I hadn't spoken to Grandma since last week, but, then again, a lot had changed since then. The operator asked, "Name please?" After giving her my name, silence lasted about five seconds. Eventually she said, "No answer." I was devastated.

The guard was waiting to take me back to the cell. He looked me directly in my face, probably wondering what was taking me so long, because I hadn't said anything since the operator ripped my heart out.

In an instant I knew exactly what I was about to do. I grabbed the phone and started dialing the number immediately. Before the male operator could ask for my name, I said, "Collect call from Divine."

I started thinking about all the nasty things I would say to Sherese, like Bitch, where is my damn money? How come you didn't tell me you were a freak?

The operator took a little longer than usual. Maybe the line had been disconnected, but static still cackled in the background of the phone, so I waited.

The operator returned to the line. "Sir, the gentleman

you just called not only denied the charges but rudely asked how to stop prisoners from calling his home. I referred him to the business office."

"I must have dialed the wrong number. Can you try it for me one more time? As a matter of fact make it a person-to-person collect call." I told him the number.

"Can I have the name of the person you'd like to speak with and also your name one more time please?"

Overly frustrated at this point, I said, "Sherese Williams is her name and the call is coming from Divine Jones."

"Hold, please."

The anticipation was killing me. I couldn't wait to give her a piece of my mind.

Feeling more relaxed, I said, "Hey sir, I think I'll have a few of those chips."

"Sure," replied the friendly officer.

Once again the operator took longer than usual.

This time when he returned to the line he said, "Mr. Jones, it is obvious that you are calling the right number, however, the gentleman answering the phone stated that Sherese will not be accepting any calls from you. There is nothing more I can do for you. Thanks for calling AT&T."

Devastated, emotionally wrecked, and abused. This is what I got for being locked up. I was already feeling lonely, and now rejected. Sherese was not only pregnant, but she now had some guy living with her and wouldn't accept my calls. She could at least accept my call. After all I've done for that hoe!

"Are you finished with your calls?" the officer asked.

"Yeah, thanks. By the way what's your name?"

"Brocton. Officer Brocton."

Now Brocton is not your average-looking guy. When he extended his hand, the dirty-blond strands stood out brightly in his hair. Even though, he's Black, he sported milky-colored skin, with high cheekbones. His pinkish lips accented his acne-filled chin. The most normal thing about him was that his medium-built frame stood about five-nine.

"Listen, I have a friend on lockdown in this wing. On my way out I didn't see him. Do you know if Niko Jenkins is still in protective custody?"

Before he could answer, two correctional officers appeared from nowhere and told Officer Brocton they needed to take me to my old cell. When I heard them say they needed to do a search and clear all of my things out, I was shocked. I didn't say a word. Before I even entered Block C, the noise of loud chatter among the inmates greeted me. *Camp as usual.* Bandanas adorned heads, a dominoes game was going on, and of course a line waited for the phones. The only thing that stood out as being different were the looks I was getting. When Equality decided to grit on me, that confirmed things. Well, I didn't care anyway. I'm getting outta here soon.

I passed Niko's old cell on my way to my former residence. To my surprise Niko stood in the corner of his cell in a daze. It was a look I hadn't seen in him before. It was almost a look of fear. I tried to give 'em some sort of eye contact. Friendly encouragement. But the officers kept nudging me ahead as if I was walking too slow. Hell, I was doing that on purpose. Basically being nosy. I couldn't tell exactly what was going on, but I hoped those two brutes with me wouldn't try to wreck my cell the way they did Niko's.

I guess I couldn't be so lucky.

"What the fuck happened to my shit?" I said as soon as I saw my cell.

The mattresses were flipped upside down and cut open. Moss from the bed was all over the place. My poster of Nia Long had been torn down, along with my pictures. And most of my toiletries had been poured out and cut open. All of my books were on the floor and Bennett was sitting there reading my letters. I tried to snatch the papers out of her hand, but got slammed to the floor.

"This is my personal shit, and I damn sure don't want you reading it."

"You should have thought about that before you decided to start murdering people," Bennett replied.

I wanted to respond but my lip was bleeding. And worse than that was the feeling of some officer's shoe sticking in the back of my neck. I lay there waiting for the cell search to be over. I didn't mind them searching my shit because I didn't do anything.

However, I didn't like my stuff being thrown around and people reading my personal business. These crazy fools are even checking the floors for a secret compartment. I guess they were pissed that they didn't find any incriminating evidence because next thing I knew, I was being thrown up against the wall. I should have known what was next when a fat male officer put on a pair of latex gloves. I yelled as loud as I could, wishing, hoping, and praying someone would walk in the cell to see me getting a rectum search. I thought those were illegal in this institution.

Even though they didn't find anything, I felt like they had won the battle. Not only did they degrade me, but left my ass feeling sore as hell.

When I was allowed to get off the floor, the first thing I grabbed was my bible. I thought Bennett was going to tell me to put it back, but instead she said,

"You need it! Read it."

With my bible tucked tightly under my arm, I headed toward the opening of the cell. A lot of commotion was going on in the recreation area. I thought, more drama to come, but fittingly two clowns danced to a video, and a few fools watched their performance.

After leaving my cell, I hoped to see Niko again. When I walked back past his cell, Deuce had his back turned, but Niko was already gone. I wish I had gotten a chance to talk to him.

I was almost to the end of the wing when Deuce tried to run up close to me. The C.O.s reacted swiftly as if Deuce were trying to shank me. I guess they'd seen some inmates who just didn't give a fuck. They might try to kill you with an officer standing right there. If you had life, I guess it didn't even matter.

Deuce was standing about ten feet from me and looked me dead in my face. Now, I had no respect for punks so I wasn't even afraid. He started pointing and mumbling so much shit that I could barely understand what he was saying. The officers were actually letting this dreadlock fool say his peace.

I asked, "What the fuck is your problem?"

He responded in his fake-ass deep voice "Niko was there for you and you stabbed him in his back."

He went on for a few minutes talking about the reason Niko was in here is because of me and how it was all my fault. He said, "Niko ended up in protective custody because of you and now he and a correctional officer are in trouble because of you. It's all you, you, you."

I had heard enough. Demons had taken over Deuce's body. Pressuring the officers to move on was like pulling teeth. They acted as though they enjoyed this soap-opera bullshit. Deuce was such a faggot and everybody knew it.

The officers didn't even take me all the way into protective custody. They waited for Officer Brocton to open the gate then he took over.

He asked, with great concern, "Why didn't you bring back any of your personal belongings from your cell?"

I started to describe how all of my things were thrown on the floor and how my books and magazines were ruined. He stood casually, with his arms folded. Not once did he blink. He said, "That's what happens when cell searches take place."

He knew exactly how things worked around here. I thought I could use a friend like this.

"How did you know my cell had been searched?" I asked.

He replied, "There is a murder investigation going on. It's procedure for the murdered and the suspects to have their cells searched for any clues that might be helpful in the case."

"Officer Brocton, I didn't do it."

He hesitated and then spoke slowly. "It's not my place to judge you. I'm here to protect you."

Feeling good, I said, "Thanks, man."

"You got it. So often inmates think we're all such bad people around here."

"Nah, not me."

"I'm just doing my job," Brocton said, pulling out a wad of money. He counted silently as he flicked each bill.

"Who said you can't make money in corrections?" I asked with a sly grin. "You like this job, don't you?"

"Kinda sorta," Broction said, folding his money into his pocket.

"Is this what you had planned for your life?"

"What do you mean?" Brocton asked, starting to become annoyed.

"Well, did you go to college?"

"Nope. Did you?" Brocton snapped.

"Yeah, I did, and look where it got me."

"Most C.O.s don't have college degrees. It's a waste of time and money if you plan on working in here. It only helps you if you want to become a superintendent or a warden."

"You're probably making side money anyway," I said trying to slide my comment in innocently.

"What are you saying?"

"Nothing. I was kidding around." I ended the questioning session realizing I could be messing up my connection.

Brocton confirmed our friendship when he said, "Oh, about your friend you were asking about. I just took him to the showers. I'm positive he'll be here for a while."

Not knowing a great deal about protective custody I started asking questions on the way back to my cell. I found out that over here everything was done separately. You ate, showered, phoned, and slept alone over here. I wouldn't wish this feeling of loneliness on anyone. I actually thought nothing could be worse than losing your freedom. Before coming over to this side, I was upset at seeing how inmates got themselves incarcerated and then acted as though they were at camp for a few years. Now, I would love to be on Block C watching TV, listening to my Walkman, or going out to play ball. I was just wishing I could be back with my homies and everything could be back to normal.

11 Somebody Still Loves Me

The clicking sounds from the locks became louder and louder as the gate slowly opened. Everything over here was so unpredictable. I didn't know whether it was time for my shower or what was happening. Well the gate was open, but I didn't see anyone. C.O. Curtis the tenured guard who worked this unit was posted at the desk eating doughnuts. I would be willing to bet he'd been a slouch his entire thirty-two years working here. I should get to know him a little better considering he's here the majority of the time.

If I had my watch, I would know what time it is. At least I knew it was Saturday, and the year was 2000. I'd just sit here and wait.

Rain beats on the roof of this place so hard, it sounds like someone is throwing rocks at this shithole. I couldn't hear the rain on Block C. I guess because another tier covers the top of my floor. I walked toward the miniature square window located at the top of my cell. The only thing I could see was the dreary sky. Even though I knew it was morning, darkness prevailed.

A tall correctional officer stood in the entrance way to the cell. He asked, "Why didn't you come out the cell when the gates opened?"

"Nobody said to leave. I'm tryna to be a good house nigga," I said.

"You have a visitor, Mr. Funny Man."

"I do?"

"When you decide to come out of here we can get going."

"I need a few minutes to tidy up!"

I was so excited! I figured it was Grandma considering Sherese was a knocked-up freak. Nobody else would be coming to see me anyway. I didn't have time for a shower, but I brushed my teeth as quickly as I could and put lotion on my face. I definitely don't want Grandma to see me with an ashy face, or dirty ears for that matter. My clothes were a little wrinkled, but they'd have to do for now!

I walked through the iron gates and turned to the end of the block. C.O. Curtis stood waiting for me. Of course I wanted to see if Niko was in his cell and whoever else living over here for now. I kept looking to my left at the cells as I walked straight. The first cell I walked past was home to the guy directly next to me. I heard him crying last night. *He's a geek.* He almost looked sick. This joker probably weighed less than a hundred pounds.

The cell next to him was occupied by a Jamacian guy with a head full of dreadlocks. I think Jamaicans are so cool. I thought about getting dreads once, then I changed my mind.

Oh shit! There he is, standing close to the front of his cell. Maybe he knew I was gonna walk this way. He probably wanted to talk to me about everything that had been going on. I went to grab the bars, thinking I would put my face as close as I could. I wanted to say something to Niko without everyone hearing us, but when I put my head near his, he turned and walked to the other side of his cell. He wanted to get as far away from me as he could. He had his back turned with his hands stretched out on the walls. He was shaking his head back and forth. Maybe he wanted to tell me something.

"Niko, Niko!"

Curtis didn't give him a chance to respond. He pulled me through the doors to put me in chains. I hated this part. The only good thing about all of this was I'm on my way to the visitor's center. I couldn't wait to wrap my arms around Grandma. I knew that would cheer me up a little.

When I finally make it to the entrance of the visitor's center, I don't see Grandma. Maybe she was all the way in the back (the VIP section). I knew I had to be searched and have my shackles removed. My hands and feet were chained. It was hard for me to walk, but I was still trying to peek through the door. I wanted to see my grandmother badly!

C.O. Riley appeared at the door. I hadn't seen her in days. Her refreshing smile made my day. And gave me a woody.

"I'll take it from here," Riley said, pointing her finger for me to follow her.

I was so focused on her luscious lips that I only moved slightly, then realized I was still chained.

"Officer Riley, you forgot to take my shackles off!" I yelled.

"Oh! I'm sorry, honey, when you're in protective custody you have to see your visitor in chains. It's policy."

"Policy!"

"Yes, policy," she said, nodding sadly.

"I don't want my grandma to see me like this."

"There's really nothing I can do for you, sweetie. You're really going to be upset when you see how you'll be visiting."

I spotted Grandma. She was sitting off to the far right in front of a small cell. A cell with bars that was just large enough for a chair and one person to sit in. I remembered seeing inmates in those cells on previous visits. I always thought they were harmful to their visitors. I had no idea I would be receiving my visits like this.

Three cells were placed directly next to one another. Hodge was in one, shackled and talking to his visitor. Must be his aunt or a family member. I hoped it wasn't his chick looking all homely. The one on the other end had some guy sitting there I hadn't seen before. He must be from another block.

Grandma was sitting right in front of the middle cell. It was bad enough that she had to come here to a place like this. Now she had to look at me in chains. I was unable to put my arms around her and kiss her cheek; I'm distraught. I knew she was wondering why my visiting privileges were different now. There's no way I could tell her I was in protective custody just because some people thought I had murdered someone!

I inched toward her, ashamed and humiliated. Her back was facing me. She looked like she was thinking hard. One thing's for sure, she'd kept herself up mighty well. Looking like she was born from royalty. Her smooth newly wrinkled skin glistened. Her gray armadillo hat matched perfectly with her knee-length black-and-gray dress. I'd never seen her wear that dress before. She was still wearing those damn knee-hi stockings that wouldn't stay up.

Her legs were crossed and she was sitting straight up and dignified. Just imagine, an eighty-two-year-old woman looking that good! She didn't even notice that I was right behind her.

When C.O. Riley turned the key to unlock the visiting cell, Grandma leaped to her feet and draped her arms around me like I was a package.

"That's against policy, ma'am!" C.O. Riley stated in a firm tone.

Grandma sat down immediately and folded her heavy arms around her purse. Riley escorted me into the cell. The gate shut and Riley left us alone. I was in the middle of these two fools, and therefore, conscious about what I say. The moment was sort of tense. I really don't know where to start. I'm wondering why she was looking at me this way.

Before I could even speak Grandma said in her southern tone, "Divine, what'cha done that would 'cause you to get visits this way?"

"Nothing, Grandma."

"You musta done something."

I simply shook my head.

Grandma began to rant. "Then why you in a cage? I reckon this is a mistake too," she said, pointing directly at me.

"I'm in protective custody because there's an investigation going on. I'm a suspect in a murder. There's a slight chance someone might want to retaliate against me, therefore, I was placed in protective custody."

"Lawd, have mercy."

" I didn't do it!" I felt like I was on trial again. Only this time the sentence would be far worse. I'd disappointed Grandma.

"I know you didn't, baby," she mumbled.

Her big brown eyes watered. "Please don't cry," I said.

It hurts me when I let her down. She took out a piece of crumbled-up tissue from her purse and blotted at her eyes.

"Grandma, Sherese is pregnant by someone else. I've been trying to get in touch with her, but she won't answer my calls. I need you to get in contact with her. The faster, the better considering she's got my money."

I expected her to act differently. I knew she never really cared for Sherese or wanted me to associate with her. I would've bet all the money in my account she'd say, "I told you so" or "she was no good." She didn't make one negative statement. Hell she didn't even seem upset.

"Baby, whatever ya need me to do, I'll do," Grandma sniffled. "I reckon, it'll all work out."

"I also need you to contact Mr. Brothenstein as soon as possible."

"For what? I neva did like all dat legal mumbo-jumbo."

"Sherese wrote me a letter saying she sent me some important documents from my lawyer. I never got them. Tell him I need a copy of those documents immediately. Have you gotten anything from him recently?"

"No, siree."

"Also, tell him not to communicate with Sherese any longer about my case. He was talking to Sherese more than he's been coming to see me. Hell, he hasn't been here in four months."

"Watch yo' mouth, boy."

"Yes, ma'am."

"I'll get on top of yo mess right away," Grandma replied.

Holding my head down, I said, "There's one more thing I need to tell you. Niko is in protective custody also. I think he actually murdered the guy that I'm suspected of killing."

"Ummmm...mm!"

"What's that supposed to mean?"

"Divine, I've tried to keep you way from trouble since you's a lil' boy. I've done the best I can. Now, it's time for you to start makin' some responsible choices. I've stuck by ya through thick and thin. Not only did ya land in prison, but now ya caught up into murder and hobnobbin' wit' a murderer!" She never raised her voice at me. *I'd really done it this time!*

We talked until the end of the visiting hour, mostly about what my day was like in here. I told Grandma that I didn't really like going to the church service on Sundays because the preacher didn't teach about the bible. He mostly prayed for forgiveness. All religions worshiped together except the Muslims. Grandma was really interested in the Muslim behaviors. She said she knew a few Muslims who didn't eat pork. And she was still trying to figure out why.

What I didn't tell her was that most of the guys around here are claiming to be Muslims while they're locked up, but believe me, that will all change. As soon as they're home a month, they'll be ordering pork chop sandwiches on a regular basis.

I hated to see her go. When C.O. Riley gave the five-minute warning, I started to tell Grandma how much I wished I could go home with her.

She cut me off by putting her finger up to the cell gate, like hushing a small child. She said, "I'm gonna take care of e'rythang ya asked me to. I want ya to do one thang for me."

"What's that, Grandma?"

"Ask for forgiveness the next time there's a service here, and remember you're blessed."

"But I didn't—"

"Ya hear me, don't ya?"

"Yes, ma'am."

She said, "I stil luv ya," and walked away with a slight limp, without even turning around.

Weird. It was almost as if she didn't believe me. Naw, that couldn't possibly be the case. I'm her baby and she loves me.

I had to wait a while, which seemed like a lifetime for all the inmates to be searched and dismissed back to their cells. I was just sitting and watching how everybody wanted to be a player. Raheem, Science, and few of the other fellas on Block C nodded, but not in the same way I used to get looks.

I was really embarrassed sitting here in this damn cage. Life was already humiliating enough in here. What could be worse? Then I looked over at Hodge, who had told his visitor all about the scams he ran on people from the football pool. He was obviously proud of that shit. That's all he talked about for his entire visit. He was real loud like he didn't care who heard him. I paid him no attention, but he was looking me right in the face. I wish someone would let me out of here.

I didn't want to sit here any longer than I had to. Before I knew it, Hodge started talking. I just wasn't sure if he was talking to me or not.

"You know, you and I are a lot alike."

I turned my head slightly to see if he was talking to me. Surely he was. I didn't respond. I was hoping someone would be taking me back to protective custody shortly. I hoped I didn't have to see him over there.

Next thing you know, his cell was being opened and he was leaving. Thank you! Before he left he turned to me with a smirk. "We both like to be sneaky and conniving, don't we?" he said.

Of course I didn't answer that bullshit. I just turned my head.

12 Board Meeting

What in the hell is that horrible scent? That shit smells like a slaughtered pig house. Damn! It can't be the food from this morning. Those trays should've been taken out the wing hours ago. Whatever it is, it's making me sick.

I tried to focus on reading this awful book the guy gave me when he came by with books from the law library early this morning. This book is not only boring but uninformative.

Officer Brocton appeared in front of the cell. He just stood there chewing on a straw.

"Hey, Brocton, what's that atrocious ass smell?"

"Hell if I know. Let's take a walk," he said.

"Where?"

"Just follow me."

"Can you be trusted?" I joked.

He laughed. Then nodded for me to come toward him. In suspense I walked closer, slowly because this was strange. I wanted to know where we were going and what the hell that disgusting smell was.

He whispered as quietly as he could, "Mathematics

wants to meet with you. I'll be back to get you shortly. Act like you need to go the library. I'll be the one to take you."

He was still chewing on that damn straw as he walked away. I didn't even know he knew Mathematics. One of my small furry friends ran across my foot. This shit is ridiculous and too frequent. I shouldn't have to live under these conditions.

I started to get dressed so I'd be ready when Brocton returned. This was great, going out two days in a row. Yesterday Grandma, today Mathematics. Trying to wash my face was like pulling teeth considering how slow the water dripped from the faucet. I thought washing my face and upper body would make me feel a little cleaner based on the fact a rat ran across my foot and the aroma in here is disgusting. *Nasty-ass place.*

When Brocton showed up I was ready. While the cell opened C.O. Curtis waited at the front with chains. Did he know what's up? He shackled my feet and my arms. Sweat started to bead up on my forehead. I didn't want to end up in a worse situation than I was already in, just for meeting Mathematics. I hoped this meeting was secure.

When we were ready to move forward Curtis did not accompany Brocton. I sighed in relief. I wasn't too sure what was going to happen. As we walked I tried to make conversation with Brocton, but he wasn't as talkative as he normally is. I even asked him to see if he could bring me a pen and some paper. He didn't reply. He kept walking looking to his sides and behind him. "Hold up. Stop right here," he said nervously. But after checking the area, said, "I guess the coast is clear."

Within minutes we entered the law library. It wasn't very large. The oversized guard posted at the front sat in a chair with his arms folded. The only other person in the room was Mathematics. When he stood to give me some dap, his Oakley watch glittered. I could tell he'd gotten some new thangs since I left the block.

Brocton surprisingly started to loosen my chains. I guess both of these guys were getting paid big time. Mathematics is a bad man! Hell, he's my idol.

I sat down in front of my homie with an enthusiastic attitude, just happy to see one of my old buddies. But something was different. Something very disturbing.

Mathematics started in his monotone voice, "Man, it's good to see you takin' care of yourself."

"Yeah, I'm okay. But you, you sho 'nuf all right."

"Hell, I'm tryna maintain in here, but it's hard. You should be glad you don't have children on the outside. I'm constantly wondering who's taking care of my seeds, and how."

"Even though I don't have kids, I know what you mean."

"It seems like I'm gonna spend the rest of my life in this dungeon. Shit's so fucked up you don't know if you're gonna make it to the next day."

"Is everything all right with you and Tashonda?"

"Yep, it's like clockwork. Same soup, just a different spoon. What I should be asking is how are you. I'm sitting here pouring my heart out to you. You're the one in deep shit," Mathematics said, changing to a more serious demeanor.

"Nah, I'm cool."

"Are you really?" he asked in a fatherly tone.

"Of course. I'm Divine."

"How did you end up in a situation like this?"

Mathematics asked, looking me directly in the eye.

"I couldn't help it. When Crazy Ed was murdered, I was immediately a suspect, just because we fought a few days before his death. I didn't do it!"

"That's not what I'm talking about," snapped Mathematics. He wasn't so calm and cool anymore. He peered down into my face close enough to fucking kiss me. I wasn't afraid because I know he's my boy for life. I just wasn't sure what was actually taking place here.

Mathematics slammed his hand on the table with a loud bang. The noise aroused the attention of the officers. "I want some answers and I want the truth!"

Brocton got up and walked a little closer to us. I guess he had to protect me even if Mathematics paid him to bring me here. I'm sure this isn't a hit.

Mathematics continued, "Man, I can't count the rumors going around this place. You know you're my man but the shit I'm hearing just ain't right."

"What?"

"You and Niko are like brothers to me," Mathematics said, placing his right hand over his heart. His gaze revealed the seriousness of the rumors. "I would go down for both of y'all, but I need to know exactly what's going on."

"What are you talking about?"

"Some people say you snitched on Niko," Mathematics said bluntly.

"Man, that's crazy!"

"Nah, it's not so crazy," he said, leaning back with his hands behind his head.

I leaned back too. Mouth wide open. "So you believe it?"

"It doesn't matter what I believe."

"It does to me," I said while massaging my head.

"Let's just say, a lot of wanna-bes want you dead."

"Who?"

"It doesn't matter. The question is, is it true?"

"Hell no!"

Sweating, I replayed events in my mind. Maybe that's why it seemed like Niko didn't want to talk to me. He might believe that crap. I didn't even *know* who killed Ed Jones. I was assuming it was Niko. Probably just like everyone else was assuming. After this investigation was over everything would be cleared up and back to normal. I hoped. Because the worst thing in jail is to be labeled a snitch.

Mathematics sat there looking at me like a daddy ready to scold his child. "Divine, let's stop playing games. I'm not talking about the Ed Jones murder. I'm talking about you secretly snitching on Niko before y'all got here."

"Go 'head with that shit," I said tensely.

"Word has it that you're the reason why Niko is in here. I don't want to believe that. I want you to tell me the truth. I'll cover you but I need to know what happened."

I got extremely loud out of frustration. "You know what, I don't care if you believe me." My guilty conscious ran wild. "You know these rumors are lies. Why are people making up shit all of a sudden? These jealous motherfuckers are trying to play Niko and me apart. Now they've got you down with it!"

"If I were believing it, you might be shanked by now."

Evidently our board meeting didn't work out the way the officers had planned. Maybe we had gotten too loud and drew too much attention because the officer who brought Mathematics in was now whispering in his ear.

They had a brief, quiet conversation between themselves for about two minutes.

"Well, I think it's time for me to roll," Mathematics said, lifting himself hesitantly outta his seat like the godfather.

Upset, I raised my voice. "But, we're not finished yet."

"I think we are."

"Oh, it's like that?"

"Look, we're still cool. But, I'm now out of it. There's nothing more I can say, or do."

At this point, I'd officially been played. Officer Brocton was willing to stay a little longer but started to reshackle me. I guess this was way too much drama for him. Before Mathematics left the room, he turned to me and said, "I hope this is all a mistake for your sake. You already know that being in here is just like being on the streets. Inmates want a beef to kick off anyway. It's simply something to do and something to talk about afterward."

He started walking forward as if he had to leave immediately. I felt like he wanted to leave on that note because the officer wasn't coaxing or moving him through the door.

On the way back to protective custody, I was completely silent. All kinds of things ran through my mind. I walked with my head down. How did rumors get started about me snitching on Niko? People needed to mind their damn business. Who did Niko hear the rumor from? He'd been in protective custody the same length of time as I had.

Brocton wasn't saying a word and he was normally very talkative. I was not down with him anymore either. At this point I didn't know who I could trust.

When we opened the steel door to my new block, C.O. Brocton put his arm up to keep me from entering the unit, although that didn't keep me from seeing what was going on. There were about four officers beating the living shit outta somebody! I had no idea who. His face was buried under several pairs of patent-leather shoes. Whoever it was, he sure was hollering. His screams were echoing throughout the entire protective custody block. Officers moved back and forth, but I could never quite figure out the identity of the inmate.

I was assuming it was an inmate because we're the only ones who got treated like shit around here.

Suddenly, I felt light breathing on the back of my neck. At first I thought it was a gnat. But, when I turned to the right just a tad bit, I found a tall, slinky nurse standing there. Her dress was way too short, especially to be working in a prison.

"Excuse me," she said, brushing past us.

Immediately the officers engaged in the beat down got off the inmate as if their parents had arrived on the scene.

"I need this inmate brought to the infirmary *now*," the nurse said.

The short, fat officer said, "This piece of trash shit on himself and stored the underwear under his bunk. I've been smelling this shit for days! If we allowed him to get away with that, everyone would do that type of mess."

"Nobody deserves to be beat like this. He's a priority medical inmate," the nurse replied.

"Inmates in protective custody don't deserve to smell shit that's been sitting for three or four days."

"And understand that two wrongs don't make a right."

"Inmate—hell whatever his name is, #982542 threw up from being nauseated by the smell. Now what about that?" the fat officer said.

"So you think beating him will keep him from repeating the act?"

"I sure do."

"Then you're a bigger fool than I thought you were."

"What?"

"You heard me. Give respect to get it!"

"Oh, you'll hear about this again."

Unfazed, she said, "Take him to the showers in the infirmary." She made sure she pointed.

I was amazed to see this thin, statured woman give orders to the guards. I detected a confrontation would stir up between them, but nothing jumped off. Guards don't normally listen to medical employees, but this woman meant business. And, she didn't appear to be afraid of the officers either.

The guards dragged the guy right past me. Then I realized who it was. The little frail guy next to my cell just got his ass beat. Now I knew why that nasty smell was so strong. He was right next to me! I couldn't believe he got beat like that. He looked small and sick before he got beat. It was a wonder he survived.

Brocton pushed me forward. Of course I was being nosy, watching that nurse pull rank on those suckers. Well I doubted if she really had rank over them, but she sure was acting like it.

When I walked past Niko's cell, he was sitting on his bunk staring into space. His fists banged together with intensity. He wouldn't look at me and didn't appear to have been amused by the action that took place moments ago. I knew he didn't want to look at me but I said, "Niko, what's up?" He ignored me just like I thought he would. Brocton inched me along slowly. I watched Niko carefully, trying to make eye contact with him. He wouldn't look or say anything.

When I was close to reaching my cell I was so fucked up at the shit that was going down with Niko and me, I almost didn't notice how fucked up my neighbor's cell was. Shit was everywhere! Uhh! I wanted to throw up. His mattress was still flipped up. And in spite of everything his drawers lay under his bunk with a ton of shit parlaying on top. That's some nasty, trifling shit!

13

Reality Check

"Psst, psst. Hey slim, slim goody."

I kept hearing these weird-ass sounds like somebody was trying to get my attention. Lying on the bed made it impossible to actually see anyone. The voice was meek and raspy. I couldn't tell whether it was a male or female. I said fuck it and just ignored it. I had too much shit to worry about.

I could also hear a loud, familiar female voice in the background coming my way.

I couldn't believe my eyes! This nappy-headed woman appeared in front of my cell. I began thinking immediately. Is she here to work this unit? I certainly hoped not. Hell, I was praying at this point. Bennett had it in for me. Why was she over here? She was leaning on my cell with her hands wrapped around the bars. Her body, from her neck up was twisted because she was turned around talking to C.O. Curtis. They were perfect together: two insensitive idiots. He was asking her about how things were going on her wing.

"Crazy as usual," she replied.

"That's better than being on this boring block," C.O Curtis said.

"Let's switch places," Bennett said as they both laughed.

She started talking about all the recent fights and how she couldn't take much more. Bennett's voice softened as she looked to make sure nobody was nearby. "Some new guy is trying to run shit, and I'm having a problem getting a handle on him. I'm gonna have to use my hidden artillery," she joked bringing her voice back to normal. "I'm praying for all these guys," she said turning to me.

This was a fake broad. Little did she know, I heard it all. Lucifer himself was in protective custody.

"This is your lucky day." She smiled.

I got an instant attitude. "Why the hell am I so lucky?" I wish I could strangle this perpetrating bitch.

"I've got a package for you." Bennett bent down to pick up the brown bag sitting on the floor next to her. It resembled a grocery bag, but I knew she was not delivering food up in this motherfucker. She picked it up slowly and slid it through the bars. Curtis was watching T.V. paying no attention. This bitch could be trying to kill me.

"Enjoy."

Then she blew me a kiss as she walked away. What the fuck had gotten into her? She hated my ass and she was coming around here switching like she was fond of me all of a sudden. I put my head as close to the bars as possible to see if she was going to stop by Niko's cell. Maybe she stopped there first. Maybe he told her to send me the package.

I opened the top part of the bag, still standing in the same position when someone said, *"Psst."*

That same annoying whispering sound was coming from directly next door. I moved slightly closer to the left end of the cell. I wanted to be sure it was coming from the next cell.

"What's up, partner?" Dude sounded like he was trying out for a western movie.

I kept trying to get closer so I could see his face but I couldn't. His hands dangling from the bars were so pale. Had this guy gotten whiter and weaker since I had seen him in his cell? Oh! Not to mention when he was getting his ass whipped for shitting on himself.

I finally responded, "What's up?" in my lowest voice possible.

I didn't want anyone to hear me talking to him. I guess if one of the officers had walked by, they would have been able to tell anyway. I couldn't believe I had my entire, precious face plastered against these bars talking to someone I didn't even know. I knew I was bored. And getting soft too.

"So what you in for?" dude asked.

"Man, I'm innocent." I couldn't believe I was still saying that. I'd said it so much, I was actually starting to believe it. "I won't be here for long," I answered with a slow sigh.

"Yeah, I won't be here for long either, but I damn sure ain't innocent."

I asked, " What you in here for?"

"Well honey, two counts of check fraud and first-degree murder. I almost got away with writing and cashing other people's checks until this little bitch got in my way. She fucked everything up and got me caught. So when I got out on bail, I killed her ass. Li'l mama was too many things, but she deserved it though."

When I saw his fingers snap it brought me back to reality, 'cause I was really into this story.

Next thing you know, that fly-ass nurse I had seen yesterday was standing right in front of this dude's cell. In silence, she stared at both of us like we stole something. I'd hate to get on her bad side. She held on to a clipboard as she jotted something down on paper. I hoped she wasn't writing shit about me.

Finally she asked sympathetically, "You feeling okay?"

When my neighbor responded, "Fabulous," she walked away.

"Isn't this some bullshit! Someone has to come in here and write some shit about me every fuckin' hour. Don't nobody want to live like this! I damn sure don't! I'd rather just die!" he said.

I felt like I needed to say something to calm him down or everyone would know he was down here telling me his problems.

"Hey, calm down, kid. Maybe she's worried because of the beating you took yesterday. She's just doing her job."

He snapped back, "She doesn't care about me getting the beat down. This is an everyday occurrence. Every hour on the hour Miss Lula prances in with her white get-up on and takes notes on my current state. Tasteless tramp! They think I might kill myself since I've got HIV, but I ain't stupid. I love my white ass too much. That's why I'm here."

"Why?"

"A couple of weeks ago, I threw some piss on this asshole who was trying to make fun of me. Well, I showed his ass. The joke was on him. Or should I say, the piss was on him."

I could barely make out the rest of the story because of his extended girlish laughter. Once he settled down he continued, "The next thing I knew, I was told I was suffering from depression. And that I was intentionally trying to infect people with the AIDS virus. Huh! A bunch of nonsense. I wasn't trying to harm anybody. If you call throwing piss on some fool dangerous, then I'm guilty. They've even got me on depression medication. That shit ain't helping 'cause I don't even really take it. I learned that if you sit up and plead for it then they get frustrated and won't monitor you when it's being given. I twirl that little pill to the back of my mouth with my luscious sweet tongue and flush it when I get back in the cell. And she think she's something 'cause she got a nursing degree. Honey, I ain't never known no degree that can grant you common sense. Huh! If you think education is expensive, try ignorance. Either you have it or you don't. That's why I was able to avoid the po-po for so long."

"Who's the po-po?" I asked curiously.

"The police, sweetie."

"Oh! I knew that."

"Hey, you never told me why you're here."

"Let's just say I'm here for some similar shit like you. I mean I didn't murder anybody. But I did get hooked up into some fraud shit. As a matter of fact some big-time fraud."

"I thought you said you were innocent."

"I am, I just got caught up with a friend, but I'll be out soon. That's right," I said, trying to sound positive about the situation. "Just as soon as my lawyer straightens this mess out," I said, nodding slowly, pretending to be confident.

Hell, I think I'm really beginning to believe this shit.

Dude interrupted my thinking. "Well, I'm supposed to be transferred within the week so if you look one day and I'm gone don't be surprised."

"Why are you being transferred?"

"Honey, I told you I have HIV. The system won't allow you to stay in a regular populated block with such a disease and being a threat to everyone else. I told them I'll change. I even said, 'I won't throw anymore piss,' but they don't believe me. Cock suckers! That's why I'm in protective custody. These guards don't want me to scratch somebody's eyes out and give them the Big *H* at the same time. So I'm here until I can be moved to a prison where they have a unit for HIV-infected inmates."

I felt bad for this dude. I didn't even know why. It was obvious he was a flaming queer and besides that, I don't normally converse with people not down with my crew. Well, I didn't have anyone else to talk too, and nobody will find out, so I asked, "How will your family know you've been moved?"

"Oh! They don't give a good got damn. They wrote me off a long time ago when they found out I didn't like pussy."

"Oh."

"Honey, I'm my family's dirty little secret."

I said, "I'm sure that's not true."

"Huh! I haven't had a visitor since I've been here. Not one letter! Not one dollar! Not one birthday card! Nothing! Fuck 'em! I just hope I'm moved somewhere north. I've got a friend on the outside who can write some checks for me if I show him the ropes. You know what I mean?"

"Yeah, I sure do." All I could do was nod. I guess when

you sit in here, all you have is time to think.

Several voices headed my way. Time to end our conversation. I asked the dude his name but didn't get a response. He had started arguing with Curtis as he brought in the scrumptious evening meal. Officer Curtis asked him why he was talking to himself. Dude responded hastily with, "Fuck you."

"You wish," Curtis replied. Then he called him a faggot.

"That's *Mr.* Faggot to you."

I even thought I heard his fingers snap.

When my meat appeared at my cell I prepared for the long digestive process. As usual I couldn't make out what it was. I believe it's in the salisbury steak family, but don't quote me on it. I had to get some potatoes. That shit must be a mandate around here because at least three times a week we had potatoes. But I had a treat. A bright red apple! We normally got those every blue moon and never at dinner. This was a blessing in disguise. Can't say the same about this hard-ass bread. Who decided to make the shit so thick? Inmates cooked the food, but there was somebody high up making some fucked-up decisions! Like not putting any seasoning in the food. They could at least send some salt and pepper packets along with the plastic-ass dishes.

The only thing around here considered a privilege during dinner was getting a real fork. Who would have ever thought I would end up being excited about using a metal fork to eat with? My juice cup was metal as well, but the bullshit they mixed in the juice should be against the law. Imagine drinking what you think is fruit juice and all along it's red punch mixed with some shit to make your dick soft. It works for most people, but not all. Some inmates didn't even drink the shit. Fuck that, I'm thirsty. Besides it was not like I'm fucking anybody.

By the time I had finished my gourmet dinner I had almost forgotten about the package from C.O. Bennett. It was still sitting on the floor by the front of my cell, just where I left it before kicking it with the flamboyant faggot next door. Only now an intruder lurked around the bag. I kicked the little gray critter away and sat down to see exactly what I was so lucky to acquire. I couldn't believe it. I had a brand spanking new Walkman and some new books. Maybe Bennett felt bad because my old walk-man was taken away when I got moved to protective custody. Aah shit! A pen, paper, and some stamps. I was in business.

First thing I was going to do was write Sherese. I needed my damn money! I was going to have to threaten to sue her ass. I was also gonna write Langley, my old boss. He owed me a few favors. I knew he'd come through. He should anyway, considering he didn't get locked the fuck up.

14   Forty-nine Dollars

I chuckled, thinking about the drama that went on around here. According to Brocton, Crawford found himself in some real deep shit. Apparently, Mathematics took his ass for a trip he wasn't prepared for.

Tashonda entered Dunnridge at about 3:10 P.M. She had been in the visiting area for several hours waiting to see Mathematics. He said that some visitors came in after her, but were called first. Unconcerned, Tashonda sat patiently. She watched nearly thirty people have their I.D.s scrutinized, and names be given a clearance to pass. People from all walks assembled in the facility: old, young, sophisticated, and thuggish. You name it. They were there. Tashonda sat on a set of connected, hard, yellow chairs, which were positioned directly next to the metal detector.

She watched mothers, girlfriends, and baby mamas rush in to see their family members. The trip was long so I know some were disgusted as they got turned away for all kinds of foolish reasons. The visiting room boomed with chaos. I could just imagine the guards yelling, "Step over here!"

Brocton said Tashonda watched as one young lady was denied a visit because her skirt was too short. Ain't that a bitch. Now isn't this the time to wear something short and hoeish? *Easy access.* Anyway, another young man left without seeing his brother because he couldn't clear the metal detector. "Fuck y'all," he shouted, as he took off every possible accessory while the detector still beeped. That dumb fuck probably had something stuck in his ass.

Brocton alluded to Tashonda's good looks, got a woody as he described her tight black pants and DKNY haltertop. Fitting the script, her hair was perfect. Rolex on the arm (of course with a diamond bezel) and a set of pear-shaped diamonds gleaming in her ears. This chic is high maintenance.

As she sat, visitors continued to pour in in front of her. Crawford and three other officers were on duty in the visitors' center.

Eventually, the large influx of visitors demanded the other officers' attention. It seems they were bombarded with individuals needing clearance to enter the gate. Crawford gave Tashonda a signal. She walked through the metal detector without taking off any jewelry, not removing her shoes, nor responding to the beeping sounds from the detector. Now that was unusual considering that sometimes people transport drugs into a prison in their shoe soles, hairstyles, and even baby diaper bags.

There are many creative ways of getting stuff in and everybody knows it, officers are simply supposed to try to deter it from happening. I couldn't believe Crawford just didn't give a fuck! Before he went on with the details, I figured something was up.

Tashonda proceeded through the gate. The piercing

beeping sound continued. One officer turned to see what was going on, but assumed Crawford would handle it.

Crawford simply nodded for her to keep walking. It sounded as if at this point, Tashonda had become a pro. I could imagine her strutting through without looking back. Right then, it clicked. Tashonda had been smuggling drugs into the institution for the past three years, and hell nobody knew it. Ain't that some shit? C.O. Crawford, Tashonda, and Mathematics had a system. Apparently Crawford was a neo to the game. At first it was just Mathematics and Tashonda. They had a smooth method of moving their products through. No wonder they have those long, drawn-out, slobbery kisses.

While kissing, Tashonda would transfer a drug-laden balloon from her mouth to Mathematics. He would then swallow the balloon and retrieve it from his feces later in privacy. I guess Mathematics' ass got tired of that method and decided to up the ante. That's when he brought Crawford in on the deal. Crawford wasn't getting much money. At least that's what he told his superiors before he was arrested a week later by the Feds. They took his drunk ass out the prison in an orange jumpsuit.

Obviously Crawford didn't feel like he was making enough money or getting his fair share of the profits because he eventually tried the blackmail tactic on Mathematics. I know my boy didn't play the fall guy on that episode.

Well, when the drug ring originally started, Crawford agreed to accept a C-note every time he let Tashonda enter the facility. One hundred dollars was nothing compared to the money Mathematics was making. But Crawford was also receiving extra perks because he liked getting his knob polished. That nasty bastard!

Oh no! Not by Mathematics! Brocton said Mathematics was responsible for securing a date for Crawford and telling him where to meet the inmate. Crawford would even pay the inmates for servicing his dick. By the looks of it, everyone involved seemed to be getting their needs met. Well at least they appeared to be satisfied.

Not only was Crawford making money off Mathematics, but other inmates as well. He soon earned a reputation for taking bribes and bringing shit on the inside.

As time went on, Crawford started making slick remarks to Mathematics implying that he would stop letting Tashonda get through the main gates without being searched. He knew that every time he let Tashonda through with drugs valued at two thousand dollars on the street, Mathematics would double that. Therefore, being the greedy sucker that he is, he kept asking for more and more money. Hell, he never thought about giving Mathematics any money for setting up his freak dates, yet he wanted more money for getting Tashonda inside safely. Ain't that a motherfucker?

Now Crawford must not have known who he was fucking with. Mathematics would never let a measly low-budget C.O. stop his operation or punk him into an increase. He knew Crawford would keep asking for money so Mathematics decided to set him up.

Raheem was one of the inmates who gave Crawford a blowjob on a regular basis. It's crazy because he's a tall, bulky brotha, and presents himself as if he's unlikely to be gay. Mathematics told Crawford where to meet Raheem. But, he also sent an informant to Lieutenant Graham to say two inmates would be at a particular spot conducting a drug transaction. Graham believed it because the information was coming from one of the trustees. That was real skillful of Mathematics to choose someone trustworthy. When Lieutenant Graham found out about a possible drug transaction, he had the Feds brought in to be at the location. What Graham didn't realize was that he would see Crawford getting his knob slobbed by an inmate.

The location Mathematics designated was a room on the backside of the kitchen. With Mathematics' connections, he had arranged to have the room unlocked. Raheem showed up first. Unless it had been recently renovated, that room was cold, dark, and wasn't conducive for romance of any kind. I remember the concrete walls being dark green with old wobbly chairs stacked on top of one another in the center of the floor. I could visualize the two old crates in the right-hand corner facing the door. They were large enough for two federal agents to hide behind unseen. Brocton told me that Raheem took down a chair and sat down waiting patiently for C.O. Crawford to come. After about five minutes, footsteps tapped cautiously. Crawford's keys jangled slightly as he approached his conquest. Slowly the door opened, making creaking sounds like it needed a little oil. It was so dark that neither Raheem nor the Feds could see Crawford's face until he walked right up to the stack of chairs. Crawford wore the mandatory C.O. uniform, but as normal, his was grungy looking. His blue pants were half ironed with a double, uneven crease, accompanied by his tattered wrinkled shirt, which hung down near his huge black belt.

According to Brocton, Crawford walked up to Raheem and slowly pulled his hand from his pocket. He handed him two twenties and nine one-dollar bills. He started removing his belt by pulling the strap over far enough for the hook to unloosen. He unzipped and moved closer to Raheem.

Crawford then asked, "Is your appetite wet yet?" He told him to put his money away and to come closer.

Raheem moved his head closer to Crawford's crotch. He anxiously grabbed Crawford's piece and on target, stroked it with his mouth. The officers laid low a moment, then from behind the crate jumped out and read Crawford his rights! Crawford stood in a daze, filled with shame and mouth wide open, unable to speak. Realizing he had been set up, he obviously got up enough nerve to try to retaliate. He told the Feds all about Mathematics' dealings inside the prison. He excluded the parts about how he'd contributed to getting the drugs in. Along with this, Crawford got so desperate, he even threw in information about activities of crooked officers.

Graham told the Feds that Crawford probably said those things about Mathematics to get himself off the hook. They totally disregarded the other comments. Graham was already in deep shit with the warden about the increased drug problems on Block C. He was hoping the Feds would arrest Crawford and keep on moving.

However, following routines, the Feds searched Mathematics' cell. They didn't find any sign of distribution of drugs and didn't really know what to believe. Nonetheless, they did find a puzzling letter. It was obviously written in response to a love letter that Mathematics had written. The letter was somewhat apologetic. Seemingly, he wasn't acknowledged when he met face to face with whomever. Also feelings about being together at a later time and place were discussed.

I was confused until Brocton explained that C.O.

Garcia was responding to a love letter that Mathematics had given her. Could she be so stupid? Rookie C.O.s are so vulnerable. Why would she even respond to a letter from an inmate? And I definitely couldn't understand why she would sign her name. I hope Mathematics didn't get transferred for this. She was either under investigation or fired. Everybody knew jailhouse rules. Anything an inmate gave an officer should be reported and turned in. I mean anything, from a shoelace to a cupcake.

Well if you ask me, I thought Garcia was a little freak anyway. She acted innocent, but why was she called into Lieutenant Graham's last week? And, now to add insult to injury, they found a letter in Mathematics' cell involving her. If I was the superintendent, I wouldn't ever let her enter the facility again. Freak! She should have been called at home and told not to return. It was crazy around here!

When I heard about what happened with Crawford, I couldn't believe a guard would actually pay an inmate forty-nine dollars to suck his dick! I mean you're in a prison where inmates do that shit for free! Why couldn't Crawford satisfy his needs outside the facility? Just think, if he was convicted he could spend two-fourths of his life, just like me. They were going to make an example outta his ass.

It might be good for him to see how the other side lives. Mathematics did a good job setting his ass up. I guess Crawford underestimated Mathematics because he's an inmate. He forgot that all an inmate had was time—time to think of ways to beat the system. There's nothing else to do. Now I see exactly what Mathematics meant when he said, "You wouldn't believe the shit these officers are doing up in here."

Now as for Raheem, Brocton said things didn't look so good for him either, considering he and Squzzy had a fling going on. When Squzzy found out Raheem was tasting on Crawford, he cried like a bitch. Riley tried to console him, but nothing would help.

"How could he do this to me?" Squzzy cried.

"Sweetie, just do your time, and you'll forget all about him."

"But, I love Squzzy," he said, slamming his arms to his side, hitting both legs.

"I know," Riley said as she stroked Squzzy's back.

Squzzy stomped away with folded hands, and Shaunte following. Now, *that's* loyalty!

15   Anticipation

Eleven days had passed since I had gotten any mail. The last piece I got was when Grandma wrote me to let me know she had gotten in touch with Mr. Brothenstein, and that he was working on getting me out as soon as possible. He was obviously having a problem getting the original judge in my case to agree to what she had promised me. Grandma also said I should be receiving a copy of the transcript he sent Sherese, but nothing had come for me yet.

Officer Brocton is in a real good mood today. Maybe he got a little trim last night. Listen to him, whistling and singing like he hit Lotto. He'd been hanging around my cell for the last twenty minutes telling me about everything that had been going on in Block C over the past week. He knew a lot of the dirt. I was quite lucky to have an ally like him. He was a good dude. I only wished I could tell him his breath smells like some dog poop!

"Man, shit's in an uproar on your block," Brocton said, shaking his uneven head from right to left.

"What's going on?"

"Well, your man Bishop is taking over. All kinds of beefs have kicked off."

I was shocked. Bishop was running things! He and Niko were going to bump heads when Niko got outta here. I was still gonna be down with my main man no matter what. We always said we were brothers for life. No matter what happens. You know, like soul mates.

"I knew Bishop was crazy when I first met him."

"Well, he's beyond crazy now. He's splitting up crews and causing all sorts of mess."

"He's cool. His bark is bigger than his bite."

"I hope you're right 'cause C.O. Warren is ready to get permission to transfer him to Block E."

Bishop wasn't that bad. Maybe people just didn't know how to take him. I hope he didn't expect me to be down with him because he helped me get through my panic attack over Sherese. I appreciated the kindness, but it was not worth betraying my crew.

Brocton said, "Bishop has been working out, tryin' to get buffed."

"No shit!" I said, surprised. I couldn't imagine his little midget ass buffed.

"I think that's why he's been running around like a little tyrant. Now, he's got his own crew. From what I heard, Science, Rafik, and Bones appear to be with him tough."

"To each is own. That shits on them," I said.

"The tier has been locked down twice since Bishop has been in control. Motherfuckers starting to do stupid shit like igniting fires with toilet tissue and newspaper. They seem to light anything that burns," Brocton said.

"We never did no dumb shit like that. They deserve to be locked down," I said.

"It will be interesting to see how Bishop and Niko get along." Brocton smirked.

"Oh, I'm not even worried," I said, thinking in the back of my mind about Niko's current state.

"Niko doesn't say much at all anymore."

"Well, the investigation has been going on for about three weeks now, and Niko and I have been away from our crew. He might be a little depressed."

"More like deep depression. He hasn't even had a visit," Brocton said.

I was starting to agree with Brocton. Niko resembled one of those insane people locked in a padded room, wearing a straitjacket waiting to be served Zoloft. If I didn't know better, I'd think Niko knew about what happened in the court room. But, I find it hard to believe because everything I discussed with the judge was sealed. Nobody knew about it except my lawyer and Judge Lasey. Niko might be pissed off from listening to all the rumors. Or, maybe he was mad because he ended up killing Crazy Ed because of me. Shit, I hated Ed, but I never wanted him to kill him. It was not my fault. They had to eventually let one of us go. You couldn't charge two people for the same murder. At least I didn't think you could.

Brocton became suddenly tense. Standing erect he said, "I'll see what I can do."

Now what the fuck was he talking about? I hope he hadn't gone crazy. His voice and mannerism changed all of a sudden. He walked away from the cell not even finishing the conversation we were having about Niko. Fuck it! I'd finish my letter to Langley.

Brocton was talking to two other guards. I couldn't quite see who they were because he was blocking my view.

They tried to speak discretely. Brocton kept nodding, with his hands folded like he was important. I'm assuming he walked away from my cell so the officers wouldn't see him rapping to me. That's so uncool in the C.O. handbook. Do they even have one? I was tired of trying to figure out what the hell was being said. So much shit went on up in this motherfucker!

I tried to find my new pen. Excited as hell, I found it!

What's up, Langley?

I hope all is well with you. Things aren't so great with me. Not only am I still trying to maneuver out of this situation, but now I'm in protective custody pending a murder investigation. Luckily, somebody was looking out and sent me some stationery and a pen. You hardly get any privileges on this unit.

Enough about this spot. I know you'll never have to come to a place like this. I should have listened to you before. I know you're disappointed, but hopefully I'll be out of here soon. I'm counting on you to find me a job. I don't care where it is. I want to live my life right.

How come you don't ever write me? I hope you're not scared. It's over now. You could never get in trouble.

Peace out!
Divine

Brocton returned about an hour later all buddy-buddy. "What's up?" he said, like he hadn't talked to me earlier. "Chillin'," I replied.

He looked around all suspect and shit. If I didn't know better I'd think this was a drug transaction.

Almost whispering he said, "The investigator in charge of the Jones case is going to come to see you soon. He's already seen Niko."

"Should I be worried? That's good. Maybe I'll be up out of here soon."

"I wouldn't be in such a rush if I were you." Looking around, he continued,"I found out that the investigators found a transcript that was addressed to you during the shakedown in Ed Jones' cell. They were looking for clues to his murder and finding that doesn't look good for you."

"What do you mean? Doesn't look good for me? It shouldn't look good for Crazy Ed, stealing my mail! I've been waiting on that information for months."

Taking hold of his neck, Brocton said, "I think Niko knows about the transcript also."

"So," I snapped, standing aggressively.

"From what I've been told, that document has some deep shit in it that could get somebody hurt."

"Well, it won't be me." I felt nervous as hell. My goose was cooked.

"Now don't get me wrong. Niko has been really calm. It's almost like he's a different person. He didn't have any words for none of the investigators. He kicked it with Bennett briefly, and that's it. She's been getting him what he needs, I guess," Brocton said.

"Seems like he would at least want to talk to Mathematics," I said.

"Oh! He wouldn't even see Mathematics when I tried to set up a meeting spot. He just said he'd pass."

"Oh yeah? Damn."

"Yeah. Mathematics was disappointed behind that shit."

Azárel

"What's been up with him?" I asked, trying to piece shit together.

"That crazy dude got caught smoking weed. He had nerve to use the first page of the bible as his rolling paper. Now how sick is that? Cats need to know we down with all those tricks. Been there, done that! What was really bad for him was that C.O. Warren was the one who caught him. You know he got body slammed. I heard he fucked your boy's pretty little face up on the way to the hole."

I tried to sound concerned. "Damn." Mathematics is still my boy. But I could only focus on the possibility of Niko knowing about the transcript!

Brocton continued, "Plus, he was already up shit's creek for getting Officer Garcia pregnant and fired!"

I needed to know, so I asked, "Who said Mathematics got her pregnant?"

"She did."

"Damn. Does Mathematics know that she told?"

"Yeah. And as cool as he is, he told all the white shirts to prove it!"

"Officer Garcia was called into Graham's office the same morning that Ed Jones died. She appeared to be on trial for a murder beef. I should have known something was wrong then."

"To make a long story short, she's a goner!"

Once again Brocton turned two-face on me. He cut the conversation short, and a lazy grin appeared on his face. This time he didn't have a chance to ease away from the cell. Being fake, like he didn't kick it with me, he turned away to speak to someone. Whoever he was talking to this time sounded real cool. He had a slight accent. I had never heard this voice before. As the guy got closer I realized that he might not be a C.O. I don't know what connections he had, in order to be all up in protective custody. Uhm! He didn't have on a uniform, although he couldn't be an inmate because he had on a blue jacket, and since we couldn't wear blue, he was not one of us. Dressed in jeans and a polo-style shirt seemed a bit odd. He had a fresh new haircut that definitely wasn't the works of a prison cut. Somebody on the outside cut that shit. He was of Mexican decent, speaking slang from the street.

"Hello, Divine! I'm Investigator Hernandez," the short man said in the friendliest tone I'd ever heard in a damn prison as he stepped directly in front of my cell.

I couldn't quite understand what was going on until Brocton disappeared and this guy claiming to be an investigator out of uniform was in my cell. He was trying his best to be down. But, no matter how you dress or what slick talk you use, an officer is still the enemy—except for Riley and Brocton of course.

After walking back and forth around the room he finally decided to speak. "I've got some good news and some bad news for you. But first I've got to tell you, Homes, I've heard some positive things about you."

"And. . . "

"I heard you graduated from college, had a nice career, and come from a good family."

"Get to the point."

Changing his approach, Hernandez said, "Homes, the point is, it seems like you had a pretty good life on the outside. One that I recently found out, you're trying to get back to. If your little deal works out with the judge, you'll be set. However, you have to make it out of here first."

I grabbed both sides of my head and out of frustration,

yelled, "What are you talking about?"

"Homes, let's stop playing games."

"No, you're the one playing games."

"May I sit down?"

Not waiting for a response, he sat down on the edge of my bunk. With his hands rubbing his knees he continued, "I know you snitched on Niko during your trial! Niko also knows."

My eyes got big as hell as bile rose in my stomach. My life was fucked but I didn't say a word.

He was trying to see my reaction but I just stared into space. He continued, "Ed Jones got a copy of the transcript by accident. He knew you were a snitch and that's why he attacked you a couple of weeks ago. Niko was furious with him and wanted to see him dealt with anyway so when Jones approached him to tell him about the transcript, I guess Niko retaliated on your behalf instead of listening to what he had to say. The rest is history. I guess Niko handled his business."

"How do you know all of this?"

"Some of this is speculatory, but most of it's solid. I'm the best damn investigator around. Now, I want to help you."

"Why the fuck would you want to help me?" Pacing and nervous as hell, I wasn't quite sure why this shit was happening to me. I was smarter than this. I could handle mine.

"I want to help you because I know you can make something of yourself on the outside. Besides, you might be able to help me. I've dug up all your background and secrets. I really don't want to see you get extra time for Ed Jones' murder."

"But, I didn't do it."

"I know, you're innocent, Homes," Hernandez stated sarcastically.

"Oh, you've got jokes."

"Even though the murder happened on the inside, it will be treated as a new outside charge. Just think about going to court all over again."

"But I didn't do it. Besides, you just told me Niko did it."

"I said *some* parts of my theory were speculations."

The madder I got, the louder I got. "You probably have no clue as to what happened to Ed. You're looking for somebody to pin this case on."

Bending to scratch his ankle, he continued, "Listen, this internal investigation is just about over. The state police will be coming in a few days to make a formal arrest based on my investigation. I've got inmates lined up to snitch and give me any information about Ed's murder. They're sending notes through C.O.s and trying to help themselves any way possible. So don't tell me I don't have a strong investigation. Before Ed died, you and Niko were his only enemies. Now I'll be back tomorrow, hopefully you'll be ready to come clean. Maybe we can work a deal. I'll help you, and you know you'll help me. I'm sure you know what I mean. You've played this game before."

He had his back turned to me while waiting for the officer on post to let him out the cell. He looked like a big dude standing there. But I was sure I could handle him. I knew Niko would!

16

Exposed

I can't understand why I'm acting like everything is gonna be okay. People are shanked, even killed, for being known as a snitch. I can't imagine being laid up in the hospital, or for that matter laid in a casket. I can see Grandma now, crying and sobbing through Reverend Grey's message. "Oh, he was a good-hearted boy whose soul is now at peace," he would say. "All of us will remember him as a loveable, successful young man, with many talents. He is survived by his grandmother, Sister Ella Mae Lewis, a pillar of our community." Then, Grandma would sob some more. I'm sure Grandma wouldn't dare let Reverend Grey mention my time here at Dunnridge.

Sherese would probably show up to pay her respects. I bet she wouldn't bring my damn money though. She'd probably walk to the front pew like she was weak, bending over fakeishly to hug Grandma. I'll tell you one thing, if I don't get my money before I die, I'm coming back to haunt her ass. As a matter of fact, I'm coming back to haunt all the motherfuckers on Block C.

I must have dozed off because all I could hear in the back of my mind was mail call! I'm so use to running to the podium excitedly to collect my shit, I almost forget I was in protective custody, locked down twenty-one hours a day. I saw C.O. Curtis strut over, taking his sweet time. Anxiously, I waited while he moved in slow motion. He could care less if anybody in here got anything. He continued to sift through the mail like he was at home separating junk mail from bills.

He stopped at the Jamaican dude's cell. "Tanks, man," he said.

Then he stopped in front of my flamboyant neighbor's cell and just shook his head. I don't know what's been going on with him lately. He hadn't been as talkative, but I couldn't worry about that right now. As Curtis moved closer to my cell, I got goose bumps. I was just hoping I'd get what I'd been waiting for. He handed me an envelope, which I immediately began to tear open.

"Shit, I got a damn paper cut," I said as I sucked my finger in an effort to make it feel better.

Shaking off the discomfort, I was determined to see what was in store. The envelope was demolished by the time I unfolded the paper. The two pages stared me straight in the face. When I realized it was a handwritten letter, my eyes immediately refocused to the bottom of the page. It was a letter from Stacey. How nice. Just bad timing. I began to read:

Dear Divine,
I hope everything is okay with you. I've been thinking

about you a lot lately. I enjoyed our visit a few weeks ago. You seem to be a really nice person. All the good ones are always taken (smile).

Tashonda is coming to see Mathematics next week. I was wondering if you want me to come also. If Sherese is coming I understand. I won't take it personal. My mailing address is on the front of the envelope. Use it!

With loads of love,
Stacey

As soon as I finished reading Stacey's letter, Curtis reappeared at my cell, shoving a huge manila envelope through the bars. I jumped. This was it. It had to be!

The package looked like it had been through hell. Postage had been stamped all over the envelope. Four dollars worth at least. On the outside was a return address. My lawyer's address! I took my index finger that had a fresh new paper cut and jammed it quickly between the seams. There stood a thick stack of papers. At least twenty to thirty pages. I backed up toward my bed to sit down. This would take a while. A cover letter had been written from Mr. Brothenstein that stated:

Dear Mr. Jones,

I will be on the premises to see you Tuesday, July 4, between the hours of 9:00 A.M. and 2:00 P.M. Familiarize yourself with the following documents and be prepared to discuss the agreement.

Sincerely,
Mr. J. Brothenstein

I fumbled through the many pages, looking for the transcript from the private meeting with the judge. I quickly got frustrated by the countless forms, transcripts, and motions. I slowed down, thinking and proceeding page by page. Why would Brothenstein be coming to see me on a holiday? Yes! This must be a good sign. Obviously he had such good news, he had to see me as soon as possible. I can't wait!

I found the portion of the transcript that I needed. Studying the document as if each page were under surveillance, I read:

STATE OF VIRGINIA
CRIMINAL COURTS
June 13,1995
Reporter: Sheila Cooke

Clerk: Let it be stated, this will be a sealed document, and previous transcripts related to this case have no bearing on this private meeting.

Judge Lasey: Just what is all this mess?

Defense Attorney: Your Honor, my client is not denying participation in this crime, however, he strongly feels he was not the person pursuing the crime spree. In addition, it is his hope that he can lessen his sentence by bringing out all the true facts in this case.

Judge Lasey: How do you plan to do that? The trial is over.

Defense Attorney: He wants to redeem himself by implicating his co-defendant and revealing the whereabouts of all monies embezzled.

Judge Lasey: How does your co-defendant feel about all of this, Mr. Jones?

Divine Jones: Ma'am, he doesn't know. I feel it's my duty to tell the truth, even if it means I have to do some time myself.

Prosecuting Attorney: All of this appears to be a waste of taxpayers' money. Mr. Jones is obviously revealing information now to shorten his sentence. It is the belief of the state that he conspired along with Mr. Rhaphic (Niko) Jenkins to embezzle as much of the funds of U.S. Savings and Loan as he could. Consequently, he and Mr. Jenkins should be punished equally.

Defense Attorney: Although, my client was a participant, he was not the aggressor. I believe he should be given a chance to speak in this setting.

Judge Lasey: Sentencing has already been imposed. What is the purpose of honesty at this point?

Defense Attorney: My client would like to receive some leniency from the court in exchange for important information, which will prohibit similar embezzlement at financial institutions.

Divine Jones: Also, ma'am, if I might add, I can lead you to the whereabouts of a large portion of the money taken.

Prosecuting Attorney: This is unacceptable. This man deserves twelve years, just like Rhaphic Jenkins. My office is not willing to negotiate. Mr. Jones was uncooperative during the entire trial. That's my final position.

Judge Lasey: I will agree to bringing Mr. Jones back before my bench in five years, provided that he does give the required information to return the majority of the funds embezzled. What was the figure?

Prosecuting Attorney: Approximately one million two hundred and six thousand dollars.

Judge Lasey: Mr. Jones, if we can retrieve fifty percent of that money with your help, I will bring your case back for review in five years. At that time if you have not gotten into any more trouble and have good prison behavior, I will dismiss the remainder of your time. That means you will be a free man in approximately five years if all goes well.

Divine Jones: Thank you, ma'am. Thank you.

Ugh! I lay on my bunk reflecting on what I just read. What was I thinking? How could I have been so foolish? With my conscience eating me alive, I replayed different scenarios of how things could have gone, over and over. I couldn't stop thinking about what would have happened if. . . or if. . .

Flashbacks of Niko and me at the trial kept entering my mind. I could still see Niko's face when our sentence was read. I should have taken the twelve years like a man, but instead look at me now. And the sad part is, I couldn't change what happened. What's done is done!

Besides, it's not all my fault. I never even knew I could talk to the judge in a private setting. That was Brothenstein's idea. So he's somewhat liable too. He was the one who told me exactly what to do. I just did it. Should I take all the blame alone? No! Plus, I never expected the judge to freeze all Niko's accounts. That wasn't my intent, because that was my money too. I figured I could tell my side of the story to earn some brownie points, and that would be it. I soon found out, it wasn't that easy. The legal system is some bullshit! I got fucked, right along with Niko, and the state still made out, recovering more than six hundred thousand dollars of the money we boosted.

All that work for nothin. Well, not really. Once Judge Lasey said, If fifty percent of the funds were returned, she would bring my case back up in five years, I had my plan ready for action. Since Niko had several accounts, I decided to expose pertinent information about the account with a balance of roughly six hundred twenty thousand dollars.

Niko still had about two hundred thousand left in cash and other accounts. That's not including money he was making from side scams.

He could've had more money than that, if it hadn't been for his "die broke" lifestyle. Niko always said, "Spend what you have now, or someone else will be spending it when you die." Trust me, he lived by his motto.

I mean, this man bought so much shit, it was ridiculous. He spent big money daily. Because of his spontaneous personality, he went from buying a car one day to flying off to the Bahamas the next.

See, I just chilled. I spent a little here and there. My main focus was working and keeping the heat off us. But, no matter how hard I tried to cover up what we were doing, you see where we ended up. Grandma always said, "Good overrides evil." I should've listened!

17 Change Is Coming

"Now that my ass is on the line, so is yours!" Lieutenant Graham said. His face was beet red with sweat beading up on his forehead. "I've got to take some drastic measures, even if it means firing some of you lazy fucks!"

Brocton said the meeting got heated. He described the way Graham paced, banging his fist on the desks after roll call. I guess shit was about to hit the fan. He said the room went silent.

Forty intimidated correctional officers sat scared, listening to an irate Lieutenant Graham. I can just imagine him ranting and raving about the reprimand he had gotten from Warden Weaver, in reference to the increase of drug use on his block. By no means was Block C the only one with drug problems, but it was the only concern of Graham's.

I bet Graham was pissed as he fussed, "The warden has known about this and has been disturbed for quite sometime. Now he's getting heat from the state. This ultimately means the heat is now on us! And I do mean all of us! Basically, we're not doing our jobs." He told the C.O.'s that he made a request to have Investigator Hernandez come in to assist in curbing the drug activity around here. "He's going to be an integral part of our staff," Graham explained.

Brocton said he walked through the middle of the aisles, eyeballing officers. Most wouldn't even look him in the eye. Everyone sat straight up in their seat as Graham got closer.

Corning sat in the front, taking attendance, looking like a schoolboy. To everything Graham said, he nodded. That's pitiful. He worships the ground Graham walks on. For his sake, I hope he makes lieutenant soon. Or all that sucking up will be in vain.

Brocton had me trippin. He said C.O. Brown was extra funny. Not once did he look at Graham, or pretend like he was interested. I couldn't help but think about how he tried to rough me off during the random drug test. I guess he was trying his best to get some money out of me too.

Apparently Bennett caught a bad case of scareditis. From what I understand, she sat there in a daze, twisting that damn ring around her finger. She wasn't paying attention at all, but I assume it didn't matter, because, when Graham walked past her, he looked right down in her face and kept on moving. He's real hands-off when it comes to her. It's sickening.

Graham's voice got even louder as he continued to fuss. "As a matter of fact, some of us are a big part of the problem. Don't you *agree*?" he said angrily, putting fear in some C.O.s' hearts.

Nobody spoke a word. The officers were looking around, trying to see if he was speaking to anyone in particular.

Banging on the wall he said, "Hello, is anybody home?"

C.O. Curtis sat slouched with cheek in hand, unthreatened by Graham's psychotic outbreak. He'd been here almost as long as Graham and was definitely his elder. "Some officers are more than a part of the problem. They're involved," Curtis said, getting things started.

With a wrinkled forehead and popped eyes, Graham said, "Well, we have to catch them and hit them with criminal charges."

I laughed when I found out Warren tried to earn brownie points. He had the nerve to say, "I've actually seen an officer with cocaine in her lunch pail, but I ain't saying no names." I know the C.O.s snickered when Graham sarcastically said, "Oh! so now you want to give information and no names. Thanks, but no thanks."

Warren, shrugging and embarrassed sucked up with, "Okay."

Graham finally calmed down a little. Resting on a brown wobbly stool he looked around at each officer carefully before speaking. He bent slightly and rubbed his forehead. "I know we can't stop all drugs from coming in this institution, but we can cut it down on Block C. Over forty-five percent of our population is here for drug charges. So they know exactly how to get the drugs in. We need to figure out a way to reduce what's coming in."

Brocton said, Graham got buck. Standing up again he said, "This place is like living on the streets! Drugs keep finding their way on our block. Does anybody have any suggestions?"

Then he handed C.O. Riley a piece of chalk, not giving her any instructions. Riley stepped to the chalkboard.

I could picture Graham snapping, "If we're going to

work together, let's start now! Does anybody have any suggestions?"

Two hands went up as if the C.O.s were back in elementary school.

Riley's voice trembled as she said, "More random drug testing?"

Graham nodded and signaled for her to write it on the board.

I laughed out loud thinking about these punk-ass C.O.s sucking up to Graham. "Do a better job checking quarterly packages," someone said from the back of the room. Graham rewarding his ass-kissers, said "That sounds good."

Brocton told me Graham discussed the yard and how more and more inmates were beginning to walk around glassy eyed. He's known for quite some time that the yard is a big problem. He just couldn't figure out how to fix it.

Chiming in, Investigator Hernandez said, "We've got inmates always willing to give us any information we need. Use them!"

Everyone started noddin. Riley wrote on the board *Use Snitches*.

Hernandez added, "The visiting room is the biggest problem."

"That's right. Girls hiding shit in baby bags and diapers," Curtis said.

Hernandez's response made me cringe. He said, "I say we change the rules. Anytime a visitor is caught bringing something in, let's prosecute to the fullest and cancel *all* visits for Block C inmates for a few weeks. This way, if the whole unit feels the pressure, they'll start snitching."

Once again most of the officers agreed. And Graham was happy.

Brocton said the motivation for some escalated. Others sat as if they knew they weren't going to do a damn thing. Shit, just as much money can be made in prison as on the streets.

Smith put his arm up and blurted, "The laundry room and the kitchen. Those areas need to be watched more closely."

"Yeah, it's real convenient for making transactions," Riley said.

"Everywhere is easy access around here," Bennett said, finally coming to life.

"So, what do you suppose we do?" I could almost hear Graham's tone of voice change from strong to weak when he responded to Bennett.

"Umm, I don't really know," Bennett said.

Graham winked. "Keep thinking about it, and let me know."

"Okay."

From what I'm told, by the time Graham walked to the front of the room, he was in high spirits. He said, "I think we're off to a good start. I'm going to make a huge poster to post in the sergeant's office with all of our suggestions. Remember them. Stick to them and make some changes. Also, spend some time investigating. Try to figure out who seems to have the money around here. Then check to see what funds have been logged in under their accounts. Be creative! Do whatever you've got to do. I want our unit to be the best. Other units are feeling the pressure as well as us, but I don't know what they're going to do about it. I like my job! It's what I live for. What about you?"

"Yeah, yes, sir," most said in unison. Mumbled conversations proceeded.

"You may be dismissed."

Nobody wanted to be the first to get up. Brocton said he made the first move and others followed. As they rose, quite a bit of whispering still went on. Different people had various opinions about what was going down. Riley grabbed a sheet of paper to copy the suggestions off the board. Most officers exited toward the sergeant's office, which was connected to the meeting room.

"Hernandez, I need to see you for a moment," Graham stated.

Sitting on the edge of the desk Graham told Hernandez to talk to some of his trusted inmates to develop a list of the major suppliers around the unit. Riley listened, but didn't say a word.

Brocton lingered around, to get more info, even though he was the first one out of his seat. He then noticed a large percentage of his coworkers packed in Corning's office. He decided to join them.

The sergeant's office has always been like Grand Central Station. Workers congregated, filled out paperwork, and handled administrative tasks. From all his talk, I guess Graham's lecture motivated them to get right on the job. C.O.'s studied the board where all the inmates ID cards were posted. Every inmate on C block had a picture made just for the board. The ID cards provided officers with pertinent information such as their inmate numbers, date of incarceration, and sentence length.

Apparently, the way the officers were pointing and gazing at the pictures, it was almost as if the ID cards hadn't been looked at by anyone before now.

Brocton said Warren was on joke time when he snickered, "Hey, look at Squzz. He was actually a man when he came in."

His comment sparked major laughter in the room and initiated more interest in the ID's.

"Look at Science. He used to keep himself up," Riley said.

"Hey. Where's Niko's card?" Warren asked.

Riley, Warren, Smith, and Bennett all examined the board carefully for Niko's card. It wasn't there!

Warren turned to Corning, who was now working at the computer with Brocton, and said, "Did you remove Niko's card?"

"No."

"It's not here," Warren said.

"Check behind the table. Maybe it fell down."

I can imagine all those fools checking to see if Niko's card had fallen down off the board. Corning stopped typing on the computer and turned completely around in his swivel chair.

"Brocton has a great idea," Corning said. Everyone stopped and looked directly at Corning.

"What's that?" Warren said, green with envy.

"Why not use the inmates' files to our advantage?"

"And. . . " Warren said.

"Brocton, you tell them," Corning boasted.

Now, Brocton might be bending the truth a little bit, trying to pump himself up. He told me he remained silent, like he had done something wrong, but Corning insisted.

Hesitantly, Brocton said, "Well, if we look up everyone's file, we can find out why they're here. It might give us some clues as to who had previous drug connections."

"That's smart," Riley said.

No one else said anything. Warren continued to look for the ID.

Brocton said Corning decided to test Black's name—
Edward Jacobs. Everyone gathered around the computer,
anxious to see. When Black's picture appeared on the right
side of the screen, the picture size was nothing compared
to the length of charges on the left.

Corning ran his finger down the screen, reading the
category of each criminal charge. "Assault with a deadly
weapon, armed robbery, gun charge, assault with a pistol,
multiple gun charges," he said.

"Well, Mr. Jacobs has been busy. And not just with
drugs," Corning said.

"He's a known drug user," Smith blurted out.

"Keep an eye on him," Corning said.

Everyone nodded.

"All right, the party is over," Corning said, grabbing his
cap and closing out the program. "Let's do this more often,
and remember, investigate!"

I became famished after listening to all Brocton's mess.
It was interesting, but I had my own problems.

18

A Fool in Love

Strangely Bennett has been hanging around Niko's cell frequently. Obvious to everyone, she has a much-too-close relationship with him. Oddly, she doesn't care about hiding it anymore. Her coworkers are starting to give her suspect looks, and some horrible rumors have been circulating. For starters, C.O. Garcia told Graham she saw Niko and Bennett kissing. That was her attempt to get the heat off her ass. Therefore, nobody really paid attention to her comment. Also, rumor has it, that whenever Bennett isn't working, Niko is constantly making collect calls to her house.

Giving Niko her number has to rank number one, as the stupidest shit in Dunnridge. And the way she hangs around protective custody makes it visibly clear that something is going on. She has no business being in protective custody anyway. This isn't her assigned unit. I wish she'd take her sloppy ass outta here.

Although, one good thing has come out of her hanging around Niko. He must have told her to give me those supplies she brought to my cell. At least he was still looking out for me. I couldn't wait until we saw each other face to face. We're boys, and I was sure we'd work everything out. Whatever he read in those transcripts, I'll explain. All the details aren't in the transcripts because the files are sealed. So no matter what Hernandez is saying, I am positive Niko doesn't know everything.

He must not be too mad. I'm sure it is Niko who sends me the newspaper every morning. When I wake up the paper has been slid right under my cell. It's just like the paperboy delivering the Sunday morning edition. Only difference is, I can't go out front to get it. Niko knows I loved to stay abreast of what is going on in the world. You know, I can't live without the business section. And I especially love the horoscopes. I truly believe in all that shit. Some people think I'm crazy, but then they ask me about their horoscope. You see I'm a Leo, born August 11. Leos always have promising horoscope sections. For instance, today mine reads. . .

You have a wonderful personality and you're a very logical thinker.

You often take advantage of situations where someone isn't thinking. You will be paid well for talents and production. Relationship intense, might get too hot. August will bring romance to your life. Money will change hands —fight for your fair share.

"Mail call," C.O. Brocton said as he walked down the aisle.

Brocton said a few words to Bennett as she was on her way out. She must have figured she should be leaving now.

Brocton was nearly two feet from my cell when he stopped to have a few words with my faggy neighbor. All at once, Brocton's carefree demeanor changed to distress within seconds. He stood helpless with his mouth wide open as if he had gone into shock. He yelled, "Bennett!"

Bennett, near the end of the unit, turned to ask, "What's wrong?"

Brocton was speechless. He pointed his index finger at my neighbor's cell, dropped the mail, and backed up against the wall. I continued to stick my head through the bars. Bennett had already gone inside the cell, and was no longer in my view.

"Oh God, he's foaming at the mouth!" Bennett yelled.

I screamed, "Brocton, call for help!"

Maybe dude was having a seizure, but at least Brocton was outta his trance and calling for help.

Before I knew it, there were three officers in the cell and based on the conversation, I knew my neighbor's fate. Bennett said, "I'm not cutting him down." One of the other officers described the sheet that he had tied to the heater vent. At the top of Bennett's voice, she said, "Brocton, you do it, it's your wing."

Even though Brocton had gotten himself together, he was still saddened by the self-inflicted hanging. Able to finally walk in the cell, he told Bennett that when he first saw the inmate, he was still alive. And, that the look on his face was as if he had changed his mind. But, it was too late.

Moments later, the body was taken out, and the block was clear. The mail lay on the floor, but no one was around to give it to me. The C.O.s were obviously busy, and I didn't want to seem insensitive, so I chilled.

About an hour had passed before Brocton returned. He didn't have much to say, but looked as if he was in better spirits. He whistled, appearing to be normal. And before I knew it, he was back on mail delivery.

"Thanks," I said, grabbing the small envelope.

The return address was unfamiliar. However, the red lips that were kissed on the back of the seal were. Sherese was writing me? For what? Maybe the bitch realized that nigga she was living with wasn't worth a damn. I hoped she didn't think I was gonna take her ass back. Fuck her! I meant that shit! You can only treat people the way they let you. I was definitely not falling into her little trap.

If my eyes could pop completely out my head, they would. Shocked! I unbelievably looked at the receipt, showing the amount of a money order sent by Sherese. I couldn't believe my eyes, this bitch had a nerve to send me a two hundred dollar money order. She had more than eighty thousand of my damn money.

The attached note read:

Divine, I thought I would send you what's left of your half of the money. Take care! Sherese

She had to be kidding. I should have her ass arrested. I did her a favor by not implicating her in our last gig. She could at least be honest with me and give me my loot. I knew I couldn't be exact considering the money she had spent on me over the years but, I knew for sure she hadn't spent close to eighty thousand dollars.

"Jones, you've got a visit!" C.O. Curtis yelled without even getting up.

Leaving my cell, I was nervous for the first time in years. I was going to talk to my lawyer, and this meeting could mean a positive or negative change in my life. I walked to the end of the walkway where Niko's cell was located. I didn't see him at all. I turned slowly, looking all around as the shackles were being applied to my feet and hands. I hoped that weak-ass money order Sherese sent was no indication of the money my horoscope was talking about. It said money was supposed to change hands. Two hundred dollars was by no means my fair share. And I *know* she's not the person I'm soon to be romantic with.

On the way to the visiting facility I thought about all the things that could possibly happen. Would I be released in the next couple of days? Would I have to go back to court to see the judge? Would I be denied everything that was promised to me? What would I do my first day out of here? I was driving myself crazy.

In the visiting area, I was taken to a room off to the right from where the general population sat. I felt real important. Why? There was nothing important about being a convict.

The room had a glass window, open to the inside of the visiting center, so I could see Brothenstein sitting there, fiddling with some papers. This man had not changed since the day I met him. He was still sort of chubby, with a circular face. He wore a dark blue suit with another one of those boring ties. He should leave that assignment to his wife or secretary. He probably would get more respect if he dressed like a top-notch lawyer.

His haircut is ridiculous. Or should I say his lack of a haircut is ridiculous. It's too long for a man anyway. He's

always moving it out of his face. He's too old for that shit.
I could see him with half of a bald head. Or completely
bald would be better than that stringy mess!

And oh! The way that man sweat was inconceivable.
Even in the winter months. I could remember going to court
in the dead of winter, and he'd take out a handkerchief to
wipe the sweat from his face. Well, he was at it again.

I was really upset with his appearance and shouldn't
be at all. He had bent over backward for me. When I was
initially arrested, my bond was so high that I thought I'd
never get out. He used his connections to have the judge
reduce my bond so Sherese was able to post bail. Come to
think of it. . . he'd never doubted me.

When I entered the room Brothenstein stood enthusi-
astically, with a huge grin on his face. We shook hands and
he pulled my chair out signaling me to sit. He still had that
firm grip. The grip that said to me—everything is going to
be okay. All right, I know I'm dead wrong, but didn't he
make enough money to get his teeth fixed?

I really like this guy, I had to keep saying it to myself
so I wouldn't think any more horrible thoughts. But, he
could at least get them cleaned! Uh, okay, okay, okay.

"Divine, sit down," Mr. Brothenstein said.

I sat, eager to get down to business. Clearly he was
running the show. I didn't know whether to make small
talk or simply shut up.

"Divine, I hope you reviewed the transcripts I sent
you."

"Yes, sir," I said, feeling like I had regained respect for
others.

"Well, I guess you realize that this agreement was made
between you, me, and Judge Lasey."

"Uh—huh."

"The worst part of this whole deal is that Judge Lasey is no longer servicing Criminal Court."

I almost fell out of my chair! My whole world had been turned upside down.

"How is that possible? This is my life we're talking about. I snitched on my buddy in order to make this deal happen! And I think he knows it! As a matter of fact, I know he knows it! If I don't get out of here soon, I'm gonna die! Literally!"

"Calm down, son," Brothenstein said, placing his sweaty palm on my shoulder. "I didn't say you won't get out. I'm just laying all the cards on the table. I've been in contact with Judge Lasey, and she's willing to speak to another judge friend of hers handling the cases in Criminal Court."

I couldn't believe my eyes. Hopefully I was mistaken. No, I wasn't. Tashonda walked past the window to my visiting room. Glancing at me, she dropped her head. She had been crying and took a slight resemblance to a battered woman. Unraveled, her hair was far from her usual pin-up. If I didn't know better, I'd say she fought ten people. Her eye liner had started to run down her face from the tears. When I realized her hands were behind her back and hand-cuffed, I stood. This was serious. I watched closely as she was being transported out of the visiting room where two county uniform officers were waiting on her. These weren't correctional officers either. This shit was real!

How did this happen? Did another officer snitch on Mathematics? Maybe even an inmate?

Brothenstein was sweating intensely at this point. I had completely forgotten that he was telling me about my life.

I had forgotten about my deep problems.

"I hate to bring this up, but I need another payment from you," Brothenstein said, facing downward.

"Money!" I snapped.

"I'll need some to set up the continuation with the new judge," he said.

"I've been sending you money over the past five years, and for what? Look what I'm getting in return. I'm still here."

"Divine, you're a good guy, but I've got to pay my staff for filing motions, pulling transcripts, and making phone calls. You need these services to be handled on your behalf in order for anything positive to transpire."

"Uh-huh," I said, shaking my head.

"Trust me," he stated, peering into my face.

I said, "I'm trying. Although, it's starting to be difficult."

"I'm even here for you on a holiday."

Brothenstein started packing up. I knew his time was valuable, but damn. He could have at least stayed a little longer. I was not ready to go back to that hole-in-the-wall yet.

He patted his forehead with his pricey Armani handkerchief before saying, "Ask Sherese to send the payment to my office as soon as possible."

"I thought Grandma explained everything."

"That's right, she did say she would be handling everything for you."

Wiping his sweat again he sighed. "Ms. Lewis is going to be able to take care of the bill, isn't she?"

"Of course."

He knew I was lying. He set his briefcase back on the table. I guess he wanted to stay awhile now. When you start fucking with a man's money, that's when he wants to be serious. He put his shiny patent-leathers on the chair, patting his knee. He closed his eyes. And the room went silent for nearly two minutes. I didn't mind. That was more time for me to stay here.

"Are you and Sherese still together?"

"Hell no."

He waited a moment before speaking. "Remember when I defended you in that case where Sherese and Niko were supposed to be your codefendants back in 1993?"

"How could I forget?"

"Well, how come you took the rap for her role in the deal?"

"She was my girl and I was a fool in love."

"Well, she needs to be there for you now."

Picking up his briefcase he prepared to leave. He waited at the door for the officers to notice that he was ready to exit. He didn't even turn to say he was leaving or that the conversation had ended. Right before the guard unlocked the door he said, "This advice is free—if I were you I'd make Sherese think her name will be implicated when you return to court if she doesn't help you with your legal fees. I'm sure she still has money left."

He was gone with a twinkling of an eye, sweating all the way out the facility. That dude was sharp. I'd never talk about his teeth again.

19

Spillin' the Beans

Before I called Sherese with my swindle of bullying her into paying my lawyer some money, I needed to think about what I was doing.

Okay, although Brothenstein helped me out on that case, he didn't realize I was the mastermind. He thought Sherese came up with our brainiac idea.

See, it all started after Sherese and I had gotten serious. Well, after she realized she couldn't live without me. I fell in love with her from the start. Niko kept telling me not to get serious about her because she was so shady. I didn't care, I liked her style. And let's face it, she had street smart. She had more common sense than book sense. I was starting to think that wasn't so bad.

Niko told me that Sherese once set up some guys for him. Robbing them was a part of his big plan. He just didn't know how until he met Sherese. He knew as soon as they met that she was the one. Niko thought that since she knew the guys would be pistol whipped, duct taped, and possibly murdered, maybe she wouldn't go through with it. *She did.*

Ever since that deal, Niko hasn't really trusted her. He said she'd do the same thing to us for the right amount of money. He also said I shouldn't want a person like that to be my number one girl. Fuck it! I wanted her. She excited me! Niko didn't trust her at all.

I wasn't too sure how to approach Sherese with this news. She wouldn't accept my phone calls and she was definitely not coming to see me. I could ask Grandma to go to her house, but then Grandma would know everything. I didn't really want that to happen. Maybe I could send her a letter and hope her new man didn't intercept it. I didn't even know where to start or how to end. All I knew was I needed her to send Brothenstein some money. He didn't even say how much he needed. I was assuming from my history with him that five thousand dollars would be acceptable.

"I've got it! I'm a smart mother fucker," I said while giving myself dap.

I was gonna ask Brocton to send Sherese a letter certified mail from outside the facility, I thought. That way she wouldn't know it was from me and she'd have to show ID in order to get the letter. This way I'd know she got it.

I started pulling out my collection of supplies and began writing Sherese. Before I knew it hours had gone by. I told Sherese I was going to implicate her in every illegal activity I'd ever committed. I went on to say how I didn't appreciate the two hundred dollar money order, and that I would be expecting her to send all my money to Grandma.

I revised the letter over and over, making sure I said all the right things and that my grammar was appropriate. Not that Sherese would know anyway. I was trying to finish up before Brocton came on post. I wanted to be able to give him the letter before lights went out. I hoped Sherese would take this seriously and would be scared as hell. She needed a little fear in her heart.

"Bitch," I said loud enough for Brocton to hear.

He was standing in front of my cell, shaking his head as if he were disappointed in me for talking to myself.

I wasted no time. I walked directly over to him with the unwritten paper in my hand. "I need a favor."

Standing straight up, Brocton paused examining me from head to toe. "Oh yeah," he finally answered.

"Yeah." Why would he fake on me?

"What you got for me?" Brocton asked.

"Oh, so you're acting brand new. I don't recall you acting like this before. What's up?"

"Listen, Divine, you're cool people, but I've got to make a little paper too. I work this shitty-ass job and the pay ain't good. Besides, I generally get paid by someone around here for helping you even though you don't actually pay me."

"What?" I said, with my mouth hanging open. I didn't understand that at all, nor did I have time to listen to the explanation he was about to give. "Brocton, I'll pay you fifty dollars to do the easiest thing you've ever done in here. It's not much, but it's all I can spare."

Brocton all of a sudden lit up. Relaxing the muscles in his face that had been balled up, he smiled. "Man, my fault, I'm just having a bad day."

"It's not even illegal," I said, returning the smile. He loosened up as I began, "I'm gonna make this as short as possible."

"I've got a few minutes, I guess." Brocton looked

around, making sure none of his player-hating coworkers were watching.

"Okay, you already know all about Sherese."

Brocton smirked. "The girl who's pregnant with someone else's baby and won't accept your calls."

I nodded and said, "Yeah. Well, about five months after we had been seriously kickin' it, and I do mean seriously, she started working for this marketing company. I don't know how in the hell she got the job. Maybe it was her personality. Anyhow, she wanted to share everything about her new job with me. Every aspect of working was new to her. She would call me at work with the craziest stories. She was mostly proud that she was finally able to land some bona fide, real—what you and I call legal—employment.

"Well, one day we were phone boning while she was at work. Someone so rudely interrupted us by calling into her firm. I was on hold for about nine minutes. I was pissed, but tried not to show it. You see, we had a date that night and I didn't wanna fuck that up. When Sherese came back to the phone she apologized over and over. She told me all about the phone call and remarked how people call and place orders over the phone for loads of money. On bullshit I might add. Being curious, I inquired how they paid for the orders. When she replied with credit cards, I started getting a few ideas. I wasn't quite sure if they would work, but the concept was definitely in my mind."

"How long is this gonna take?" Brocton asked, looking out for unexpected guests.

"Not long," I said. "I told Niko about the possibility of getting some credit card numbers from Sherese, but he wasn't really interested. He was down, but couldn't figure out a profitable way to benefit from that type of hook-up. He was all about getting paid for murdering someone, robbery, or some old rough-neck shit.

"As time went on I kept throwing different ideas Sherese's way. We were madly in love! Sometimes during pillow talk Sherese would tell me the high limits on most of the credit card orders she had taken. I told her to start writing down some credit card numbers in order to be ready if I thought of a scam. Being the thieving person she is, she got up to get her purse. Next thing you know she pulled out two sheets of scrap paper with about eight credit card numbers. Can you believe that shit? Each number was written backward with an expiration date at the end. I laughed at the fact that she was always on top of the situation.

"Hanging out with Niko one day, it occurred to me that maybe I could buy loads of expensive clothes with the credit card numbers and sell them on the streets at half price. Everyone who Niko knew was into expensive gear. That's where I figured he would be helpful. Sherese would get the numbers, I would make the purchases, and Niko would have the connections to sell the shit.

"As weeks passed by, I was somewhat distraught that we had this plan, but had no way of implementing this brilliant idea. The major problem was that because we didn't physically have the credit card we couldn't go shopping for clothing. We either needed the credit cards in hand, or we needed an inside connection. Essentially, our scam called for someone who would punch in the numbers manually, without having the actual card.

"At first, I thought, who would be stupid enough to do that? No one. Then I figured, everyone has a price. I felt I was being considerate by letting somebody else in on the deal. I just wasn't sure who it was going to be. I told Niko and Sherese to be on the prowl for anyone that could make things happen for us. Especially, someone who worked in an exquisite shop. Exquisite, I thought—that's pushing it! They hardly know people with jobs.

"That's when it came to me! I thought hard about how I would ask Conrad Owlings—Mr. Straight and Narrow— to help me."

"Who in the hell is that?" Brocton said, agitated. "Is Conrad in Dunnridge?"

"Nah."

"Is he locked up at all?" Brocton asked, baffled.

"No, but he's an important piece to this puzzle. Conrad and I met in college. We had nothing in common except the fact that we were both from Virginia. Conrad is average height with a slender build. He has always worn, and still wears, a pair of square nerdy glasses. I would have never guessed he would still have those same glasses. His voice is high-pitched and he articulates every syllable. It's almost nauseating to hear him talk. He spends so much time enunciating each word, you get tired of listening to him.

"He was reared by both parents and lived in an upscale neighborhood. I mean his bedroom was larger than the average home in my neighborhood. His mom's a dentist and his dad's a lawyer. That type of environment puts pressure on you to be a nerd. However, it didn't have any effect on the type of career he chose for himself. He graduated with a degree in business and became the manager of a Foot Zone at one of our local malls. Now, I'm not one to judge, but when you come from a background like that, you need to represent. Hell, my job at U.S. Savings was better than that. I just assumed he would have done better than most of the people we graduated with. His persona purely made you feel that way.

"Although, a bore on campus, I believe he thought he was a gift to the ladies. He loved to impress people at any cost. That's why I thought he would be down from the start. He liked for people to think of him as being down with the in crowd. He always cared about what people thought about him."

"Divine, give me the condensed version!" Brocton said.

"When I was certain that he was the one, I had to think about how to do it. I decided to go to the mall where he worked. I chose the late evening because I figured if I was one of the last people in the store we could talk privately. Or if that didn't work, we could at least exchange numbers. I worked it out by meeting Sherese at the mall one after- noon after I had gotten off work. We walked around browsing, window shopping, sort of hanging out. When we walked past Conrad's store, I immediately got anxious. I don't know why. I hadn't done anything.

"We walked around the small but heavily inventoried store. There weren't many items to choose from. Loads of sneakers lined the wall. Sherese was fingering through some sweat gear on one of the racks while I was eyeing a few pairs of kicks I thought I'd look good in. I wanted Conrad and me to make eye contact so it would look like I happened to run into him. Every time he finished with a customer I moved his way. He sure wasn't a good salesperson because it took him fifteen minutes to ask me if I needed some help.

"Conrad's face nearly blew up when we he realized it was me. He even hugged me! A manly hug, no faggy shit.

We started kicking it about old times, where I live now, where he lives, our jobs, etc. Before you knew it Sherese and I were the last customers in the store, if that's what you want to call us. I was perplexed about how to ask Conrad about making purchases without a credit card, so I decided to buy something small, so if all else failed I could pay cash. Of course in my mind, I wanted to throw about twenty pairs of kicks on the counter and whip out one of my credit card numbers. I threw two pairs of socks on the counter.

"When Conrad said, 'That's all you're getting, man,' I got nervous.

"'Yeah.' I pretended to look for my credit card. I patted my back pockets and intensely looked through my wallet. I should have won an Oscar for my performance. I seem to have left my credit card at home. I know the number. Do you think you could enter it without the card?"

"Ummmm," he hesitated. Then he said, "Sure."

"I rattled off the number that was written in the palm of my hand. Do you need the expiration date? I was trying to make everything sound legit.

"No. Sign here.

"Deciding what name to sign was rough. I didn't want to put my real name, but I knew Conrad would know if I signed a fake name. So I signed my name as sloppy and shady as possible so you could barely make out the name. I made sure the 'D' was written large and clearly so Conrad wouldn't have any doubts.

"He was clearly ready for us to leave at this point. He kept walking toward the gate of the store that had been pulled almost completely down for the last half hour.

"Here, take my card and call me sometimes," Conrad

said, handing me his business card.

"I don't know if he wanted me to be impressed, but I in return handed him my business card and replied, "Let's hang out sometimes. Call my secretary and leave a message."

"Now I did have it going on at my job, but I damn sure didn't have a secretary of my own. The four people working in the finance department shared the same secretary, but I wasn't about to let Conrad know that!

"As soon as we were clear of the Foot Zone, Sherese started lightly punching me in the arm, gritting her teeth. I thought I had done something wrong until she said, "Why the hell didn't you at least get me a pair of tennis shoes?"

"I told her I wasn't quite sure how everything was going to work out. My plan was to talk to Conrad outside the store within the next few weeks to get a real operation going on. My aunt Delila always said, If you gonna steal a car, make sure it's a Benz.

"So I knew I had to make some real money if I was going to do some bullshit like that. Big mistake!

"About a week later, I ended up telling Conrad about the entire plan. Surprisingly, he was down. Thinking back, I truly believe he thought it was going to be a couple pair of shoes here and there. He really couldn't see the big picture. Sherese was down the whole time, never doubting any part of the deal, although, she made it clear she wanted her cut. She felt like the credit card numbers were the most important part of the operation. She wanted half! Can you believe that bitch?"

At this point Brocton was fidgeting, looking around. I knew I needed to get to the end quickly. I desperately needed this letter to be delivered. I was totally sidetracked by thinking about his comment. Who would be paying him to look out for me? Niko don't fuck with him like that.

Looking at his watch, Brocton said, "I'm gonna have to hear the rest later. Give me the letter."

"It's not finished yet, but come back in about twenty minutes. It'll be ready."

I handed Brocton the letter thirty minutes later with a smile on my face. "Put a bogus sender's name and address."

Taking a moment to glare, he said, "I've got one question. Is this the reason you and Niko got sent up the river?"

"Hell no."

"Let me guess—you never told about Sherese's involvement."

"Man, all I can say is I was in love."

Brocton said, "All I can say is you were stupid."

It seemed like Brocton was interested in the rest of the story. He had already spent way too much time around my cell. So I quickly continued my story. "Things went slowly and smoothly at first. I would go in the store and purchase three or four pair of kicks at a time when Conrad was working alone. Niko would sell them on the street and we would split the money. I had to give Sherese half of my cut. So you can understand why I needed to increase production with this scam."

Brocton nodded, giving his undivided attention.

"Conrad started to get nervous after about a month. He didn't feel comfortable with me and Sherese coming in the store to get shoes and sweat gear on a regular. Whenever Sherese went in alone she would come out with way too much stuff, so I stopped Sherese from shopping and simply gave her a cut off what I was getting. She was holding all the money we made anyway. She should have been satisfied. We had made nearly sixty thousand dollars.

"Conrad definitely wasn't satisfied with the way things were being handled. I should have figured the Foot Zone would eventually be a problem. He said his district manager was concerned about the inventory. Unfortunately, I was able to convince him that everything was going to be okay and that there was no way he could get caught. I don't know why he believed me. If I had listened to him, we probably wouldn't have gotten caught.

"In no time that business venture became so profitable even Conrad would ask when was I stopping by again. He was only making a flat fee of one hundred dollars every time I came in the store. He was pulling in about three to four hundred dollars a week, tax-free. That's a lot to a store manager. Plus, this went on for months. Everyone was happy. I even started taking back a couple pairs of shoes using a fake name and address to get a refund check. Of course I had to have Conrad's help, but Sherese and Niko knew nothing about that.

"Everything seemed fine and dandy. What we didn't know was that before the scam, Foot Zone was averaging about six thousand dollars per day in sales. Once we started buying merchandise with the card numbers, sales went from six thousand to twelve thousand daily! Everything was going swell until Conrad's district manager, Cynthia, noticed a huge increase in daily sales. This woman is like the don of retail sales. Customers would walk in the store browsing and leave with sneakers, matching sweats, socks, hat, and anything else she could sell. She was a petite hyper little woman, always persuading people to buy! Sell, sell, sell, that's all she thought about. Making quotas, crunching numbers, and changing displays was her life.

"Anyhow, she was hungry for a promotion and knew that consistent increased revenue in that store would do the trick. At first she slyly questioned Conrad to see if there were any days in particular where he had a large-volume day. Of course Conrad had no idea why she was asking. He was happy just because she was pleased with what was going on with daily sales, not to mention, the fact that the corporate office was elated. They wanted to know what was making the Foot Zone all of a sudden so popular. They were happy about the increase in sales, but wanted to know what was making it happen. I guess they wanted the same success to continue at other locations as well. Cynthia was so interested in how to keep the high-volume days, she decided to analyze days with the most sales. She had given her bosses the impression that she was the reason for the increase in volume for that particular store, therefore, she had to make sure the store continued to prosper.

"Cynthia decided she would analyze the sales from the previous months to pick out the high-volume days so she could work those days in the future. She ordered an audit to assist her in this venture, saying it was needed for the success of the store, but it was a personal venture for her. She had no idea what she was about to encounter.

"Once the auditors realized there was an enormous amount of charges that had been run manually, they started register tapes from the beginning of the year. The auditors were alarmed at what they had found and notified corporate security immediately. Once corporate saw that for six days straight there was a total of sixty charges run manually from the same store, and by the same person, it was obvious fraud was present! After contacting the credit card companies and through further investigations, Conrad was read his rights as he turned his key to open the Foot Zone for the last time."

"So he did get some time," Brocton said.

"Just a little. He was such a punk! He sang like a bird, squealing on the entire operation. He told on me, Sherese, and Niko."

"This is way too much," Brocton said, baffled by the information.

"Sherese, Conrad, and I were charged with grand larceny. Being the soldier that I am, I said that Niko had nothing to do with anything. I took the rap for Sherese too. She claimed she already had a check-fraud charge and couldn't afford to go down again. She cried, telling me all about what the judge said he would do if she ever crossed his courtroom again. The prosecutors still wanted Sherese, considering she actually worked for the marketing firm. Hell, she was the one who stole the credit card numbers. Nonetheless, I fell for all her bullshit and lied for her ass. I said I got the card numbers one evening while visiting her at work. I made up this long, drawn-out story about how she didn't know anything about the numbers. I don't think the prosecutors or the judge believed it, but, they had me to pin the crime on, so it didn't even matter.

"So you see, I saved that bitch! And Niko's ass too. . .

"I'm not really sure how much time Conrad got. Our case was dragged out in court for months. The lawyers kept getting extensions and more extensions. It dragged on for so long that I never had a chance to finish that case. I ended up getting into more trouble and ended up here."

"For what?" Brocton asked, shaking his head.

"That's a story within itself, man."

Brocton snatched the letter from between the bars and snapped, "I thought you said you were innocent. You got me feeling sorry for you!"

I couldn't even respond. I had spilled the beans and talked Brocton to death.

"And, where is my money?"

Raising my voice, I said, "I just got some money, I need to make sure it's in my account already."

"I see, you want services you haven't paid for yet."

"I'm gonna pay you! Besides, I thought you were my boy."

"I am. You better have my money though," Brocton said as he exited with the letter.

20
Cuttin' Up

That's strange. The cell doors screeched as I heard squeaking noises like someone was coming in. It was dark as hell, and as still as a mouse. That's how it is over here—silent and lonely! All you could hear were your thoughts. And if they were unstable, consider yourself marked insane. It had to be around three in the morning. It was not time for chow. And I could barely see anyone. I hoped I was not getting ready to be interrogated again. I was sick of this shit, and plus I was tired! I spent most of my day writing to Sherese and spilling my secrets to Brocton.

Lifting my head about a quarter of an inch took all my might. I sat up just long enough to see if I could catch a glimpse of anyone moving around. Maybe my cell was opened by mistake. Or maybe the guards wanted me to come out. Fuck that. If they wanted me to come out, they should've said so. I lay back down to get comfortable again. Before I could get in a relaxed position, it felt like someone was coming close. I lifted one last time, feeling leery about my surroundings.

A stinging sensation ran through my entire body. It was the most excruciating pain I had ever felt! I was being shanked! I tried to get off the bunk to fight back. The room was so dark, I could see only a figure. A man slammed at my chest. I lunged off the bed. My left leg was somehow stuck. I tried to give myself a push. But no power was left.

Someone yanked my leg. Two people were now in the room. The pain! I couldn't think. I didn't know if I was shedding tears because it hurt so bad or because I didn't know if I'd survive. But, if I didn't help myself, I was gonna be dead real soon.

With the tiny bit of energy I had left, I forced my arm up to grab the shank. Nausea gripped me. I tried to pull the object away from my chest. It felt like a long rod or an icepick. I didn't struggle for long. I'd been stabbed at least ten times. My heart raced and my breath faded slowly. My screams weren't helping any, because nobody was even saying anything. Where was everybody? Where was the guard?

My entire body fell to the floor. One of the attackers started to drag me across the floor. I could vaguely see a light coming from the C.O.s' desk across the room. I couldn't hear anyone! And the guys never made a sound since they've been in here. I thought it was over. Rapid strokes dug in my abdomen.

I screamed, "Nooooo!"

My field of vision went blank. I started seeing dark shades rolling through my mind. I lay on the floor, lifeless. Everything went blank.

⚷

I lay on the floor motionless. People talked in the

background. I couldn't quite make out the voices. My fear got the best of me. Every organ and vein shuddered. I was terrified! Were the voices from the guys that did this to me? Had someone found me? I tried to move my arm. No feeling at all. I then thought about trying to move my leg. Rapid footsteps clattered my way again. If I lay like I'm dead, the attackers wouldn't waste their time trying to finish me off. I made sure my body lay stiff as a corpse. I could feel them getting closer. Someone was right over top of me! I felt my arm being lifted in the air, then someone began to speak. Next, I heard more feet swiftly running into my cell. People were now standing all around me.

"Will he make it?" an unknown voice asked.

"I'm not sure," another said.

Someone screamed, "Hurry, Hurry!"

I started to wail. I cried like tomorrow would never come. I blurted out a sound no one understood—my way of saying thanks. I kept sniveling and sniffling. Snot and blood gushed from my nose and it became increasingly more difficult for me to breathe.

"One, two, three, and up," two paramedics said as they put me on the stretcher.

They were in full swing as they pushed me down the hall. One guy talked on a walkie-talkie while the other one worked on me. From their conversation, these guys were worried. I was queasy and losing a lot of blood.

"Do you copy!" the paramedic yelled over the whopping sound of the helicopter.

"That's a negative. Come back with that."

"This is medevac unit 116. We're in route transporting a patient with abdominal injuries, chest injuries, and severe blood loss."

"Copy. What's your ETA?"

The paramedic paused. "Ah, we should be there in approximately four minutes. We're leaving from the Dunnridge Correctional facility."

"Come back with that," the emergency room technician said.

The paramedic waited a few seconds before repeating. "I said I'm bringing in a patient from Dunnridge Correctional— "

"We do not accept patients from Dunnridge. You need to go to County General."

"County General? This man is dying."

"They handle all inmates needing outside care. I can call ahead for you if you'd like."

"No thanks," the paramedic responded in a sorrowful tone.

The paramedics talked and decided not to call County General. They didn't want to be denied and didn't want anybody dying in their care. They quickly redirected, and landed at County General four minutes later without prior notice. As soon as the door of the chopper was opened, the group of doctors started reviewing my situation at once.

It was so noisy, and everybody was talking at the same time.

As soon as my stretcher hit triage, about four people began to work on me immediately. One person was taking my vitals, and someone else ripped my T-shirt open.

"What happened to this guy?" one doctor exclaimed.

"Apparently he was stabbed in the chest and the abdomen multiple times!" a nurse yelled from across the room.

"It appears we have no choice but to do laparoscopy surgery," the surgeon said.

He had only looked at me for thirty seconds. How the hell could he decide that shit? I was so out of it, I couldn't speak up for myself.

"Prepare the O.R.," the surgeon said, walking away. "Also, he'll need a blood transfusion. He's lost way too much blood."

I breathed deeply, trying to stay calm. It hurts like hell every time I took a breath. I grunted a few times.

"He's got cuts everywhere," one examiner whispered in disbelief.

The health practitioners looked at my body as if they had never seen anything like it before. I got angry that I had even survived.

The examining doctor responded, " What's worse is the fact that the knife tore completely through his triceps muscle and numerous veins."

He turned swiftly and asked, "What is this young man's name?"

"Ah. . . " one of the nurses said as she grabbed the chart.

"Divine Jones."

The doctor looked down into my face and spoke sincerely. "Divine Jones, you've been hurt very badly, son. Lucky for you we've got the best darn surgeon around, and we're going to do our best to get you through this. Just hold on, buddy."

Tears welled once again. This was the first time I felt

like I could make it. I might live! But, for what? I might
not be able to walk again. I might end up as a paraplegic.
Once again, I began to sob hysterically. I couldn't believe
I've been cut up like this.

21   Here We Go Again

I listened as Riley and Warren conversed about the intimate details that led to my near-death experience. They stood outside of the infirmary door where I lay in ungodly pain. The door half cracked, I could hear it all.

"I can hardly believe all this shit is happening around here," Riley said, sideways positioned toward Warren.

I guess they figured I was in a deep sleep, so it was safe to speak openly. I squinted as Warren began to respond.

Shaking his head in disbelief as he continued the story, Riley listened in awe. She could not believe what she heard.

"How do they know she was there?" Riley asked.

"Blood," Warren said, clearing his throat. "I can't believe she was that stupid to get caught with blood on her shirt."

Who in the hell was he talking about?

"Are you sure?" Riley asked with her hands on her hips. "I can see Niko doing that, but not Bennett."

The hairs on my body stood. I could not believe my ears.

"It's the truth, hon. Your girl is on her way to crossing over to the other side of the gates. She claims she didn't actually stab Divine."

I almost forgot my state. My neck and shoulders hurt as I attempted to sit up. I knew there was a slight chance Niko and I wouldn't be as tight as we used to be, but I didn't think he would stab me! And Bennett? Didn't she know thou shall not kill is a commandment? Warren turned slightly in response to my movement. I needed to hear more, so I froze.

"She said someone else did it, and she walked in. But C.O. Curtis was on duty, sleep I might add. When he woke up, he saw Bennett and Niko walking back toward Niko's cell."

"Oh, and how did Niko even get out of his cell?" Riley asked.

"So let me get this straight. Even if she denied participating in the shanking, she thinks it's okay to let Niko out of his cell? Bullshit! What in the hell got into her?"

"Love," Warren said.

"Well, love got her ass into some shit."

"Niko isn't saying anything at all. He's guilty as hell."

I lay agonized as I took in this new information. So my boy did this to me?

"He had blood plastered all over his clothes, was sweating like a pig, and was caught out of his cell! What more is needed?" Warren said confidently.

I shut my eyes quickly hoping Warren did not see me as he turned in my direction. Riley's eyes followed.

"He's one lucky kid, that Divine. I can't believe after having surgery only eighteen hours ago, he's now back here to recover with our people. At first, the doctors thought it was more serious than it really is. He'll be okay. He's a lucky kid. If C.O Curtis hadn't found him when he did, he'd be in hell by now. They tell me he was whining and crying like a baby," Warren said with a smirk on his face.

"He must have been stabbed up pretty badly if he had to be medavaced," Riley said.

"Shanked forty-eight times, hon."

"Warren, you're cruel. You seem to be getting enjoyment out of this shit!"

"It's a life we're talking about here," I wanted to scream!

Warren continued, "That's what happens when you fuck people around. Now, I don't particularly care for that piece of shit Niko, however, I do feel his pain. I would've shanked his ass too."

I cringed. Damn they knew everything!

"What are you talking about?" Riley asked.

"He's been whooping and hollering about his innocence, and come to find out, he's not so innocent. As a matter of fact, he's the reason why Niko ended up here."

"You lying!" Riley shouted with her mouth hanging wide open.

"You see why I said I don't blame Niko."

"Damn!" Riley lightly shouted. "But, I still don't see why Bennett would get herself caught up in all this drama. I mean this is her job, her livelihood. She's fucking that up over Niko."

"Riley, you are way too naive," Warren said. "You would probably do the same thing for your fiancé."

"Fiancé!"

Fiancé! Niko and Bennett. Oh snap! I nearly fell out of bed.

"Yeah, fiancé," Warren repeated. "Bennett and Niko are engaged to be married."

"I can't believe this."

"Yeah, that funny-looking ring Bennett wears is her engagement ring from him."

Niko? Engagement ring? My mind tripped. I couldn't believe what I was hearing.

Warren continued, like he was reading the script from some soap opera. "Everything is starting to come out. As soon as it was said that C.O. Curtis saw her leaving out of protective custody when Divine got stabbed, other officers came out of the woodworks. Everybody has a story to tell. Lieutenant Graham's office has been packed since the incident happened. Officers from all shifts and all blocks keep coming up with additional information."

"I didn't even know Bennett was under investigation by Graham's office," Riley said.

"Me either," Warren replied. "I just found out today, obviously. Divine filed a complaint form on her last month."

"How come I haven't heard anything?" Riley replied, upset she had been left out.

"Because you're a Goody Two Shoe." Warren laughed.

"I never tried to be a goody-goody. I thought Bennett, Ms. Holier Than Thou was the goody-goody. Now I'm realizing she's a fake. Walking around here putting on a façade like she's better than everybody. Hell, she's engaged to a damn inmate. When the hell did she think they would get married?"

"My sentiments exactly," I said under my breath.

"Niko's not getting out anytime soon. Especially now," Warren said.

Puzzled, Riley asked, "Has Niko been formally charged?"

"Not yet. I think Hernandez is waiting to talk to Divine."

Talk to me! In this position? Couldn't I at least get well? Getting emotional again, tears poured.

"Bennett has already been fired for even being on the protective block, however, her indictment will be based on the investigation," Warren said.

"They don't need an investigation. Her ass is guilty. And stupid, I might add!" Riley said.

"Yeah, but when the state comes in to make a formal charge, it's based on our inside investigation."

"The heat is really going to be on us now. We've had way too many stabbings and two deaths within the past three weeks."

"The state boys are supposed to be here tomorrow to formally charge someone for the murder of Ed Jones. I don't know what Hernandez has decided, but if it's Divine, God help him!" Warren said.

All of a sudden, I heard what sounded like people walking near the door. Riley and Warren stopped talking immediately. Their voices grew closer.

"Good evening, Captain Hart," Riley and Warren said simultaneously.

Nurse Jean, the same nurse I had seen in protective custody zipped past all three C.O.s. She walked directly to my bedside, checking my stats. She appeared to be about my age. Whenever I even moaned, she increased my pain medication and patted my forehead with a wet cloth. She was kind of cute too. That is, for a white chick. I think the warden has his eyes set on her. That's probably why she talked so firmly to those officers beating that faggot. She knew Warden Weaver had her back.

Moving closer to my bed, I saw clearer visions of Warren, Riley, Hart, and Nurse Jean. Putting on a performance, I held my eyes closely together, Blinking every now and then.

"How's the patient?" Captain Hart asked.

"Resting," Nurse Jean snapped.

"I mean is he recovering well?"

"As well as can be expected. The bed rest will do him some good," Nurse Jean said while checking my blood pressure.

Turning to Riley and Warren, Hart whispered, "There will be a mandatory lockdown in place for the next twenty-four hours."

"How do you want to handle the food situation?" Warren asked.

"I don't give a fuck if they ever eat!" Hart snapped, getting louder. "People are gonna start dropping like flies if we don't maintain full control. Especially now while all this mess is going on."

Riley and Warren just looked around. They didn't say one word. Scared I guess. The white shirts have that kind of effect on people. Whatever they say goes. The problem is, they aren't going to be around when these motherfuckers start going wild from being on lockdown too long.

Moments later, I heard footsteps. Recognizing the spanish accent, I knew Hernandez was near.

"Hello," he said. "Captain, can I have a word with you?"

My caretaker capitalized on the moment. "Great, everyone can go," she said, moving toward them as they all backed out the door.

Thank God! I had some privacy. I knew Hernandez and Hart conversed outside the infirmary doors. They spoke in soft tones, but could be heard slightly. My nurse attended to paperwork, checking me now and then. I played back a million things in my mind. Unable to rest I had my eyes open when Hernandez reappeared at my side.

He asked, "How is our patient doing?"

"Fine," Nurse Jean said.

He continued to make small talk, without getting a response from Nurse Jean. She was serious about her job. Everything had to be perfect. As a matter of fact, she rarely left my side.

Shifting his weight, he studied me carefully. Hernandez stood silently. Did he feel bad for me? Or did he not know what to say? I was still heavily sedated and wasn't much in the mood for talking anyhow.

"How ya doing, buddy?" he finally said.

"Uh. . . okay," I grunted.

He moved a little closer, making eye contact, before he continued. "So you've got yourself into a little trouble."

I didn't respond. What the fuck did he mean, I got myself into trouble? I didn't remember asking to be shanked. I didn't ask to be cut open or operated on.

Nurse Jean bent her lip to meet her nose. She stood closer to me like a mother protecting her baby. With one hand on my leg and the other on her hip, she glared into Hernandez's face.

"Look, Homes, I feel bad for you, I really do," he said. "However, things are only about to get worse."

"What. . .do. . .you. . .mean. . . ?" I asked, slowly spacing my words seconds apart. It hurt like hell to talk.

"Well, once you've recovered enough to go back on the

block, you will either be charged for Ed Jones' murder or
you'll be back on Block C to face the other inmates.
Homes, I guess I need to tell you, people are upset.
Everybody knows you set Niko up. Nobody knows who to
trust. Some people were glad you got stabbed up. They
think you deserved it. Ya know what I think?"

I just stared at him. I really didn't care what he
thought.

"I think you did what you had to do in that court room.
Niko would have done the same thing given the chance.
I'm not trying to judge you or anybody else, but I do think
Niko killed Ed Jones, and I don't want to see you taken
outta here and charged for his murder. That's about
another fifteen years added on to your time."

"I. . .didn't. . . do. . . it!"

I little by little started balling my knees up to my
stomach. I grimaced in pain.

"You need to leave, sir," Nurse Jean said in a raspy
voice.

"Miss with all due respect, I'm trying to keep this man
from being taken outta here by the state shortly. He might
be charged with murder if I don't get a chance to clear all
of this up now. Do you want that on your conscience?"

Nurse Jean put her hand over top of mine. "Mr. Jones,
do you want to continue this conversation?"

I looked at Hernandez, then back at Nurse Jean and
nodded. "Yes."

"Good, because I support you one hundred percent.
We can help each other out." Hernandez's brows raised.
"Right!"

"Right." I spoke softly.

"Listen, Homes, we can eventually charge Niko and

Bennett for stabbing you, after we scare Bennett into snitching."

"Bennett and Niko?" I said as if I didn't know. "How did they get in my cell?"

Hernandez cleared his throat. His hand touched my shoulder like we were the best of friends. "Bennett showed up on the protective wing while the officer on post was asleep. Bennett opened your gate and Niko's. We have no idea if Niko made the shank or if Bennett brought it to him."

"Is that bitch locked up?" I strained.

"Not yet. She's being held for questioning. She hasn't admitted anything yet, but she will. Trust me. I haven't been focusing on her because I wanted to clear your name. The way I see it, you need Niko to be gone in order for you to even survive in Dunnridge. And I need to be rid of a major drug pusher—Mathematics. All I need you to do is make a sworn statement that Mathematics and Niko told you they killed Ed Jones. We'll make everything else stick.

"In addition, I'll write the judge on your case, informing him or her that your help has been a key component in a murder investigation. I know your lawyer is going to get you out soon. But at least while you're waiting to be released, you'll be safer without Niko and Mathematics."

Caressing my temples, my eyeballs rolled up and down in my head. Confused and scared, all kinds of thoughts went through my mind. Did Mathematics want to see me dead too? What if I didn't say they killed Ed Jones? Would I be charged with his murder? When in the hell was Brothenstein getting me outta here?

I looked around suspiciously, making sure we were the only three people in the room. "What if I just snitch on

Niko, can I get the same deal?"

"No deal! It has to be Niko and Mathematics."

My lip twisted as I thought. I really didn't want to say Mathematics said he killed somebody when he didn't. But, I also did want him around to stab my ass up. I was lucky enough to be lying on this table now.

Hernandez told me he would be back in twenty minutes for my decision.

I stopped him and asked, "If possible, I need to call my grandmother. She has no idea what has happened to me."

"Yes, she does, but I'll get her on the line for you."

Ain't this some shit. He whipped out a cell phone and asked for the number. Before I knew it, Grandma was on the phone boohoooing, and I was upset too. I didn't have any tears left to cry. I told her I was going to be all right. She said she would be here to see me soon. She also said Brothenstein told her Sherese called him, and he would be working a deal with the judge real soon. That's all I need-ed to hear.

My mind was made up. I was doing it! I'd come too close. If I didn't implicate Mathematics, I might not make it in here. No sense in my lawyer doing all that hard work for nothing. I could vaguely hear Grandma talking non-stop. I had no idea what she was saying. I interrupted her, "Grandma, I love you. I'll see you soon."

Hernandez closed his phone and began to walk away. I stopped him in his tracks. I didn't want to wait a minute longer.

"I'll do it."

Hernandez's acne-filled face lit up like a lightbulb. "Good, Homes. Very good," he said, nodding.

He was happy and I thought I was happy. Nurse Jean

was still sitting there putting cold packs to my forehead. Maybe we'll exchange numbers, so when I get out we can hook up. Warden Weaver doesn't have to know!

Hernandez jetted, saying he'd be back with the paperwork that I needed to sign. I yelled out as loud as my weak stomach would allow, "Make sure there's a spot for me to write that I saw Bennett stab me too. I don't want that bitch getting away with shit."

Hernandez laughed it off. Nurse Jean asked if I was feeling up to all of this.

I told her, "I've been down this road before." She just smiled. *I think she's in love.*

⌐━☆

I awakened from a good night's rest, feeling groggy. The room clinched a chill that made my body shiver. Airy and spacious, I was beginning to feel lost between these aqua-green walls. How long would I stay in the infirmary? "Think warm," I chanted under my breath.

The extra dose of medication held me captive. Nurse Jean thought it would be best.

Being highly drugged didn't interfere with my ability to make out the image coming through the door. Head slightly spinning, I looked up.

"Hey champ, how ya doing?" Brocton asked.

"Dizzy," I said, turning for a complete view.

"You up to chatting?"

"Sure, if you're doing all the talking," I said, slurring a few words. "I'll listen. That doesn't require energy."

"You wanna hear the latest?" Brocton asked.

"Sure, why not."

"Twelve hours ago, your boy Mathematics stepped out of his cell like he was dressed for a cabaret. As usual, he tried to stay calm. But, his shoulders were hunched and his head hung low. Instead of his familiar nonchalant persona, worry embraced him."

I was trying to understand how he could hold his composure, knowing he shouldn't be in this situation. But, Mathematics will never let 'em see him sweat. I guess when you've got ninety-nine years, it really doesn't matter what happens next. However, this man was being charged with an additional felony, and from what Brocton said, still a perfectionist.

"Man, I couldn't believe that his beard was neater than someone on the streets. Face all clear, and manicured from head to toe. He was supposed to be in an orange jumpsuit since he was going back to county to be indicted. But, obviously somebody high up allowed him to wear street clothes. He had been charged with drug solicitation and accessory to the murder of Ed Jones."

I don't know why I was feeling a touch of sadness. I guess I felt kind of bad because I knew he didn't do it. But damn! What was I supposed to do? I was caught between a rock and a hard place. No sense in getting soft now. The good part about it was Mathematics probably has no idea I was involved. Hernandez said he would probably just be transferred to another facility because he was an accessory to the murder and not the killer.

Brocton went on, "Dunnridge's finest filled Block C, like they were going to a concert. Inmates whispered, stared, and some were even gathered to see what was going on. You could tell Mathematics was popular on the block because most people were pissed off about what was happening to him. Just think, some have lost a trusted drug connection. And some C.O.s are losing side cash. For others, it didn't matter. They had seen many come and many go. He was just another number."

"Ooh. . ." I moaned.

"Mathematics held his head down without emotion, as he followed Hernandez through the cold metal doors." Seconds later, Bennett appeared, after being escorted from a holding cell. Her hair was nappy as usual. She resembled Scary Spice," Brocton said as he laughed.

I gave no response. I had lost my sense of humor.

"Divine, you should be glad, after what she's done to you. I bet she don't think she's so hot anymore. Word on the block is she had been interrogated sporadically for more than twenty-four hours. You know that's illegal, but what the heck is legal around here?"

I blinked in agreement. I was glad her ass got the inmate treatment. I hoped they ripped all her shit off and finger searched her ass. To tell the truth, I hoped they simply degraded her stuck-up ass.

"Can you believe after all that grilling, Bennett never snitched on Niko?" Brocton asked.

"I believe it."

He said, "The interrogators tried everything from she'd spend the rest of her life in a prison for women to maybe even letting her co-inmates know she used to be a correctional officer. Nothing worked! She denied everything and was willing to take the rap for Niko. When her locker was searched, they found Niko's missing I.D. card inside her purse."

"Why would she take his card?" I asked, straining.

"Who knows? The card has no benefit to her or Niko.

Maybe she had taken it to keep his picture close to her."
Brocton joked. "Or, maybe she wanted to show him off to
her friends."

Or maybe that bitch just didn't have all her scruples, I
wanted to say.

Brocton said, "After hours of questioning, she finally
admitted to being on the protective custody wing, but only
to check on Niko. She lied with a straight face, saying she
wasn't the one who opened Niko's cell. Of course Warden
Weaver didn't believe her. She had a nerve to say the officer
on duty opened it by accident while she happened to be
visiting Niko."

Bullshit! I thought. Did she really think someone would
fall for that? At least she could have been more creative. I
always knew she wasn't that smart anyway.

Although I hated her, I had to give her props because she
stood by her man, I thought, wanting to laugh. She probably
told all those motherfuckers, she loves Niko. And has loved
him with all her heart since she first laid eyes on him.

"Hey, and get this," Brocton said. "When Graham
made a comment about her deserving better than Niko, she
flipped out. She said she has no life without him. Now,
she's already going to jail for attempted murder and still
bucking at Graham. Some nerve," Brocton said with disgust.
He glanced at his watch, stunned by the time. He shared
more then hurried back to his duties.

I was definitely not surprised that Graham felt sorry for
Bennett. But if it were anybody else, he would've called the
state boys in immediately, without any interviewing,
questioning, or interrogating. His spot was soft for her. I
guess he realized, she was really in love, and had lost all
hope.

Didn't she know that the entire population, officers and inmates, would be talking about her and Niko's relationship? They'd probably be in the newspaper by the next day. I mean, let's face it, this shit was wild! The outside world was going to get a kick out of this. Did they have wedding plans? It's ridiculous for me to even think about this mess.

Refocusing on what Brocton told me, I snickered. Who came up with the bright idea of arresting Niko, Mathematics, and Bennett all at the same time? This shit was like a soap opera. I think the head dude in charge for the state was trying to be funny. He probably enjoyed the performance. It was like a comedy and a tragedy all in one.

From the story I got, somebody decided to walk Niko right past Bennett. I guess they wanted to see what kind of looks the lovebirds were gonna give each other. They hadn't seen each other since they shanked my ass. I guess dude didn't anticipate Bennett struggling to get up close to Niko. She was standing about a half a foot away from him when she reached out and stroked his face. Her hand was quickly pulled away by officers. Niko didn't react at all. He was pulled away hastily. Tussling a bit, Niko tried to maintain his tough-guy reputation.

Apparently, the way Brocton described it, he had a treacherous look on his face. Almost as if he wanted to kill. He never said a word, but it was written all over his face. People are still scared of Niko! *I'm not. Besides, he can't do much anyway, he's handcuffed.*

Bennett was the only one still receiving special privileges. Niko had six guys surrounding him after Bennett was pulled away. They walked him out like he was really somebody. Shit, I knew Niko better than anybody in this motherfucker. For real, he's not as ruthless as he wants everybody

to think. I mean he could fight, he'd shot up a few people
when he was on the street, and he shanked a few people,
including my ass. But that ain't shit! I didn't know why I
put his ass on a pedestal all these years. I guess friendship.
Feeling sorry for the brotha. But, that's okay. He had
fucked up. I wouldn't have to worry about his ass until
about 2022. That's what he got for fucking with me.

I should have seen straight through him. He was using
me for my brains and knowledge. He wasn't smart enough
to pull any real shit off by himself. And, if he was gonna
shank me, he should've been smart enough to kill me. Or
at least his fiancée should have told him.

Obviously, he didn't consider me as a true friend. Just
think, he never even told me about him and Bennett. That
wasn't the kind of information to keep from your boy!
People talking about me! He couldn't be trusted! No
loyalty at all! I was glad this comradeship was over! I'd got
some bad wounds to show for it. But I lived! I'd get respect
for that alone.

22

Help

Two weeks later, I was placed in a holding cell, waiting for my new home. I hadn't been on Block C in so long, I was homesick. This is a far cry from the protective custody unit and the infirmary. Now I can appreciate being alone, not having to share a cell, and getting personalized attention. For some reason, I can't eat, and all I want to do is sleep. This might be a sign of depression. I need to shake this shit. I don't want no damn nurses monitoring me or nobody giving me no pills. Although, I wouldn't mind a little TLC from Nurse Jean. I think she likes me. I don't mind being monitored by her, but I'm definitely not talking to a shrink. That's out of the question. I guess that's why I'm sitting here talking to myself now. I feel like an idiot, but what the hell.

I had been asking to make a phone call for more than two hours now. The C.O. sporting the jheri curl over here seems pretty busy. He said as soon as he had a chance, he'd see to it. I desperately needed to touch base with Brothenstein, just to see how things are coming along. It wouldn't be long now before he'd have my ass outta here.

How much probation time would I have? With all of Brothenstein's connections, I shouldn't get that much. Shit, he was always out playing golf with the state's attorney, having lunch with judges, and conversing with all the motherfuckers capable of keeping a man's ass behind bars. My money should account for something. I had a good feeling about all of this.

Loud voices came my way. Maybe I would get my call. The C.O. on post acted as if he had no help and loads of responsibilities. All these jokers were faking. They just didn't want to be of assistance to a brother.

Out of the blue, Hernandez appeared in front of my holding cell. He was the last person I'd expected to see. He'd been missing in action since the early part of the week.

"Man, I've been hoping you would come around for hours now," I blurted.

"Oh, really?"

"Yeah really," I said, wanting to punch him in his face. I stood slowly, still feeling a little sore from my incident. I held my side as I prepared to speak, hoping to get a little sympathy. "I'm getting ready to be assigned a cell. I've been sitting in this holding spot waiting for hours. Have you spoken to the judge?"

"No. I haven't gotten a chance to write a recommendation letter yet, but I will. I just came by to see how you're making out."

Before I spoke, I made sure there weren't any officers nearby, and, the way the holding cells were arranged, I knew none of the inmates could hear me. But, I kept my voice down anyway. "Not good. I'm gonna have a room-mate shortly. It seems like I'm despised around here. All the officers hate my ass."

"Divine, you're stressed, so everything is bothering you," Hernandez said, gazing into my face.

"I haven't even been able to make a phone call yet."

"Let me work on that for you."

I broke, "They're just mad that I was able to maneuver my way out of all this shit! I hate to boast but, I'm an intelligent-ass dude."

I was all of a sudden given a boost of energy and arrogance. I stood, paced the floor, and repeated obscenities, still keeping my low-key tone. "I got myself into a little mess, but got myself out of it too," I said. Walking around the small room in unhurried circles, I kept talking. "If I didn't know any better, I'd say they were jealous. It seems like they want my ass to stay here. I'm sorry, but I'm as good as out of here! There will be plenty of lowlifes on their way in. People who deserve to be here. Ya know, violent offenders, not masterminds like me. I'm too intellectual for this shit."

"Calm down, Homes," Hernandez said, pushing his hand up and down. "Anyway, I'm curious about something."

"What?"

"Tell me what actually happened to land you and Niko in here," Hernandez said. He had his long arms folded as if he were questioning a small child.

In full swing, I blurted, "Man, I shouldn't have gotten into this situation. Grandma told me about associating with scum—people with no jobs, no ambition, and no common sense. See, I messed myself up trying to put Niko on to white-collar crime. I should've left his ass right on the street to be the rough neck he is. But noooo. . .I tried to show him how clever people beat the system all the time."

"Aahh, so it was you."

I sat down, preparing myself to tell my side of the story. I started slowly, sort of reluctantly. "Well, I was the brain-child that thought of the idea. Niko went too far and didn't want to stop."

Rubbing his forehead and needing further explanation, Hernandez said, "All I know is that large sums of funds were embezzled."

"It all started when I was given the authority at my old job to open new accounts. Langley, my boss, had faith in my ability to get things done. He started giving me the authority to handle large business transactions, and multi-million dollar accounts. I told Niko that he could come into my branch with a fake ID and open up a bank account with fifty dollars. He had no idea why, and really wasn't interested until I told him there would be lots of paper coming soon.

"I remember the first account he opened in the name of Franklin Moody. I don't know where he dug up a name like that. Once he opened the account, it was then my job to find a way to deposit funds into the account." I paused.

"Hold up. Let me understand this clearly. Did I just hear you say you were the one depositing unauthorized funds into a fake account?"

"That's right."

Hernandez paused. His mouth hung wide open. "I thought Niko was the villain."

"Man, are you gonna listen, or what?"

"Continue. I'm still unclear about how everything went down."

"Once Franklin Moody had an account, I wrote hundreds

of false banks checks from account holders with large balances. I figured they wouldn't notice a few dollars missing here and there. They were accounts owned by wealthy, busy businessmen. Those small checks from hundreds of people added up to thousands of dollars. The checks were deposited into the fake account, and I simply monitored the account for weeks until it reached somewhere near twenty thousand dollars. That's where Niko came into the picture again. He would come in to close the account and receive all cash. Just think, I was the one who had to close the account and verify funds.

"The plan was to continue opening and closing accounts, using the same method until we smuggled a hundred thousand dollars. We had opened a real account in Niko's name, Raphic Jenkins. This account was where Niko was supposed to deposit our earnings for us to split when we reached our goal."

Hernandez interrupted, "So, why were you able to make a deal with the judge? It seems to me you were the man with the plan."

"I'm just intelligent like that. Besides, nobody put a gun to Niko's head."

"But you've been singing the I'm-so-innocent song for so long now, I even started to believe you."

"Everybody says they're innocent."

"No, I'm starting to believe you really think you don't deserve to be here."

"I don't."

Waiting to hear the rest of the story, Hernandez asked, "So what happened? Obviously things didn't work out as planned or you wouldn't be sitting here today."

"We had gotten in way over our heads. Before I knew it

we had embezzled roughly one million dollars. Although, in our account, we only had near four hundred thousand dollars. Niko had either been spending like crazy, splurging on bitches and cars, or setting up his own stash. I told him not to bring any additional attention on us. I stuck to the plan! I didn't buy shit.

"Another monkey wrench was eventually thrown on us. My boss Langley was getting suspicious. He had gotten a few complaints from people who had watched their accounts more closely than I thought. One particular businessman had a printout showing two checks displaying the same check number. Langley credited the guy's account, but immediately started snooping to find out what I was doing.

"He approached me one evening after work. He said he didn't tell anyone what he discovered, but he was worried that he would be caught up if this ever came to surface. He also told me he admired my brilliance. Once admitting he would have never thought to do what I did, he begged me to continue working with him. Langley's only requirement was for me to stop the fraudulent activities instantly, and never do it—"

"So how did you get caught?"

"We didn't stop."

"I thought you were so smart, Homes."

I shook my head reminiscing. "The money was so good, it was too easy. Once Niko found out that Langley knew and didn't say anything, he thought that was our ticket to making millions.

"He waited for Langley outside his apartment late one evening, and gave him an envelope with thirty thousand dollars cash. A note was included that read this is a token of our appreciation. Thanks for looking out. From that day forth, Langley never said anything else about the fraudulent checks or what had happened. He never mentioned receiving any money from Niko either.

"About three months later, Niko and I had stolen more than 1.5 million dollars. I couldn't believe it. We could have been real millionaires! Consequently, Niko felt like he was in charge of the money. We had spent over time, nearly half of it. It was mostly Niko though. Whenever I wanted to buy something or get some cash, I got the third degree. But, trust me, he spent freely.

"Before we could evenly split up the money in the account, we got busted! I just knew Langley squealed on us. I thought he was upset that this was going on right under his face and he wasn't splitting the profits. But when we got taken in, Langley was being interrogated also. The authorities thought he was in on it too."

Hernandez clapped his hands. "I'm impressed," he said. He's probably wondering why he never thought about pulling off some stunt like that. The room went completely silent for about sixty seconds.

Hernandez finally asked, "Don't you take any responsibility for your situation?"

"Something like that."

Pausing as he stared me in my face, he searched for the right words. Without delay, I edged him on, "Be straight up, if it's something you want to say, *say it*!"

"Oh, I will, Homes, just not now." Hernandez hurried from the cell.

I called out to him, "Damn, I didn't take the money from you!"

He turned back, giving me one last look. With his lip

twisted, he gave me the impression that he disapproved.

Knowing he was upset, I didn't want to drag it on any further.

He departed, bothered. But showing good character, left me with words of encouragement: "Cheer up, I'm sure everything will work out."

My mind worked overtime. Why was everyone against me? Hernandez was some shit. What happened to all that you-help-me, I'll-help-you bullshit? He didn't seem like he was so eager to help now. I knew he'd better take care of his end of the bargain. I took care of mine. Honor is what it's called. Fuming with mixed feelings, my mind became cloudy.

I almost didn't hear the guard saying, "You've got three minutes, son."

I slowly came out of my trance.

His voice got louder as he spoke each word. "I'm in a hurry, so consider this phone call a favor!"

"Thanks, man," I said in an appreciative manner.

"I'm not your damn buddy."

Walking past him, I realized this wasn't going to be easy. Why did I have to be over here with this nigga dripping Jheri curl juice? *Where the hell is Brocton when you need him?*

Once I got to the phone, I had flashbacks of when I first came in. The holding cell is for inmates waiting to be assigned to a cell. Just think, I'm right back where I started. I shouldn't be moving backward. *I'm too good for that.*

I dialed Brothenstein's number and waited for the computerized voice to obtain the necessary information. At least I didn't have to worry about him not accepting my call. When asked my name, I said "Mr. Jones."

Within seconds I could hear his secretary, Ms. Mable,

talking to someone in the background.

"Hello?" I said anxiously.

"May I help you?"

"Yeah, I need to speak to Brothenstein."

"He's not in. May I ask who's calling."

"If you don't know who's calling, why did you accept the phone call?"

She paused, at a loss for words, then said, "Would you like to leave a message?"

Muffling sounds came over the phone, as if Ms. Mable was covering the mouthpiece. Was she talking to someone? I vaguely heard weird noises.

"When will he be in?"

"I'm not sure, sir," she said patronizing me.

"Tell him Mr. Jones needs to talk to or see him right away. It's urgent."

The muffling sounds came again, before she said, "Mr. Brothenstein will not be in the office this week."

"Bitch, you just said you weren't sure when he'd be in, now all of a sudden you got a wealth of information!"

"Well, I've never!"

"And—"

All sounds had completely ended. I looked up to see the C.O.'s hand pressing down on the metal receiver. He had stopped me right in the middle of giving Ms. Mable a piece of my mind. She must think she could jerk my chain. It was some wicked shit going on in that office, and I knew it. No sense in trying to call back. This C.O. didn't want to work with a brotha at all.

I banged my hand on the cell before stiff ass opened it. When the doors shut, I had a chance to mull over everything. Maybe I had gotten too carried away. Ms. Mable probably had other business she was trying to take care of. I shouldn't have disrespected her like that anyway. She was somebody's grandma. And, I knew I'd fuck anybody up messing with mine. I'd call back tomorrow and apologize.

23

Thank goodness I was out of that holding cell. Who would've ever thought I'd have a cell on Block C to myself again? Although, I was told not to get my hopes up high. Space is tight, and I would either be getting a new roommate, or moved to another cell. This was temporary, but I was gonna make the best of it. Besides, I wouldn't be here too much longer anyway.

Because I was lacking personal items, fixing up my cell was unnecessary. I no longer had my pictures of Sherese or Grandma. I no longer had my bible and financial books, which were my prized possessions. And, for now, I didn't even have my stationery and Walkman from protective custody. Brocton told me it would take a few days for those items to transfer over here. So for now, I had to suffer a bit of boredom.

As usual Block C was noisy and chaotic. Camp was in session as I walked through the unit. The day was going by quickly. Already 11:00 A.M., and the showers would be closing soon. I hadn't had a shower in more than two days, and one was well needed. I decided to gather my things, and head for the showers. Since I didn't have a chance to go to the commissary, I didn't have any soap, deodorant, or lotion. That meant, I would have to use the institutional soap until I could get some of my own. I would be short in the deodorant department. I had a little bit of paper on my account. At least enough to get me what I needed for now. Hopefully, I'd be going to the commissary soon.

I headed out of my cell, dressed in my no-name Tims since I didn't have any shower shoes at the moment, an oversized T-shirt I had been wearing for days, and my dingy, baggy pants. My clothes were so dirty and funky, they'd probably stand up on their own when I took them off. A lot of guys walked to the shower with their towel wrapped around them. Fuck that! I had my clean drawers wrapped up in a towel, and the borrowed institutional gear draped over my arm.

In the recreation area, everybody was out and about. I acknowledged anybody who was cool with me with a nod. Some nodded back; others turned away. The smell of weed filled the air. A few C.O.s looked like they suspected some-thing, but didn't make any moves. Everyone on duty was pretty lenient.

It was common for the day room to be packed. C.O. Riley stood all the way to the far end, her back up against the wall, but she couldn't see me. I decided to walk closer to her so we could make eye contact. Shaunte and Squzzy mingled around Riley, having their normal girl talk.

"Riley, c'mon, girl, bring me a perm."

"Squzzy, I told you. . .no."

"Why not? You know how hard it is to stay beautiful."

Riley chuckled. "You'll make my day."

"Well, since we make you laugh so much, bring my friend a perm," Shaunte said.

"I can't do that."

"Yes, you can."

With raised brows and a twisted upper lip, Riley said, "Let me get this straight: You want me to lose my job over a perm?"

"Girl, nobody said anything about you losing this piece-of-shit job," Squzzy said.

"You deserve better anyway," Shaunte interjected.

"All right, girls, that's enough, I've got to go."

"Pleaseeeeee," Squzzy said as she fell to her knees.

As Riley was making her escape from Squzzy, we made eye contact.

"Hi, C.O. Riley," I said with the biggest grin on my face.

"Hey."

"You still lookin' good," I said.

"Thanks. See ya later."

Riley took flight. Damn. Had she turned against me too? Only about six people were socializing around the day room, but more than five people lined up, waiting for the showers. It was customary for people to be lined up outside the shower area if it was full. Only six people could shower at one time. But, I hardly expected so many people this late in the day. The guard standing outside the shower area looked like he was one of those by-the-book C.O.s. He stood straight as a board waiting for the next inmate inside the shower area to bang on the window, so he could come out. Then he unlocked the door, and sends the next person in. Two people came out at the same time, and only one person went in. I decided to call Brothenstein back first.

I rushed to the phones, which were luckily intact. Before dialing, a touch of wisdom came over me. I decided to use a different name when calling to Brothenstein's office. Once I spoke to him, I'd then apologize to Ms. Mable.

As I dialed the number, thoughts entered my mind about a counterfeit name to use, Leroy Johnson.

When the computerized operator asked for my name, I sort of chuckled when I said, "Johnson, Mr. Leroy Johnson."

Ms. Mable obviously knew it was some inmate calling, otherwise, who else would be calling collect? When I asked for Brothenstein, the woman's voice on the other end of the phone didn't sound like Ms. Mable at all. She put me on hold for a moment, and returned only to say, "What did you say your name is again?"

"Mr. Johnson."

She paused briefly. "Have you already retained Mr. Brothenstein's service?"

"No, ma'am, but, I would like to."

"Hmm, hold on a moment."

While I was on hold, I was trying to figure out the best way to handle this. This woman was being extremely helpful, but I knew, Brothenstein was definitely there. Before I had enough time to come up with a master plan, she was back on the line.

"Mr. Brothenstein said he is unable to take on any new clients right now. He has referred you to a Mr. Goldstan, attorney at law. I have that number for you, if you're ready."

"Tell Mr. Brothenstein, this is Divine Jones, and I need to speak with him pronto."

"Sir, who are you?"

"Tell him what I said. I know he's in there."

She put me on hold again. This time it took more than five minutes for her to return. They were probably getting their stories straight. Some people can't even lie accurately.

The woman returned to the phone with a few disappointing statements. First, I knew she was lying, when she said, "Mr. Brothenstein had to rush out for a court date." It was almost noon, and courts would be out of session for lunch soon. I'm a criminal, I know that kind of shit.

Then she ended by saying, "We are still waiting on a payment from Sherese or a family member."

I was devastated when the phone clicked. I didn't know what to do, or think.

Walking back to the showers, I was cheerless. I had absolutely nothing to be happy about. I was getting all kinds of looks. Both eyes of disgust and pity watched me as I moseyed by. Just think, I don't look the same, my clothes are dirty, and I can't even walk as hard and swift like I use to.

As I approached the showers, I was relieved to see only one person in line. The stiff C.O. yelled, "Two more minutes," which meant somebody had been in there too long.

Moments later, a bang came from inside the dressing area wall. Somebody was ready to exit. I would be up soon. When the door opened, the tall officer said, "It's about damn time. You shouldn't have a drop of dirt on your body."

The guy in front of me grabbed the door and entered before it could even shut. I could see him vaguely through the window located behind the officer. It was the type of glass window that you could only see images. I guess that's good, so punks couldn't see people undressing.

The spotless male exiting was quite familiar. He gave
the stern officer a half a smile and a slap in the hand. He
loosened up quickly. When the guy walked past me, we
both caught each other's eye. It was one of Ed Jones'
people! He kept on going, not really paying me any attention though. I was glad! I didn't want to fight anyone. I
simply wanted to be clean.

The next thing you know, another bang on the door.
This time three people came out. It didn't really matter,
'cause I was the only one in line anyway. At least you got
a little privacy around here. No one had to escort you in
the showers, like you're a fucking child. They didn't even
bother you, other than the time limit when inmates were
waiting. When the doors opened the steam streamed out.
I stood by the dressing area to take my things off. As I
surveyed the room, only two other people occupied the
shower area.

I was trying not to stare too hard. I didn't want anyone
to think I was a punk or nothing. I was just so paranoid.
Ass naked, I picked up my towel and entered the shower.
The steaming hot water felt so good all over my body.
The intensity of the water came down extremely hard; it
felt like I was getting a massage. I closed my eyes and let
the water beat on the back of my neck.

My name was said softly. When I opened my eyes, I
stepped away from the showerhead, looking for a way
around them. Black and two heavyweights from Ed Jones'
crew were blocking the only exit out of the showers.

If Black was rolling with these guys, that meant trouble
for me. Had I been off the block that long? How did this
trio hook up?

The naked guy from Ed Jones' crew had been showering with me, and I didn't even know it. He started walking around turning on all the showers, at the strongest speed. The officer's back reflected through the imaging window. He still stood straight, facing the general population.

I quickly looked at my surroundings. *Please God, let me escape.* I was trying to figure out what I could say to Black. After all, we were boyz.

I didn't even know Ed Jones' folks well enough to cop a plea. Hell, I don't even know their names. The one who was fully dressed was the same guy I had seen leaving when I came in.

"Black, c'mon, man, we're better than this."

"Yo kid, I thought you were on the up and up."

"I am. Let me explain!"

"Too late!"

Resembling the Bride of Chucky, with a strange look on his face, Black charged the first move. He came at me like greased lightning. Before I knew it, I had taken three blows to the jaw while being knocked up against the wall.

I was pulled to my feet and held up by the muscle-bound naked man, ready to take my manhood. I hadn't fully recovered from the stabbing. Defending myself was out of the question. *No way possible.* The unclothed man wrapped his arms firmly around my neck. He had me in a tight headlock. Bracing myself to be shanked again, I yelled as loud as I could.

My screams for help went unanswered. I begged Black, over and over. Then, out of the side of my right eye, I could see the other clothed guy unhook the buckle on his belt and slowly slide down his pants.

I screamed.

When his belt buckle hit the floor, my heart raced even more.

Within minutes, he penetrated me with rage. His words kept ringing in my ears, over and over.

"I know you like it, don't you?"

"Don't you?"

"Don't you?"

I was totally unable to answer.

Tears flooded my eyes and kept me from seeing anything. The grip on my neck let loose and a powerful stroke at the side of my mouth came smashing through. A few of my teeth were knocked out. I fell to the ground, only to have my head lifted up by Black. His hefty hands were gripping the back of my neck, like I was some junkyard dog. I was being sodomized. I had no choice but to submit. I could vaguely hear the guard in the front say, "Six more minutes."

At that point, I had no idea when this would end.

I lay on the floor unbothered and uncovered for more than thirty minutes. I was in fetal position shivering uncontrollably when finally Sergeant Corning came in to close down the showers. He rushed over to me immediately.

"Are you okay?"

"Umm, no—I guess," I said with frequent snivels.

He helped me to my feet and inched me over to the dressing area. A towel was wrapped around my once again battered body. When I turned to look in the mirror, I was so ashamed. What had I become?

My face had dark purple marks accenting my eyes. I had a cross between swollen cheeks and a broken jaw, combined with two missing teeth.

Corning asked, "Who did this?"

I answered, "I have no idea."

"C'mon."

I lowered my voice and head even more. "Seriously, I couldn't see a thing."

What was the point? I no longer had anyone who would retaliate for me. I had already been violated and dishonored as a man. Nothing could be worse.

Corning helped me through the door. Only two people stood around. They tried not to even look at me while another guard positioned me outside the shower door with a towel halfway wrapped around me. The stiff officer originally on duty remained on post with a blank stare.

Corning asked with authority, "How did this happen?"

"I don't know," the shift officer said, like his memory was a complete void.

Coming to my defense, Corning said, "Do you work this post?"

"Yeah, but I didn't think anyone else was in there," the C.O. said in an uncaring manner.

"I'll let the lieutenant handle this one," Corning said.

"Fine with me." He smirked.

Even though I had an escort back to my cell, I inched step by step to delay my arrival. I wasn't sure who I could trust. Things just weren't the same. I knew who I had to call on!

Once in my cell, all sorts of thoughts ran through my mind. I fell to my knees reciting 2 Corinthians 1:3,4: "Praise be to the God and Father of our Lord Jesus Christ, the Father of compassion and the God of all comfort who comforts us in all our troubles." I couldn't believe I remembered that scripture so clearly. I prayed steadfastly for more than an hour. I prayed for so many people, regardless of what they had done to me in life. I talked to my Father about mistakes I'd made and begged for forgiveness. Even after all I'd done, I know He still loves me, and I know He'll comfort me. Even though I've been in here, I still know He's a forgiving God.

I shed many tears as I vowed to work on being a better person and to change my ways.

The first step I took was to write Warden Weaver revealing the truth about Mathematics. The lies I told about him had been on my conscience for a while. But, I guess I needed to hit rock bottom to do something about it. Besides, it was never my intention to betray him. It was bad enough that Tashonda ended up leaving him to transport drugs for some Brazilian guy she had been dealing with. If she had stayed devoted to Mathematics, she probably wouldn't be locked up now, serving fifteen years for drug possession. Nonetheless, I think it will all work out for Mathematics. Weaver is a great warden, he's about as fair and decent as they come. It is my prayer that after this letter is read, Mathematics' punishment will be rescinded.

My prayers went on and on until I was exhausted. Before I finally closed my eyes, I ended with the Lord's Prayer.

8—⚷

The next morning, I was led to Captain Graham's office. The strange part is, I wasn't even worried. It didn't matter if they wanted to charge me with murder, drugs, or rape. I had lost my self-respect and manhood. Being ashamed to walk through a prison facility is definitely a problem.

I stood before Graham. Luckily, I had gotten my new institutional clothes delivered a few hours earlier and looked a little bit cleaner on the outside. The inside is another story. Nothing could ever make the filthy feeling I had about myself disappear.

Graham sat at his desk upright biting the tip of his glasses. His face tight, his mind so far away he barely even noticed me. He flipped through a stack of papers as I waited patiently. His entire look had changed. His buttons didn't scream for mercy now that he's lost a few pounds. His brand new pair of eyes, did him some justice, adding style to his appearance. I guess life has been good to him. Graham made captain about three weeks ago and was honored by Warden Weaver during a state recognition ceremony.

Peering through his thin-wired glasses, he finally acknowledged me. "Divine, sit down. We've got a few issues to discuss."

I sat down at a reduced speed, reluctant about putting pressure on my ass. "What's the issue?" I asked in a low voice.

"Well, I was informed about a situation with you and a few other inmates yesterday."

"Nothing happened."

"Oh, something definitely happened," Graham stated.

"Graham, what do you want from me?"

"I want the truth."

"About what."

"Ohhhh!" Graham yelled, beating both fists on his desk and standing.

Graham walked around the desk. Kneeled down close to my face, placed his hand on my shoulder, and spoke in a softer tone. "I know something happened illegal. To keep my ass off the chopping block, I now have to call your closet relative to report the incident."

"What incident? I told you nothing happened!"

"There was a homosexual act going on in those showers! I have no idea who started it or why you have bruises. One thing is for sure, I've got to inform your family that you were involved in some mess. Otherwise, they'll try to sue us later."

"No she won't."

"Who is she?"

"Grandma."

Picking up the receiver Graham asked, "Do you want to call her, or shall I?"

"Well, if you want me to, I'll call, but I don't know what you want me to say."

Placing the phone down, he allowed me to do the honors. "Fine, there's the phone. Start dialing."

I haven't used an old phone like this in such a long time, I thought as I lifted the receiver.

"Dial 1, the area code, and the number," Graham said, as if he were unsure about whether I remembered what to do on a regular phone.

When I heard Grandma's tender, caring voice, a warm feeling came over me.

"Grandma."

"Yes, baby."

"It's Divine."

"Well, siree, I didn't recognize ya voice, besides I'm use to ya calling collect."

"I know. I was able to call from the lieutenant's—I mean Captian's— office today."

"Lawdy, is that good or bad?"

"I'm okay, Grandma."

I paused trying to prolong telling her about the rape as

long as I could. Graham was staring down my throat the entire time, using hand movements to encourage me to spill the beans.

"So how you doing, Grandma?"

"Well, I can't get around like I use to. Quite frankly, my health is failing, but I'm blessed."

"What's wrong!"

"I've been experiencing a lotta vision problems, drowsiness, and I've lost lots a weight."

"Did you go to the doctor?"

"Yes, siree."

"What did the say about all of this?"

"Well, I might have diabetes 'cause whenever I don't eat I feels bad."

Captain Graham had no idea what Grandma was telling me when he snatched the phone from my ear.

"Ms. Lewis, this is Captain Graham." Pausing for a moment he continued, "I'm fine, ma'am. I'm sorry to interrupt, however, Divine has been involved in some sort of homosexual altercation. I'm not quite sure who was involved or who initiated it. The situation will be investigated. . . . Hello, ma'am." With the receiver pressed to his ear, he listened. "It's our policy to notify a family member when something like this happens. Well, you don't sound too good. I'll let you speak back to Divine."

My stomach churned like butter. "Did she say she didn't want to speak back to me?"

Placing the receiver back on the base, he said, "No. She just said she wasn't feeling well. And she'd talk to you later."

"Man, I can't believe this!"

"Calm down."

"I can't calm down. She needs me for once in her life, and I'm here."

Graham opened the door to his office. Corning was waiting to escort me back to my lonely cell. I stepped out the doorway feeling even more depressed than I did before making the call. My life was at an all-time low! Nothing could be worse!

24   Home Sweet Home

After almost three months back on Block C, I was feeling like Molly the Maid. I had just finished picking up a few things from the commissary: deodorant, shampoo, tuna fish, cookies, chips, greeting cards, batteries, and cigarettes, of course.

Leaning back on the washing machine waiting for the first load of clothes to finish, I prepared to open a letter from Brothenstein. I had just about given up on any hopes of getting out. At this point I was prepared to serve the remainder of my six years and four months. I now consider this time as a blessing in order for me to get my life right.

I was a little apprehensive about opening the letter because I had been calling Brothenstein for the last three month, and had gotten no response at all. His secretary even gave Grandma the cold shoulder when she tried to call. He could have at least acted like a professional and returned the calls. Crooked-teeth ass! All that money I'd given him over the years, and the thanks I get is desertion.

Thoughts immediately ran through my mind about my vow I made to speak only positive words. It just wasn't working. I guess I needed more time to perfect myself. It's hard not to curse, but I'm getting better. The Lord knows I'm only doing it because I can't help it.

Over the last two months, I'd started realizing my situation was pretty much hopeless. And, I'm sure that getting this letter wouldn't change anything. I couldn't decide whether to open it or not. It could just be a bill.

I held the unopened letter up high, examining it closely. I set the remainder of my clothes on top of the machine and took off my scarf. I don't know why I felt like I needed to look appropriate before reading.

Once I started reading, I couldn't believe it! Brothenstein was apologizing for never getting back to me. Basically neglecting me. He said Sherese never paid him anything. She called a few times pretending like she was going to come up with the money, but never followed through. Her child's father Langley said he was willing to help also. He said he went way back with me and wanted to help, but never did.

Brothenstein also said he thought it was mighty strange that some guy with the same name, Langley, wrote the current judge on my case. He told her all the details about what really happened while I was working at U.S. Savings and Loàn. He even sent documents with my signature opening fake accounts.

In addition he told her that Niko was the follower and I was the immoral one. Not only did he say Niko wanted to stop and I kept robbing the accounts, but also that I told the whereabouts of Niko's money and not mine.

I glared at the letter. How could anyone be that disloyal?

Just think, after all I'd done for Sherese and Langley, they were shacking up together. Not to mention Sherese is pregnant by him. When was somebody gonna tell me? And, the mere thought of Langley writing the judge. Why would he want to push me into a deeper hole than I was already in? Fuck it! Just throw the dirt over me now.

Was I such a bad person? It seemed to me, he was the awful one. He wasn't even man enough to accept my collect call and tell me he was fucking my girl. And then, turns around trying to be Mr. Righteous, writing the judge. Fuck this sh—. Catching myself, I thought, forget this mess. I tossed the letter onto the laundry table.

If I could only turn back the clock, things would be quite different. For starters, Sherese wouldn't have gotten away clean like she did. Second, I should have implicated Langley. Hell, he knew exactly what was going on. Now, instead of them serving time, they' were back in Portsmouth playing house. Big mistake on my part.

Now that I think of it, I've made alot of slip-ups. But, getting involved with Niko had to be on the top of my list. He was destined to be a failure from the start.

Brocton found out that Niko is now serving a mandatory sentence of thirty years in Rockwell, a maximum-security facility in Cartersville, Virginia. The sad part for Niko is, because of the abolition of parole in the state of Virginia, Niko will never be eligible for parole. Therefore, if you do the crime, you do the time. I smiled.

Things aren't going that great for Niko in Rockwell. Brocton's friend who works there says he's trying to run shit already, but he can't. There are way too many hard heads, all in competition for power. The funny side to his story is he's already scouted out a young, vulnerable C.O., who by the way, sports a gold ring on her finger. That sounds just like Niko, no loyalty at all.

Since he left Dunnridge, he has only responded to one of Bennett's many letters. He told her she was in no position to help him anymore and that he didn't want to have anything else to do with her. It was over!

Instead of writing Bennett, he'd been wasting energy sending me threats, both through people and the mail. He said I should consider myself dead. Yeah, right, all the way from Rockwell.

Brocton said he tried to use his old power to get a few C.O.s to handle me, but that's not gonna happen. Things have changed around here. I've got someone protecting me!

I thought about why I got protection and didn't want to mess that up. It's taking me way too long to perform my duties.

"Damn!" I yelled. Outta soap powder again. This is a poor-ass jail. They're always out of everything. Either they're low on cash or these fucked-up C.O.s never refill anything. Can't wipe your ass when you need to because there's no toilet tissue! Sometimes I got to walk around with stinking breath 'cause some slow-moving officer won't replenish my toothpaste in a timely manner! I should drop these damn clothes right on C.O. Warren's desk. Better yet, I need to find some damn soap powder.

I need to stop and pray now, because my mouth is getting outta hand. But then I thought—I don't want no beefs for not washing these boxers. I quickly walked towards Warren's desk, which was nearby.

"Warren, man, what's up? The machines are out of soap powder again."

"Yeah," Warren replied.

I just stood there. I was trying to control my anger because he knew I was pressed to wash. Otherwise, I wouldn't be standing there with two loads full of under-clothes in my arms. With Warren simultaneously humming and ignoring me, I thought I was on my own. He took his long leg slowly off the desk and raised himself out of the chair. That's exactly why he'd be a C.O. for the rest of his life.

"Follow me," he said in an unhelpful tone.

I'd already wasted thirty minutes. I grabbed the washing powder from Warren and started the second load. I then quickly began folding the fresh, clean boxers from the dryer. I folded each piece of clothing individually, and was particular about the crease in each one.

Although, I needed to hurry back, I took my time to make sure everything was perfect. Bishop was finicky about how our clothes got cleaned and folded. While grabbing the two pillowcases, a touch of hatred entered my heart. Shouldn't I be allowed to sleep with padding? I thought about asking for permission to sleep with one of the pillows on my bunk. Then, I quickly dismissed the thought, and set my mind on a different course.

Hell, I still hadn't cleaned our cell. The toilet in there was viscous. I needed to get on my job. I didn't want Bishop to start no shit with me! I'd been trying to keep him happy lately.

If it weren't for Bishop, I'd be stabbed up by now or even dead. Over the last few weeks, shit's been kind of calm, but still awkward. All my old crew has turned against me. What's left of them anyway. Everybody's acting brand new. Trying to chump me everywhere I go. Bishop got my back though. That incident that happened to me before he started looking out for me would never happen again! He assured me of that!

Hell, I'm a kept man. Whatever I need or ask for, I get. Bishop supplies all our needs. I can't believe how he's gotten to be the big man on this block. He's running everything. Anything you need, he's either got it or can get it. That li'l nigga is like a celebrity around here. He's got everybody fearing him—the white boys, niggas, and Mexicans. You name it, they ass is scared! Not me though I'm lucky as hell. Motherfuckers know not to touch me. Bishop will definitely run pipe in their asses. I guess when people found out he was in for raping men, that probably added to the terror. His little short ass is strong. Holding down big grown men. He's not ashamed of that shit either. He'll tell you in a minute how many dudes he raped. His rap sheet is lengthy. But, he doesn't look like he could rape a grown woman. I remember when he first came in, I would've never thought rape!

He's definitely been looking out for me for a while. All that precious information Brocton was giving me over in protective custody was the work of Bishop! And Brocton got paid well. Clueless, I really thought Brocton was my friend.

All those times I thought Niko was sending me the newspaper, it was Bishop. Oh! Let's not forget, that package Bennett brought me with the stationery, new books, and the Walkman, compliments of Bishop!

Bennett only did it to keep the heat off Niko. She never really liked Bishop anyway. But, at this point who cares? She fucked up when she tried to kill my ass. Now she's doing twenty years, charged with conspiracy to commit murder. I guess the judicial system wanted to make an example out of her because she clouded the public's trust in our correctional institutions.

The worst part of it all is that she ended up losing contact with everybody. At first, she wrote her church and got no response. But, when she wrote to family members who had disapproved of her relationship with Niko and received no response, she cracked.

Her crazed love for Niko and the rejection from him,drove her crazy. She now resides in the psychiatric ward of a women's correctional institution, taking the heaviest possible dose of Prozac.

See, that's what happens when you fuck with me. I told you, I'm the man. I've bumped into a few hurdles along the way, but I've survived.

One thing is for sure, I never thought I'd be getting pumped in the butt by a dude. But after a while, you get used to it. Bishop is keen on safe sex, so most of the time we use rubbers, and if those are scarce, we use a rubber glove. I just go with the flow, 'cause Bishop is all I've got.

I don't even get visits anymore. Grandma is too sickly to visit. The doctor says she's got Type 1 diabetes and needs to take better care of herself. She has to take multiple insulin injections daily. In addition, physical activity is limited, and a healthy diet is necessary. Also, her doctor told her to keep her stress level low. That's why she didn't want to speak back to me a few months ago after Captain Graham told her about the rape. The stress was upsetting so she decided to get off the phone.

Type 1 diabetes is serious. I didn't realize you could possibly go blind or have your leg amputated! She says she doesn't worry. She's got Jesus, and she's still praying for me too. Sometimes I wonder if my situation has added to her stress. I mean, it hurts her to see me in here like this. And, now the thought that her baby will be here another six years probably hurts her. She tries to be jolly when we talk on the phone, but I can see straight through that façade. How can you be jolly when you spend your whole day taking insulin?

She writes me every now and then. But as far as mail goes, Bishop checks all my mail, so he let's me know if she sent me something. He says staying on top of my mail is for my own good. He's trying to keep me out of trouble. At least he relays all the important information, like when Mathematics wrote to say thanks. He said Mathematics ended up being transferred to another minimum-security facility without any extra time. For once, I felt good about my character.

Two hours had past, and all the laundry was done. Now, time to clean our cell. Walking back to our little home, I started to think about how my life could have been different. Where did I go wrong? Even though my mom was a disgrace, I had the best upbringing imaginable. A loving grandmother, good schooling, and the love of God in my heart. It all went downhill when I met damn Niko and Sherese. I should have seen those devils coming. My grandma told me. I just didn't listen. I could have been a stockbroker or the next Donald Trump. Instead, my only job is to clean this damn cell.

"Divine, get your punk ass in here and braid my hair!" Bishop yelled.

I ignored his evil tone, jetted in the cell, apologized, and grabbed the comb and grease off the top bunk. My bunk of course. I never thought I'd be sleeping on the top.

Bishop immediately started grilling me. "Where have you been?"

"Washing."

"Did anybody step to you?" Bishop asked.

"Nah." I smiled, avoiding eye contact.

"Why you so damn happy?"

"No reason."

Treating me like a criminal on trial, he asked, "What was in that letter from your lawyer?"

"Like you don't already know."

"Don't get smart," he said, positioning his hand for an open-hand slap.

"I'm not." In a timid voice I continued, "It was just an explanation about why he hasn't gotten back to me."

"That's it?"

"That's it."

Instead of getting overly excited for nothin, or thinking about how my life has changed over the last six months, I commenced to greasing Bishop's scalp. I don't mind braiding his hair. He protects me, and I keep him looking good. Not a problem. *You wash my back, I wash yours.* As I parted his hair, I thought, *this won't take long.* Then I'd make the bunks and wait patiently for my deliverance.

About the Author

Azárel is a native of North Carolina and currently resides in Maryland.

Her first novel, *A Life to Remember*, provides the opportunity to show her readers that everyone can change.

Azárel received her bachelor's degree from the University of Maryland Eastern Shore, and earned her master's from Bowie State University in 1999.

After teaching in the Prince George's Country school system for five years, Azárel decided to become a writer. Changing the lives of those in unfortunate situations inspired her to launch Life Changing Books. Presently she is working on her second novel, *Bruised—A Family Tradition*.

As a wife and mother of two, Azárel enjoys spending time with family and friends and lending support to children in need.

A Life to Remember
a novel
by Azkrel

Order yours TODAY!

$15.00
Maryland residents, please add 5% sales tax.

+ Shipping/handling............$3.50
(U.S. Priority Mail)

Make check or money order payable to: Life Changing Books
(please do not send cash)

Life Changing Books
PO Box 423
Brandywine, MD 20613

Purchaser information: *(please print)*

Name_____

*Address*_____

*City*_____

*State and Zip*_____

*Number of books requested*_____

Total for this order $_____

Additional copies may also be ordered online at
www.lifechangingbooks.net